THE BROTHERS

RUSH

alternate edition

PENELOPE BLACK

RUSH ALTERNATE EDITION

THE BROTHERHOOD
BOOK 2

PENELOPE BLACK

For the underdogs.
I'm rooting for you.

PLAYLIST

"In A Black Out" by Hamilton Leithauser + Rostam
"Medicine" by Daughter
"Smells Like Teen Spirit" by Nirvana
"Misery Business" by Paramore
"Sweetness" by Jimmy Eat World
"(Love Is Like A) Heatwave" by Martha Reeves & The Vandellas
"Hateful" by The Clash
"There's No 'I' in Team" by Taking Back Sunday
"bloody valentine" by Machine Gun Kelly
"Dreams" by Fleetwood Mac
"Hey" by Pixies
"My Body Is a Cage" by Arcade Fire
"Earned It" by The Weeknd
"Out Of The Woods" by Taylor Swift
"exile" by Taylor Swift + Bon Iver
"Praying" by Kesha
"Cornfield Chase" by Hans Zimmer

1

ALAINA

I WAKE WITH A GASP.

Consciousness doesn't arrive slowly. It's a snap of your fingers. One minute, I'm in the back hallway of O'Malley's, and the next moment, I'm jerking awake.

It takes me a moment to realize that I'm hot—really hot. My first thought is that our air conditioner is out again. I look around, expecting to see my dorm room in New York City before I remember that I was staying in Boston with my mom's new fiancé's family. Everything is kind of foggy, but those details are irrelevant when I turn my head and see the inside of a van. My fingers start tingling, and my mouth falls open in shock. A sudden cough wracks my body with the movement.

Everything hurts. Sharp pain lances across my head, centering around my hairline and temple.

"What happened?" I know I said the words out loud, but I can't hear them. A sliver of panic zips down my spine, and I squeeze my eyes shut.

It smells like a campfire, only less roasted marshmallows and more sharp chemicals.

With one hand, I push off the floor to sit up and touch my ear with the other. I feel something wet on my fingers—blood. Everything is muffled like I'm underwater, and the smell of smoke is getting stronger.

My brows crease and goosebumps cover my arms. I don't understand what's happening, but I try to push down the panic that's creeping up my throat.

Where's Wolf?

And Rush?

Or Sully?

Movement catches my attention, and I see bright-orange flames through the front windshield. They ensnare me with their hypnotic sway, and I lose precious seconds in their deadly trap.

Oh my god. They're coming from the hood of the van.

Urgency floods my veins and adrenaline kicks in and forces me to move. I scramble up to stand and hit my head on the ceiling. The impact knocks me back a step, and I trip over something and land hard on the floor. My tailbone takes the brunt of the impact and my elbows sting, but it's the least of my concerns when I see what I tripped on.

Or should I say *who.*

A guy dressed in all black—including a black ski mask rolled partially up to reveal a brown beard—lays motionless next to me. Before I have time to do anything, a guy with red eyes gets in my face. He's dressed the same way as the guy I just tripped over, and fear holds my body in a vice grip.

I can't hear what he's yelling over the roaring in my ears, but my fight-or-flight instincts kick in as I remember him from the back hallway of O'Malley's.

When he bends down and checks the guy next to me for a pulse, I seize my opportunity. I scramble around, get to my feet, and run toward the back door. I make it two steps before someone tackles me from behind.

My chin slams into the floor of the dirty van, and blood fills my mouth. Stars dance before my eyes, and I shake my head to get the ringing to stop.

He wrenches my arms behind my back, and I thrash around and kick anything my feet come in contact with. Sweat rolls down my face as the air in the van turns sweltering. I feel something wrap around my wrists, and I feel myself detach from my body.

I'm reduced to my base as a human being, and I know that I'm not ending my days on this Earth trapped in a fiery van.

It takes a moment for the sound to filter in, but I can hear myself screaming. It's the loudest noise I've ever heard come out of my mouth, but I can't stop.

Stopping means that I'm giving up.

Stopping means I'm resigning myself to this fate.

Stopping means that I'll never see three pairs of intense, stunning, captivating eyes again.

So I don't stop. I can't. *I won't.*

I scream and I claw and I kick anything that I touch.

I turn fucking feral.

"Jesus fucking Christ. Will you hand me the goddamn syringe already? If we die in here, then we don't get paid," the person wrestling with me yells, but I don't give his words a second of my time. I need every second I can get.

I hear someone answer, but I can barely make out the words over my screaming and the lingering ringing.

From the corner of my eye, I see a syringe, and I redouble my efforts.

"Remember, you brought this on yourself," he hisses in my face, spit flying to my cheek. He grabs the syringe from the outstretched hand and brings it down hard on my neck before tossing it to the side.

It takes all of ten seconds before my muscles betray me and

stop working. Five seconds later, I fight to keep my eyes open as the red-eyed demon of a man gets in my face.

"She's done. Let's go before they catch up to us. If they catch us, we're fucking dead, and I'm not dying because Smitty can't fucking drive."

I hear the creak and groan of metal being pushed open and feel my body carried out of the van. The last thing I see is the dark sky as someone carries me from the flaming van to a waiting car.

2

RUSH

"SOME MOTHERFUCKER CAME into our town, into our bar, shit on our authority, and stole our goddamn girl!" The words come out in a torrent of rage, exploding into the still kitchen air by the last word. With my arm stretched out, I swipe it across the table, and everything crashes to the floor. Coffee mugs full of room-temperature coffee shatter and spill liquid everywhere. Loose papers flutter to the floor, some landing in the coffee puddles. My jaw ticks at the mess on the floor, but my rage won't let me take the time to pick it up.

Palms flat, I brace myself against the table and breathe in through my nose with my eyes on the wood grain in front of me.

I wait until I'm sure I can speak without wanting to destroy everything in my path. "I don't care who we have to bribe or kill, we're finding her, and we're bringing her home." I glance at my brother. His jaw clenches, but his face remains carefully blank. He rakes his fingers through his dark-blond hair and stares right back at me with those cold blue eyes of his.

"We'll find her, brother."

7

"Soon, Sully. She's been gone too long already. And I won't be held responsible for what happens to those who stand in my way."

"Aye, soon. I'll check-in with Wolf." He pauses for a moment, his stare probing before he turns on his heel and silently leaves the house through the patio door.

I'm sure he's cataloguing every small fissure in my usually impeccably controlled front. The temporary lapse in judgment that had me dumping the contents of the table is all the evidence he needs.

But he's not as infallible as he thinks. I remind myself that he's only known about Alaina for days, not weeks like Wolf. And not a year like me.

Though that's not quite true, is it?

He had Alaina, and he didn't even tell us about her. I think about the way she tastes, and I don't blame him for it. If I'd found her years ago—back before our pact—I can't say I wouldn't have done the same thing. Something as sweet as her is precious in this life, and I'd have done anything to preserve it.

I still would.

I stand up and swipe a hand through my dark-brown hair, striving for order in the middle of chaos. I track Sully's progress as he cuts through the backyard and hangs a right toward the back of the property and the carriage house.

Impatience has me contemplating a visit to Wolf or one of the other trusted guys we have in the rooms in the basement of the carriage house. I want to hear firsthand who the fuck planned this attack on my family.

It wasn't a random attack, of that I'm sure. O'Malley's has been protected under the Brotherhood since before I was born. The only real question is if they targeted my girl specifically or if they snatched the first girl at random?

Fuck.

Some distant part of me recognizes that at some point I'll have to tell my brothers about my history with Alaina—at least part of it. I'm not sure that I need to detail how I've been watching her for the last year just yet. They might get the wrong . . . impression if I tell them now when tempers are high and logic is low.

The vibration of my phone instantly has my attention. I whip it out of my pocket and answer it before I even check who's calling. "Talk."

"Boss. I need something more to go on. It's a needle in a haystack, and I'm wasting time aimlessly searching. I've checked all our feeds on the usual suspects, and I don't see anything out of the ordinary," Buzz, the Brotherhood's other tech specialist, says, his voice threaded with exasperation.

"Not the Italian?" I still don't trust Matteo. He's hiding something. Could mean anything from a little bird stashed away to standard multi-tier paranoia. But trusting my gut has saved me countless times in the past, so I'll continue to reserve judgment on him until he shows me otherwise.

This life is built on secrets and favors. Some men don't know how to handle their secrets, and your only hope is that you don't get sucked into their orbit when they implode. Because they almost always do. It's never a happy ending like in those bullshit Hollywood mafia movies and shows—the bad guy doesn't get a change of heart overnight and suddenly decide to turn his back on everything and every*one* he knows.

No, what really happens is that some motherfucker who watched one too many episodes of *Sopranos* thinks he can run everything better. Too cocky and being surrounded by yes-men inflates his ego, and he thinks he can run everything better than those before him. But thoughts aren't really what kills the cocky motherfucker. Nah, it's the secrets. See, these little fucks get too confident and start chatting up everyone they meet. And that's their mistake.

Everyone has a price, and loyalty is earned, not given.

"Didn't you say Matteo was with you when Alaina was taken?"

"Aye. But Matteo looks like he's trying to do some spring cleaning. And we all know how that move plays out. I'm not so sure that he can pull it off without starting a goddamn revolution. For all I know, they took my girl as a preemptive incentive so I'd make a deal." I pause and feel the cruel twist of my lips as I recall how we dealt with the last person who tried to force my hand. "Do you remember what happened to Scottie?"

Buzz exhales, the noise loud in my ear. "Aye, who could forget the little prick who tried to stage a coup? No disrespect, boss, but we don't exactly have time for a trip down memory lane."

I clench the phone in my palm, my fingers protesting at the strain. When I don't immediately reply, Buzz is quick to backtrack.

"Fuck. I didn't mean anything by it. It's just—I've got a lot of work to do. If you'd let me call some—"

"No," I interrupt him. "No outsiders. You know that. And the next time you question my orders, you won't like what happens." The warning hits my intended target as Buzz mutters his apologies, but I'm only half paying attention.

I know he doesn't mean any disrespect, and while I do trust him to an extent, I don't trust anyone right now—except for my brothers. And the last thing I need is another fucking ambush.

I'm preoccupied as Buzz rattles off something about traffic cams around O'Malley's. The conversation I had with Matteo minutes before Alaina was taken plays on a loop in my thoughts. Was it a setup? Was Matteo a decoy or a *sacrifice*? It's possible that

10

his uncles found out about the plays he's trying to make, and they made their move first.

Just as quickly as that thought comes, I dismiss it. If the Italian mob wanted Matteo out of the picture, he'd already be gone. They wouldn't do some roundabout way of getting to him through me—shit, we're acquaintances, passing friendly at best.

And if Matteo was genuinely there to warn us, that begs the question: how did he know?

"Find Matteo Rossi," I interrupt him. "I want eyes on him. And I want names of his sources." I hang up before he replies.

Whoever took her will regret it for the rest of his life—however short it may be. And I will rain down a hell unlike anyone has ever seen on everyone who stands in my way.

If I make a move before I have all the information, it could cost us something I'm not willing to pay—Alaina. There are a lot of prices I've paid—like my soul—but she won't be one of them. I refuse to let her be a casualty in this war.

So I'm static for the time being, and I'm practically vibrating with the need to move. And for someone who routinely gets all the information I need and more, this lack of information grates on my fucking nerves. We just need one tiny kernel to find her.

I can find a needle in a haystack, but the only problem with that plan is that it takes significantly longer. And time is not on our side.

"Fuck," I yell into the empty kitchen.

Alaina was stolen from me right underneath my nose. These are either the cockiest sons of bitches out there or they're the most stupid. It wouldn't surprise me if they were both.

I have another play, but I hesitate to make the call. It's a certifiable ace up my sleeve, but they bring their own set of chaos everywhere they go.

The Kings.

We've been friends since childhood, and while they're not in the Brotherhood, the Kings are their own force. Every time I think about that no-women archaic rule the Brotherhood has, I want to punch someone. When I'm president of the Brotherhood council and not just the junior council, that's one thing I'm going to implement.

Shit, the King sisters are better than some of my guys in more than one area.

Maeve, Fiona, Keira, Ava, and Roisin King were trained by the Hammer himself. Joseph King wanted sons and the universe gave him five daughters—all born a year apart. I still remember the first time they came to the family barbecue.

A little girl marches right over to me, her hair a wild mess, and sticks out her hand for me to shake. "Hi. I'm Maeve King, and these are my sisters. My da kept trying for a boy, but instead, God gave him my baby sisters instead." She hooks a thumb over her shoulder to the four girls standing behind her.

I nod my head to the side. "These are my brothers, Conor and James."

"Cool. Wanna play spies? My da says I'm gettin' real good, and some-day, I'm going to be the best goddamn spy ever. But my ma doesn't like it when he says those words, and she threatens that she'll make him sleep on the couch if he doesn't clean up his language around us." She shrugs. "He never does, and she never makes him. She says she likes da to keep her warm at night too much—whatever that means." She pauses, and I don't say anything. She gave me too much information at one time, and I'm not sure what I should say. She doesn't give me long to respond before she says, "So, are we gonna play?"

I glance at my brothers, and they both shrug their shoulders in response. We're trying to master our nonverbal communication. I'm positive it'll come in handy one day.

"Sure," I say with a shrug and a nod.

Over the years, we'd see the King sisters a couple of times a year, and then less as we got older and they started their own thing. King tried to get his girls in the Brotherhood, even though he was never a member himself, but the council kept voting no.

Despite the fact that all five of them had indispensable skills. They'll be my first recruits when I sit in that president's chair.

Every so often, I get a call from one of them when they need assistance from one of us. We've never had to call in a favor.

Until now.

3

WOLF

THE HINGES CREAK as the body of the faceless guy sways with the last punch. His head snaps to the side with an air of finality that has me roaring in frustration. I spin and kick the metal folding chair into the wall.

"Fuck!"

Desperation weighs heavy on my shoulders. I rake my hands through my hair, no doubt painting it with this worthless fuck's blood. He was some low-level thug our boys caught at the port selling skin. Everyone knows we don't tolerate that shit—*everyone*. We've had him on ice for the last couple of days until we could squeeze more information from him.

I was content to let our boys have a chat with him since I planned to spend the weekend in the city, but then circumstances changed—I still can't quite bring myself to say my girl was kidnapped without flying off into a blackout rage. I thought it best I come have that chat with him.

In fact, I made it my mission to have a personal chat with each person we've got here—and everyone the boys pick up until I get my girl back.

15

I don't bother wiping off the blood spatter, but I grab the hand towel and toss it over my shoulder. I push open the metal door to the hallway and nod at the guy, Jimmy, posted up against the wall.

"Who's next?"

Jimmy tips his head to the room next to him. "This one's here compliments of Rossi. Left him outside the gate with a bow and everything."

My eyebrows hit my hairline. "Do you know who it is?"

"Said he's someone who crossed him," Jimmy says with a shrug.

"I don't take out his garbage," I grit through my teeth.

"That's what I told him, boss," Jimmy assures me with a nod. I don't have to tell our boys that I'm one wrong word away from snapping.

"He better give us something good."

He nods at me but doesn't say anything as I push open the door to the room next to him. I whistle under my breath when I see the mess before me.

"Huh. I guess someone already had a chat with you," I tell the guy in the middle of the room. I'm not surprised when he doesn't respond right away. It looks like he went a few rounds in the ring.

His arms are stretched up high, zip-tied and connected to a hook hanging from the ceiling. His head hangs low and blood drips down his face onto the floor. In a dirty, torn shirt and jeans, I don't see any visible tattoos or identifiers to give me any hints as to who the fuck he is.

Some unlucky prick, I guess.

I take a step toward him, and he lifts his head. A crazed smile takes up half of his face as he flashes me his bloodied mouth. He looks like some sort of horror movie extra.

"Ah, so you can hear me. Perfect. That makes this more fun,

doesn't it?" I take another step forward and let him see the beast in my gaze. I'm tethered to my humanity by a thread right now, and all it takes is one misstep, and everyone will be fucked. Everyone.

The last time I gave in and let my inner beast run unchecked, the aftermath looked like the set of a b-grade horror movie. As far as I'm concerned, they deserved it. Everyone knows what happens when the Brotherhood catches you breaking a rule.

I cock my head as the idea of letting my beast out to play takes shape in my mind. It does have merit.

I clap my hands and get back on task. I level him with my blank stare that I've perfected years ago. It never fails to make men spill their secrets—men far greater than him.

"Where's my girl?"

I know he either doesn't get the memo just yet or he's playing hard to get when his smile kicks up a notch.

"You don't want to know who I am?" he taunts with a cocky little smirk.

"Nah. I don't give a fuck who you are." In two swift steps, I deliver a right hook across his nose. The satisfying crunch fills the air as blood arcs across the room. "Did you know you could break your nose in several places? And each one hurts more than the previous break?" I pause and flash him a cruel smile. "But I'm sure you knew that already. I'll ask again: Where's my girl?"

The nameless guy in front of me pants, spraying blood pouring from his nose with every exhale. "Fuck. You."

I tip my head back and laugh. It's a harsh sound, and I glance at him to see that he's finally cluing in to his situation.

"I see you don't know who *I* am." I shrug with faux nonchalance. "Some people call me the VP of the Brotherhood's junior council. Some people call me the wolf. You'll know by the time I'm done exactly who I am."

Real fear shines in his eyes, and a sliver of satisfaction slithers around inside me. Sometimes it's good that my reputation precedes me. Honestly, a lot of the rumors flying around about me are total bullshit, but in situations like this, it's goddamn helpful. It means less work for me.

I glance at my hands streaked with blood—not all of it mine—knuckles busted and swollen. If Red's life wasn't on the line, I might take a breather and come back from another angle. But something primal inside me urges me to use nothing but my fists to mete out judgment on these poor excuses for men.

Today I am the judge, jury, and in some cases, executioner.

I go another few rounds of questions, none of which he answers, before he passes out.

"Goddamnit!" I shake out my hand and exhale a weighted breath. If he didn't come to me already so fucked up, I could've actually squeezed some information out of him.

The creak of the metal door behind me alerts me to one of my brothers. They'd be the only ones to interrupt me. I take a moment to recenter myself before I turn around.

"Anything?"

I glare at my brother for even asking such a dumbass question. "Do you really think I'd still be standing here if I got anything useful out of any of them?"

Sully stares at me with a scowl on his face and folds his arms across his chest. "Fuck off, Wolf. You're not the only one frustrated. Rush has been basically mute except for his check-ins."

I scoff. "Are we still pretending like Red doesn't mean shit to you?"

I walk over to the guy hanging from the rope attached to a customized pulley system hooked up to the rafters. I've got another three faceless guys in the other rooms—and five more at our secondary location in the city.

Except for this guy, Sully and I volunteered to drag all the others here, since we thought they'd be the most promising leads. So far, they haven't panned out.

Sully's saved from answering by his phone ringing. He digs it out of his pocket and my gaze zeros in on the flecks of dried blood on his forearm.

"Talk to me."

I unhook the guy in front of me, and he slumps to the floor.

"Where? How sure?" He pauses for a second. "Survivors? Bodies?" He pauses again, and I feel every muscle in my body tighten with whatever information is on the other end of that phone. "Yeah. Okay, thanks. Good work."

He ends the call and looks at me, his expression carefully blank.

"What?" The word comes out harsher than I wanted, but I'm not going to take it back now.

"That was Matteo. One of his soldiers spotted the same make and model van from O'Malley's. On fire."

My heart skips a beat before it races. "Where?"

"About halfway between the city and here, two hours northbound. And before you ask, there were no survivors on the scene, but there were bodies pulled from the wreckage. Two men from the looks of it."

I wipe my hands on the black hand towel and stride toward the door. "Let's go."

Sully stops me with a hand on my shoulder. "Hang on a minute. She's not there, man. And it's at least another three-hour drive. Our efforts are better spent here, asking the right questions now that we have some more information to go on."

In one move, I flick his hand off my shoulder, spin around, and shove him back a step. "Our girl's been missing for almost six hours, and you're telling me to *wait* after we got our first credible lead? Are you out of your fucking mind?"

I can feel the vein in my forehead throbbing with the beat of my rage. Each minute that passes without her is a slash on my already bruised soul.

Sully doesn't break eye contact. "Yes. That's exactly what I'm telling you. Call Diesel and have him fucking video you when he's there, if that's what you need. But she's not there, and if we want to find her, then we need one of these motherfuckers to talk. And I need you to help me make them *fucking talk*." He's breathing heavy by the time he's done speaking.

If I was in a better frame of mind, I would bring up the fact that he's one step away from losing it. But as it is, I'm stuck in my own hell, and I don't have the capacity for anything else right now.

"Fine. I'll call Diesel again, but you're telling Rush."

He nods once, and I step back. We both pull our phones and I send a text to Diesel with my request.

I follow Sully out of the room. Jimmy waits outside the door. "Ice him—he decided to leave the party early, and he's not done yet."

"On it, boss." He pushes off the wall and heads inside the room we just left.

I don't spare him a second glance as Sully and I head to the two rooms next door. I pause with my hand on the doorknob and look at my brother.

"Whatever it takes, brother."

He nods. "Whatever it takes."

4

ALAINA

IT'S the noise that I notice first. Or rather, the absence of noise. I've become so accustomed to the noises of the city that truly never sleeps that the lack of yelling and honking horns and blaring music feels jarring to my ears.

I struggle to pry my eyelids open, but they feel like they weigh a thousand pounds. A groan slips past my lips when I open my eyes and instantly regret it. The room spins, and I have just enough presence of mind to lean over before the contents of my stomach come up and splatter the dirty floor.

"Side effect of the sedative."

I flinch at the sound of the unfamiliar voice and flick my gaze around the darkened room until I see him partially shadowed in the corner by the doorway.

I cough a few times and spit in an attempt to clear my mouth, and when I'm sure that I'm not going to hurl again, I use my hand to push myself to a sitting position. I'm sitting on a faded blue-and-white floral-patterned couch in a floor-to-ceiling wood-paneled room. Two windows are on the wall to the left of me with drapes in the same pattern as the couch pulled closed. I don't see any sunlight spilling in, so I can only assume it's the middle of the night.

Dread pools in my belly as I glance at the man in the shadows and try to collect my thoughts over the pounding in my head.

I clear my throat a couple of times and wince at the burn. "Where am I?"

He takes two steps toward me, no longer concealed in shadows, but he doesn't get closer. In dark jeans and a black tee, his clothes give nothing away. No visible tattoos and closely cropped black hair. He stares at me for a moment as he rolls around a toothpick in his mouth before pulling a cell phone out of his pocket. I spot the gun in a shoulder holster when his arm moves to grab his phone, and an intense wave of panic licks up my spine.

I push it back down, unwilling to douse the flicker of hope I just got. I discreetly shift my weight from one side to the other to feel for the outline of my phone that I know I stashed in my pocket back when I was at O'Malley's.

Bingo.

I've never been more thankful for my love of dresses with pockets than I am right now. I'm so distracted by my victory that I miss the beginning of the conversation.

"Yeah, boss. She's awake. Yeah, I got it."

He hangs up before I can get any more clues from the one-sided conversation. If watching TV has taught me anything, it's that I need to keep him talking. Most bad guys like to brag about what they did or what they're planning to do, and hopefully, he'll slip up and give me something I can use. Somehow.

I shake my head, trying to ease the intense throbbing so I can focus. I need a plan on how the hell I'm going to get out of here.

Yes, that's exactly what I need.

Planning on how the hell I'm supposed to escape a place I've never been to surrounded by people I don't know in a location I've never been to before.

With each word, the panic grows until it's swelling so large that I know it'll crest soon and take me down with it. I'll never resurface. And I'll never get out of here.

I've watched enough horror movies to know that it doesn't look good for me in my current predicament. What I do know is that I was taken from O'Malley's, then I woke up in a van, and then I vaguely remember seeing flashes of a burning van and being carried to another car. And now here. I could've changed locations a dozen times in all those blackout moments I don't remember. And with each new location, the likelihood of rescue goes down.

Like, really down. I'm not even sure if there *is* anyone looking for me. *You know that's not true,* a little voice whispers in my mind. I swallow the acidic taste as I think about them—my boyfriends? No, that doesn't sound quite right though. Sully's not my boyfriend anymore. And the word seems too small to encompass what they are—or what they could've been.

All I know is that they're *mine.*

And they'll come for me. I know they will.

But I need to do everything I can to help. And I need to get out of this place—this situation. Once I'm safe, then I'll give into the fear draped across my shoulders and then I can take a breath to examine my feelings for three very different men.

With my newfound conviction, I square my shoulders and look at the guy in front of me. "Who are you?" My voice is clear despite the double vision.

"Tsk, tsk. C'mon, Alaina. They said you were smart, but you're not asking the right questions," he says as he taps his temple with his index finger. "No, not who am I—who are *you?*"

I still at the use of my name. Okay, so he knows who I am. I mean, that's not that big of a shock considering they kidnapped me—Jesus, what has my life turned into?

But wait a minute. He said who am I? Doesn't he already know?

"Look. I think there's been a misunderstanding, but I'm not who you're looking for. Why do—"

He interrupts me with a hand in the air in the universal *stop* gesture. "You're exactly who we're looking for." His voice is hard, impatient.

I shake my head a couple of times. "What do you want from me?"

"Ah, there it is. Unfortunately, I've already said too much. The rest you'll get from the boss. Until then, enjoy your stay at the cabin. It's a little slice of heaven away from the bustling crowds of the city. There's a lake bordering one side of the property—big enough that you can't see across it. In the daytime, of course. It's in the middle of the woods on five acres of land, so no one will hear you if you scream. Keep that in mind while you wait." He delivers my fate with a mocking smile painted on his face.

I squint and do my best to force the two of him I see into one as I try to find something to commit him to memory. I just know Wolf will want all the details as soon as he gets here.

The stranger turns on his heel and leaves the room.

I hear the lock on the doorknob click, and even though I know it's pointless, I stand up and cross the room to try the handle. It doesn't budge, and there's no lock twist on the handle on this side.

What kind of door locks from the outside like that? I shudder when I think about what someone would use a near empty room like this for.

I rest my forehead on the door. "Think, Lainey, think," I whisper.

I tilt my head and turn around to check the obvious places a security camera would be—the corners and above the curtain rod—and come up empty-handed.

Good, this is good.

If there are no cameras, then I might have a fighting chance at sneaking out.

I cross the room and tentatively open the other door. Relief momentarily settles in my lungs when a small bathroom greets me. It's barely big enough to turn around in, but it has a toilet and a sink, and right now, that's good enough for me.

I flip the switch as I step inside. Shock holds my breath hostage as I come face-to-face with my reflection.

"Holy shit," I breathe out.

My once smooth, wavy hair resembles a lion's mane, littered with dirt and debris. Something black streaks across my cheek and bruises bloom on my cheekbone and underneath my eye. The vibrant emerald green of my birthday dress mocks me with rips and snags along the bodice. The hemline is torn over one thigh, and the swath of fabric over one shoulder is holding on by a thread. Crusted, dried blood lines my nostril, but that's not what holds my attention.

I stare, transfixed by the sight of dried blood on the crown of my head.

Aside from spraining my ankle a few years ago, I've never been hurt like this before. Never bled like this before.

I slowly bring my hand to my head and probe the edges of the cut. Pain, sharp and shocking, rolls through me at the exploration, and I wince.

"Okay, Lainey. You can do this," I whisper as I hold my own gaze in the mirror.

I nod a couple of times and mentally fortify myself. I don't know what's going on or where I am, but I'm smart and resourceful and . . . and I know that Wolf will be looking for me. I just have to hold on.

I turn on the faucet and a small rush of brown water sputters out before it goes dry.

Okay.

That's okay.

I don't need to clean these cuts.

It's fine. I'm fine.

I eye the toilet and weigh the merits of using it when I remember the reason I came in here in the first place—my phone!

I curse myself for forgetting something so important and wasting time as I pluck it out of my hidden front pocket.

"Shit."

The screen is covered in spiderweb cracks, but it might still work. I swipe up to unlock it, and I'm so relieved it works I nearly sob. Pulling up Wolf's contact, I hit the call button and jerk the phone to my ear.

"C'mon, c'mon, c'mon," I chant with my heart pounding in the same rhythm.

When I don't hear ringing, I pull it away to look at the screen and my heart sinks. No service.

"Okay. That's okay. I'll just find service," I whisper the plan to myself. I extend my arm in the air, holding my phone in different corners of the small bathroom with my eyes glued to the bars of service in the top corner. My ribs protest the movement, sending a punch of pain to my side that steals my breath. But I have no idea how much time I'll have by myself, so I swallow the groan and keep moving.

I step back into the room and immediately head for the window. If I don't have service, I'll climb out the window and run until I get service. The familiar comfort of my white Vans settles my nerves as I wiggle my toes.

I've never been more thankful for my love of sneakers in my entire life. In fact, I just might sleep in these from now on.

I pause by the window and listen for movement in the house. When I don't hear anything, I glance at my phone again—still no service—and slide the floral drapes aside.

Blinking rapidly, I can't quite understand what I'm seeing. A dozen nails hold the window semi-permanently in the sill and make it nearly impossible for me to open it.

I tuck my phone back in my pocket, and I try anyway.

After sixty seconds and not even a millimeter of difference, I give up and walk the perimeter of the room with my phone in the air.

My steps are a little heavier as I make my way back to the couch. I sit down on the other side, tuck my phone away, and make sure the outline isn't visible through the dress.

Once I'm satisfied with its concealment, I let my hands fall to the cushion and try to think of my next steps. But it's hard. Every time I try to think too hard, my head aches like someone has taken a hammer to it.

I lean my head against the back of the couch and smooth my hands over the rough fabric of the couch. I fight back the cringe as my fingers run over some crusted patches on the couch.

Something pricks my index finger, and I lean over to see a sharpened pencil wedged between the cushion and the armrest.

Okay, I can use this.

I pull out the pencil and gently run my fingers along the edges of the cushion, hoping to find something else I can use. A pencil could give me a small advantage, but I need something else—something more.

Empty-handed, I slide off the couch and kneel on the floor. The only things under the couch are dust bunnies and a broken piece of the wood. It hangs on by a thread toward the back of the couch, and it takes me a moment to realize that it's part of the couch frame.

I kneel-walk around to the side and peer underneath for a better look. I flatten myself to the ground, reach my hand underneath the couch, and wrap my fingers around the splintered piece of wood. It takes a few tugs, but I finally wrestle it away and pull it out, earning myself several slivers in the process.

About the size of my forearm, thick enough that I can't quite wrap my hand around it, and a jagged edge. It's a better weapon than a pencil, but not by much. It kind of reminds me of a crude rendition of a stake.

Thank you, Vampire Diaries, for that imagery.

I'm not even really sure what the hell I'm planning on doing with either one of them, but I feel a little better knowing that I have *something* to defend myself.

I settle myself back on the couch and tuck the piece of wood between the cushion and armrest to conceal as much as possible.

Then I wait.

5

ALAINA

I LEAN on the few meditation exercises I learned from a class Maddie dragged me to last semester and work on calming my breathing. When thoughts of Maddie and Mary start to creep up, I shove them down—way down—where I can't see them. I know that if I start thinking about them, I won't be able to stop. And I need all my wits about me.

My breathing slows as I pick a spot on the wall in front of me to focus on. My phone presses into my hip on one side, and the stake presses into my other hip—both offer me a little comfort.

I've never done well with the unknown—there's a reason I prefer a plan.

Sitting in the void of possibility leaves too much to chance. And chance by its very definition is unpredictability. I like the idea of spontaneity more than I actually like it—unless it's in small doses. Getting brunch on a whim is fun for everyone. Getting kidnapped without understanding why or what's going on is the worst kind of chance. Changing locations several times by men you've never seen before without a single self-defense class under your belt could be the final stop on my journey. I've never been more aware of the fact that I'm a defenseless five foot four eighteen-year-old woman than I am right now.

I make a promise to myself—if I make it out of here, then I'm going to take chances, be spontaneous, and claim my boys. That word doesn't feel quite right. They're men. *My* men.

But first, I'll take self-defense classes—no, first thing I'm going to do if I get out of here alive is find my men and kiss the hell out of them. In fact, I may never stop kissing them.

And I'm going to hug my cousins and make sure they realize how much I love them.

But self-defense comes in a close second.

The facts are simple. I have no idea why I'm here or who took me. And I have a pencil and a rudimentary stake as my only form of defense. The odds don't look good. Luckily for me, I always root for the underdog. I had no idea that one day *I'd* be the underdog in every sense of the word.

Footsteps startle me out of my forced state of faux calm, and my heart starts to race.

I watch the doorknob turn with bated breath. A man I've never seen before shuffles inside the room. Tall and skinny with brown hair—he looks like everyone and no one.

I swallow reflexively and track his movements with my gaze, keeping my body still. Once he steps inside, he turns to lock the door from the outside before shutting it firmly with the palm of his hand.

The blank look on his face when he turns to look at me sends a shiver of fear down my spine.

He brings his deadened gaze to mine. "You're so much prettier in person."

His words, delivered with such a lack of emotion, hang in the air. Trepidation and wariness blanket my shoulders.

"Do I know you?" My words are quiet in the suddenly too-small room.

He takes a step toward me as his gaze rakes over me, and I see a flash of something too quick to name. I fight to suppress the shudder of revulsion that instinctively flares.

"I'm Sean."

I lick my lips and pause before I ask, "Where's the other guy who was here earlier?"

"You don't have to worry about him. He left." He takes another slow step toward me, and I tense. "I told him I'd take good care of you while he's gone." He takes another step toward me, and he's suddenly within arm's length. "I just wanna talk."

A spike of fear shoots through my body, my very soul protesting everything so profoundly that tremors start in my hands.

"I-I think we should wait until he gets back to talk. Don't you?"

Sean reaches out to touch my hair, and I flinch, jerking my head to the side.

"Ah, don't be shy. I'm not afraid of a little mess. And it looks like you made quite the mess here." He nods his head toward the drying vomit next to his shoes, and a smile I'm sure he thinks is reassuring curls his lips up. But there's too much mania painted in the curve of his mouth to be anything less than terrifying.

Sean sits down next to me, an overwhelming scent of gasoline and body odor assault my nose. I fight the urge to gag.

"I-ah-I think I should talk to your boss, don't you?" I look at Sean out of the corner of my eye, still facing forward.

Wait, Lainey, wait for the right moment, I urge myself. A drop of sweat slides down the back of my neck, taunting me with its swift movement.

"Nah, I don't think so. You're not going to like his plans." He places his hand on my leg, right above my knee, and everything inside me freezes. My senses hone in on that one motion. "That's why I made my own arrangements for you. And I know you're going to like what I have planned. After all, I've been following you for a while."

The pride in his voice sickens me, but I don't answer him. I don't even know what to say to that.

"I found you months ago, but I didn't tell Boss about it until last week—when you disappeared." He tilts his head. "Where did you go, Alaina? I looked at all of our usual places. I even talked to some of your friends, but no one had seen you. I was so worried about you."

The sincerity in his voice tips me over the edge, and I lose a little bit of my calm. It slips down my shoulders and fear slinks around me like a house cat.

I slowly shake my head as my fingers curl around the pencil hidden next to me and my breaths come out harsh. "I want to go home."

"Don't be silly. Your new home is with me." Sean squeezes my leg and bile crawls up my throat. "We just have to wait for the signal, and then we're heading to our new home. Together. Just like it should be. And don't worry about Boss, he's got a lot of enemies, and it only takes one little bird to whisper the right secret, and poof! He's no longer a threat," he says with this great big Cheshire Cat grin.

The mention of *little bird* sends a pang of longing and regret through me. *Rush.* My heart aches for all those little moments over the last year and for all those we could've had together. All the time I could've had with all three of them.

Rush.

Wolf.

Sully.

Oh, god, *Sully.* The idea of never reconnecting with him, of never making it right, pierces my soul.

Is this where my story ends? In a dirty cabin in the woods in the middle of nowhere? Am I going to end up on the back of a milk carton like Grace Adams did in second grade? One day she was in Ms Twist's class, and then just like that, she got off the bus on her street, but she never made it home. They had search parties for her for weeks, but no one ever discovered any clues. And her school photo on the back of milk cartons for months. But they never found her.

And I have a terrible thought—a depressing, gut-wrenching thought that realigns everything.

My dad is gone.

My mom might as well be gone.

Who would miss me if I were . . . gone too?

A tear rolls down my cheek at the thought. Logically, I know that they're looking for me.

But for how long?

What if Sean takes me somewhere else, and the trail gets too muddied, and they can't find me? Panic rises like a tidal wave with each possibility. How long will they continue to look for me before my photo fades from milk cartons and my face fades from their memories?

And maybe the scariest thought of all: What if I don't ever get rescued?

No. Just no.

This cannot be where my story ends—where *our story* ends. I refuse to let this be the last stop on my journey.

Sean squeezes my leg again, pulling me out of my swirling thoughts, and the action kicks my flight or fight response into hyperdrive. I push his hand off and lean away from him as I try to scramble off the couch.

Sean wraps his hand around my bicep and pulls me back, my shoulders knocking against his as he drags me closer. "C'mon, Alaina, I'm not going to hurt you. I could never hurt you. I'm just killing time until we can leave and finally start our life together."

I struggle in his grip as he hauls me against him, my side colliding with his chest. "No, Sean. I don't want this. Please, just let me go. You'll never see me again. I won't tell anyone!" I'm not above begging.

"Would you stop wiggling!" Sean shakes me a little by his grip on my arm. "And why the hell would I do that? If I let you go, he'll find you, and then we'll never see each other again. You'll never see *anyone* ever again." He pauses. "No, it's better this way, you'll see."

My eyes fill with tears as powerlessness fills me. I'm not bigger or stronger, and I'm at a disadvantage in this unfamiliar location. All I have in the element of surprise. And a fierce determination to live.

But I'm not sure it'll be enough.

The only thing I know for sure is that I have to try.

I stop wriggling around and focus on the feel of the pencil in my grip.

"There. That's not so bad, ri—" The sound of an explosion interrupts him, and he loosens his grip on my arm as he turns his head to look out the window. "Perfect. Two more, and then it's time."

I bolster my courage and use this interruption to my advantage. With his head turned, I bring my hand up high, grip tight and knuckles white, and slam the pointed end of the pencil down on his thigh as hard as I can.

Sean howls in pain and drops my arm instantly. I leave the pencil in his thigh and wrap my hands around the splintered makeshift stake. In one movement, I stand up, twist, and bring the stake across the side of his head. I pack every ounce of strength I have in that one hit, adrenaline soaring through my veins.

"What the fuck, Alaina!" Sean growls the words as he brings

38

his hand up to his face and pulls back bloodied fingers from where they touched his hairline.

"Oh, fuck." The words are ripped from my throat as I realize that one hit wasn't enough to incapacitate him.

He looks at me in disbelief, and if I had the time, I'd dissect the reason his gaze is laced with betrayal.

Before he has time to do anything else, I wind up and bring the stake across his head again, right over his ear this time.

He roars as another explosion goes off nearby. When he still doesn't pass out, I wind up and hit him again. But he grabs it at the last second, so it barely grazes his cheek.

He wrestles the stake out of my hands, and I take a step backward, my chest heaving.

Sean pushes off the couch, murder in his eyes. He tosses the stake to the side as he advances on me. "Why would you do that to me, Alaina? I'm *helping* you! Don't you see that? This is so we can be together!"

For every step I take backward, he takes one toward me. I flick my gaze to the stake on the floor and the pencil sticking out of his thigh. My muscles tense as I make a quick decision. I only really have one option.

I dash for the stake, and with a yell, Sean tackles me to the ground. My chin collides with the floor and blood fills my mouth. The second I feel his weight pinning me to the ground, I lose my goddamn mind.

I'm like a feral animal.

Kicking, scratching, screaming—anything and everything I can do, I do it.

I ignore my ribs that scream at me in agony and my head that pounds harder with every breath and all the burns and bruises that litter my body. I ignore everything except my one goal: survive.

"Calm down, Alaina." Rage colors Sean's words, belying his plea for me to calm down.

My fingertips graze the stake. And if I were the kind of woman who believed in miracles, I would be thanking whoever is looking out for me.

Through the grace of some divine intervention, I roll the stake toward me enough to grab it at the same moment he leans back. I scramble and roll over as I try to get out from under him when I hear the distinctive click of the safety on a gun.

I still my movements, slowly peer over my shoulder, and come face to face with a gun. A third explosion happens, this one sounds closer to us, and a bead of something wet trickles down the side of my face—I'm not sure if it's sweat or blood.

"I don't want to hurt you, Alaina. I don't understand why you'd want to hurt me?" Sean brings the handgun to tap the side of his face that I hit. "Now, I don't want to knock you out, but we have to go. So, I'm going to get up, and you're going to come with me. Okay?"

The earnestness in his voice freaks me out more than the gun in my face. Okay, that's not exactly true. But staring down the barrel of a gun a foot away from my face is as close to a mental breakdown as I've ever experienced.

In that moment, something unexplainable happens. Flashes of all the what-have-been and what-could-be moments of my life superimpose the scene in front of me.

All the late nights singing and laughing with my cousins. Traveling the world with them and my aunt.

Exploring what I know in my bones would've been life-changing experiences with Rush, Sully, and Wolf.

My dad's kind smile and the way his eyes crinkled in the corner when he laughed.

And my mom—god, the chance to connect with my mom flashes before my eyes.

Bits and pieces of my very soul fracture and fall away, leaving nothing more than a cold determination behind.

I no longer feel like myself.

I feel like some stripped-down version of humanity. The need to survive beats at me with every thump of my heart.

I keep my face carefully blank as I slowly nod. Sean pushes to his feet, but he doesn't go far as he loosely aims the gun at me.

Using my grip on the stake, I push up off the floor, keeping my gaze down. "Oh ow!" The words are high-pitched and believable when I let my arm give out, so I slump back to the ground.

"See? Now you went and hurt yourself," Sean says as he shuffles closer to me. He sets the gun on the floor beside my head and wraps one hand around my bicep and the other around my shoulder. "Alright, let me help you."

Sean starts to lift me off the floor, and before I get too far, I snatch the gun with one hand, bring it close to my chest, and wrench my body around to face him. Sean drops me, and my back crashes into the unforgiving floor, but I don't let that stop me.

I raise the gun up and fire.

Once.

Twice.

Three times.

It takes me a moment to realize that I'm screaming and shaking and crying. My ears are ringing again, and my hands won't stop shaking. Sean staggers back a step, his movements in slow motion as he brings a hand to his bleeding abdomen, disbelief written all over his face.

"I'm sorry," I cry. "I'm sorry, I'm sorry, I'm sorry." Using my feet, I push myself backward as he takes more staggering steps toward me.

He reaches for me with blood dripping from his hands, betrayal I don't understand etched in his face. Sean crashes to his knees, the sound whipping through the air like thunder. He falls forward, half landing on me and clutching my legs like the lifeline I am not.

I'm not his lifeline.

I'm his grim reaper.

After a moment, he stills, but the feeling of his lifeblood coating my legs is enough to make me dry heave. I push at him, but from this angle, it takes me more than a few tries to untangle his arms from around my legs and roll him off me. By the time I'm done, I'm sweating and shaking, but I'm not crying anymore.

I sniff and wipe my nose along my forearm, one of the few places that's not bloody, bruised, or dirty.

And then I hear footsteps in the hall. With an ease I'm sure I'm going to need therapy for, I lock everything down and raise the gun at the door.

6

RUSH

WITH THE TAUNTING melody of "Reach Out I'll Be There" playing on repeat in my head, I go through the motions of double-checking my weapons and kevlar vest for the third time.

The air is thick with anticipation, only the sounds of the woods as our companions. A half mile away, on the other side of these woods, lies ten small cabins. They're owned by a woman named Nancy Lowell, but they were recently rented by a group of bloodied men carrying exactly one unconscious girl.

The woman who checked them in, gave them their keys and then called Diesel, VP of the Blue Knights. Turns out, Nancy's Diesel's aunt. A stroke of luck in our favor. I've never been more thankful for my social butterfly of a brother who's been spending every Friday night at the Blue Knights's clubhouse for the last year and subsequently befriending their VP.

Diesel granted us the favor and went to the scene of the van fire. I watched as he video called us to show us the wreckage. My gut still churns at the image of the shell of the van, the interior almost entirely burned-out. It's imbedded in my brain, and I'm not sure I'll ever get it out. I keep picturing Alaina there—her lifeless body barely recognizable as it lies on the ground.

We don't know what happened exactly, but by Diesel's best guess, the driver lost control of the vehicle and crashed into a pole alongside the road.

I shake the details from my mind and focus on the task at hand. Wolf and Sully move to stand on either side of me with the rest of our team scattered around the perimeter—all of us stationed a half mile out. There's no way I'm letting those slimy fuckers escape my grasp because they hid out in the woods somewhere.

"One?" Wolf's words are soft in the still of the night air. It's been twenty-three hours and fourteen minutes since she was taken from O'Malley's—taken from *us*.

We made the decision to wait until dusk at the earliest to move on the cabins. During the summer months, it doesn't get dark until close to nine p.m., and we can't risk getting spotted. If one of those pricks gets a look at us slinking through the woods strapped with enough guns and ammunition to take out a city, they might panic and do something I can't fix.

So for the last three hours, that's exactly what we did. We waited.

And slowly, methodically lost our minds. Wolf was first to go, then Sully, and finally, me. I felt like my skin was crawling and the only way to distract myself from spiraling into the what-ifs was to plan.

I planned out all the excruciating ways I'm going to torture whoever took my little bird, and I'm going to fucking enjoy it.

"Aye. Invite one home for the holidays." *Take one to the carriage house.* "And have the boys take the rest for donuts tonight." *And have the boys clean up and dispose of the bodies.*

What started out as a fun way to talk in code with my brothers when my da's friends were around has turned into a

46

valuable tool between the three of us. It sounds like nonsense to anyone within earshot, but both of them know I just gave the order to bring one back home for information and the rest of the team will clean up our mess.

And make no mistake, we will be making a very big mess tonight.

I plan to redecorate these cabins in shades of crimson.

"Ready for this? Thirty seconds until go-time." Sully glances at his watch. We synchronized our watches hours ago on the drive here. In a situation like this, timing is everything. Ten seconds doesn't seem like a lot of time, but it's an eternity when you're staging an ambush and rescue.

I inhale deeply and taste rage on the back of my tongue. It's a violent combination from the three of us. "Aye. Let's bring our girl home, brothers."

"And kill everyone in our way," Wolf says, a feral grin lighting his features.

"Every. single. one," Sully says as he takes a step forward.

It's showtime.

We make our way through the forest at a steady but cautious pace. Wolf jumps over a fallen tree truck and a flashback slams into my head so swiftly, I grunt with the impact.

Sweat rolls down my neck, and a mosquito buzzes around my ear. My brothers and I wade through the overgrown piece of land in Brooklyn's industrial park.

Buzz, our resident tech guy, said the warehouse 100 feet in front of us has our shit. Considering I've been running circles around him in tech the last few months, I'm not too confident in Buzz's skills.

"That motherfucker better be right about this," I grumble.

"Face it, brother, Buzz found our shit before you did." Wolf flashes me a condescending smirk.

I give Wolf the bird. "Fuck that—"

The first notes of some song pierce the air. Wolf spins and jumps over a rotted log to land right next to our brother, Sully.

"What the fuck, dude?! Turn that shit off before you get us killed!" Wolf hisses and glances from left to right.

"Shit. Sorry." Sully holds the power button down.

Something in the air shifts, and my heart skips a beat. Dread slithers inside my veins, and my fingers start to tingle. I stop walking, and Sully walks right into me with a grunt.

"Something's not right."

Sully rubs his nose as he looks to the left, and then to the right. "What do you mean?"

"I mean, why is it so quiet?" My voice is quiet.

Wolf step next to Sully with a scoff. "Look around you, man. We're sneaking around in these shitty woods at eight o'clock on a Friday."

"Exactly. Where the fuck is all the noise? I don't hear a single goddamn cricket or branch moving." I look over my shoulder to glare at him.

"No shit, man. We don't want them *to hear us." Wolf's eyes widen. "What's up with you?"*

Sully slowly turns in a circle. "He's right, Wolf. It's too quiet."

I tilt my head. "Do you guys hear that?"

"Wha—"

"Shh!" Wolf takes a step forward and cock my head.

"Is that . . . buzz—" I tilt my head to the side to listen.

"It sounds like . . . ticking?" Wolf interrupts me.

"Why the fuck—"

"That's ticking!" Wolf yells, interrupting Sully.

My pulse thunders, and my adrenaline soars.

"We gotta get the fuck outta here!" Wolf yells, grabbing Sully and I by the shoulders and encouraging us to run.

I pull out my phone as I jump over a fallen tree and call my da. "It's a fucking trap! Get back! Get back, Da!"

"What? Where are you, boyo?" Da yells into the phone. My heartbeat roars in my ears, drowning out anything he's saying. I end the call and

maneuver around some broken metal, glancing to the side to make sure my brothers are still with me.

Today is not the day we die. And god help the rats who laid this trap. They're going to beg for death by the time we're done with them.

We're halfway back before the ticking stops.

And then the world as we knew it explodes.

"Rush? What's wrong?"

Sully's words snap me out of the flashback and I notice he's several paces in front of me. I shake my head to rid the lasting images of my brothers flying through the air with a building on fire as their backdrop. "Nothing."

"Then let's go, man. We're wasting time." Sully looks at me with an eyebrow raised and a scowl on his face.

I jog to catch up to him and Wolf, and we resume our pace. We've been walking for ten minutes, so we should see the furthest cabin on the property any moment.

An explosion cracks in the night air, and we all still our movements. The hair on the back of my arms stands to attention as I survey the surrounding woods. I don't feel eyes on me, and I've honed my instincts for just this sort of reason.

"There," Wolf whispers as he points ahead and to the right. I follow the direction of his finger and see the corner of a one-story cabin with two others right next to it. None of them are on fire, though.

We follow Wolf's lead and all head toward the cabins. I draw my gun and flick off the safety. Without a word, the three of us fan out to a cabin each. I head toward the cabin right in front of us, Sully takes the one to the right, and Wolf takes the one to the left. I don't see the rest of the guys we brought with us, but I'm not surprised. There's a reason we chose them for this.

With my back to the exterior, I inch along the wall until I reach the corner of the front of the house. I peek from behind the corner and see a small porch. I take a breath to center myself before I spin around the corner, my back still tucked against the wall and my gun raised in front of me.

A second explosion paints the summer air with thunder, and this time, I see it—flames engulf one of the cabins in the distance. Fear slithers inside my veins and urgency pounds at my temples.

Three quick steps, and I'm next to a window. I pull my arms in without letting go of the gun and tilt my head toward the window to peer inside. The drapes are drawn all but a crack, and I see the glow of a lamp. I'm on the other side of the window in one quick movement, stepping up the two steps until I'm next to the front door. I grab the doorknob with one hand and pause to listen for movement either inside the cabin or from Wolf or Sully. The crackling of the cabins burning is loud enough to cover up the other sounds. My nerves are dancing with urgency, but rushing protocol won't help anyone if I'm dead. Once I'm satisfied with the silence, I carefully twist the doorknob and the door opens without a sound.

I pause for any reaction, and that's when I hear it—sniffling.

My instincts roar, drowning out any rational thought as I fling the door open. It hits the wall hard enough to dent it, but I don't even give it or the sound it created a second thought. I spare one glance into the living room and kitchen in this studio cabin and sprint down the short hallway to what I assume are bedrooms.

Soft grunts and thumps fill my ears, and my mind short-circuits.

I don't think. I act.

I lift up a booted foot and plant it in the center of the cheap, flimsy door. The door breaks under the pressure of my boot, but it doesn't open. I pull my foot out of the hole I made and lean toward it.

It doesn't matter what I find in this room, it won't change the way I feel about my little bird. But I don't want this for her. I don't want this experience to reshape her into something I can't fix. I'm fearful of the impact on her soul.

I'll raze the entire world to spare her a second of pain.

Nothing could have prepared me for the image I find as I peer inside the hole.

"Birdie." Her name leaves my lips on an exhale.

She aims a gun at me, and if I wasn't being crushed under my need to get to her, I'd praise her. Her gaze flies to mine, but it's empty of Alaina. Her torn, dirty birthday dress, red hair wildly framing her face, tear tracks down her cheeks, leaving streaks of black mascara in their wake. Someone has broken my little bird, and that fractures something inside of me. Something I didn't realize I was capable of.

I reach my hand inside the hole and grab the doorknob to unlock it. When I don't feel the locking mechanism, I glance down. My jaw clenches when I see the lock is on the *outside* of the door. What the fuck kind of sick place only locks the bedrooms doors from the outside?

I flick the lock and push the door, but I meet resistance. I flick a glance toward Alaina and see that she hasn't moved an inch, but her eyes follow my movement.

When I push against the door again, I watch her gaze flick toward the floor and then back up to me. I push one more time from the bottom half and finally it opens a little. From there, I wedge my boot inside and leverage the door open and push whatever has been blocking it.

Finally, the door is open enough for me to slide through. I'm not surprised to see a body. I give him exactly two seconds, just enough to note that I don't recognize him, his pants are still buttoned, and he's covered in blood.

I fix my gaze on the creature in front of me. She white-knuckles an unfamiliar gun—the dead guy's gun if I had to guess.

I tamp down my inner beast that preens at what looks like a pencil sticking out of his leg.

Now is not the time to praise our little bird for her pencil stabbing skills, I reason.

Blood spatters cover her body, some dry and others still wet—fresh, and her whole body trembles, but still, she's silent.

I step closer to her, and she flinches. The action is enough to pierce another piece of my soul.

If I would've protected her better, she wouldn't even be in this situation to begin with. I'm to blame.

Well, and whoever the fuck that motherfucker is behind me, but that's for another time.

"C'mere, little bird. You're safe now. It's me." I hold out one hand toward her.

Alaina tilts her head to the left, fresh tears trailing down her cheeks. "Declan?"

Relief swamps me, and my shoulders sag. "I'm here, birdie."

A sob wracks her body, and she drops the gun to the floor without a thought. I have half a second to brace myself before she takes two steps and launches herself into my arms. "Oh my god, Rush!" Her arms wrap around my neck and squeeze. "I can't believe you're here."

I wrap my arms around her and pull her closer to me. "Of course, I'm here." I pull back and tuck some of her unruly hair off her face, so I can look into those soulful eyes of her. "I'll always find you." She blinks and another tear trails down her cheek.

"Do you promise?" Her voice is quiet, but her eyes are loud. They're bright and shining with something more than tears. Relief, maybe. Or gratitude.

"Aye. I promise. I'll go to the ends of the earth for you, Alaina."

She pushes up on her toes and presses her soft lips to mine. It takes every ounce of control I have not to push her against the wall and take what she unknowingly offers me. I lick the corner of her mouth, the taste of her blood somehow ramps up my desire.

I pull back when I hear the faint sound of footsteps. And while I recognize Wolf's gait, I don't take any chances when it comes to her. I pull my gun out, tuck Alaina behind me, and aim at the doorway. The idea of being a sitting duck in the middle of this room doesn't sit well with me, but I'm out of time and options.

Wolf glances into the room from the hallway, and I release a breath.

"We're in here, brother."

Wolf slides in the room at the same time Alaina steps out from behind me.

I reason with myself that it's a good thing that the lines on Wolf's face smooth out a little when sees her. That a weight visibly lifts off of his shoulders. It gives me hope that he's not lost —that Conor is still lurking beneath the rage and violence.

It's a delicate balance that we all learned to master too early in this life. There was never a question of if we'd join ranks—the Brotherhood is woven into my DNA going back generations. And Sully and Wolf are my true brothers in every sense of the word. There is no one walking this Earth that I trust more to have my back.

One day, that number will increase by one. One day soon.

I watch the way the object of my affection throws herself into my brother's arms. Something tugs painfully inside my chest when she sobs against him. Wolf folds her against his body, practically wrapping himself around her and tucks his head into that wild mass of waves at her neck.

I hear him murmur something too low for me to hear against her neck, but she tightens her hold on him. After a moment, she pulls back from him and looks over her shoulder at me.

I meet her gaze, and even though I know she's not ready for everything I have to give her, I can't mask my obsession. Not when I'm struggling for control. The thought of what could've happened in this shitbox is enough to send me into an early grave.

"How many in your cabin?" I ask my brother in an effort to turn my thoughts in another direction.

He looks at me over her shoulder, but doesn't step back or remove his arms. "Two. How many here?"

"Just this one," I say with a nod to the guy behind him.

Wolf glances at the body and whistles. "What happened?"

I nod my head toward Alaina, and Wolf's eyebrows hit his hairline. "We can figure that out later. Let's find Sully and the others."

"Aye. Let's get Red home."

7

ALAINA

WITH HIS HAND firmly clasped in mine, Wolf leads me out of the room and through the small cabin. I look over my shoulder no less than three times at Sean's prone form. On my fourth attempt, Rush steps in closely behind me and blocks my view.

"No more, Birdie." His voice is low as he speaks the words softly.

I feel the heat of him hit my back a second later, and something inside me settles. I glance at Rush's eyes as I place my trust in Wolf to guide me out of the cabin safely. As soon as we cross the threshold and into the summer air, another explosion lights up the sky and shakes the dirt beneath our feet. A flock of birds takes flight from a nearby tree, squeaking their displeasure.

"Rush," Wolf grits out through clenched teeth.

"Stay with her. I'll find him." Rush brushes his hand along the small of my back as he steps around us and heads toward the nearest cabin on our left.

I wrap my free hand around Wolf's arm and press my body close to his. A fifth explosion comes from the right, this one the loudest of them all. I flinch but don't say a word. I'm not sure that I'm capable of speech right now. I don't even know what I would say if I was.

"God-fucking-damnit," Wolf curses as he digs his phone out of his pocket. He punches in a few numbers and mumbles, "Pick up, pick up." Someone must pick up because a moment later, he exhales. "Oh, thank fuck. Where are you? By my count, that's five explosions—and there are only ten cabins. Our odds are not good." He pauses. "We got what we came for." Wolf squeezes my hand. "If you didn't find anyone by now, then just get the fuck outta there. We'll talk at our next rendezvous."

Without a goodbye, Wolf ends the call and pockets his phone. He taps his leg with his fingers, a fast, frantic beat. He glances at me, a quick scan across my face, and whatever he sees there has a curse slipping past his lips.

I absentmindedly wonder if his lips will feel different against mine. His hand clasped in mine feels the same—but more. It's a curious thing, really. His hand feels warm and comforting wrapped around my smaller hand, which sounds good in theory. I mean, it is good. But I don't feel good. I don't feel warm and comforted.

I feel cold and raw, as if everything I thought I knew about the world has been ripped away like tissue paper, leaving the real world in all its violent, burning glory on display. The layers of humanity I naively placed on every person I met have been peeled back to reveal the beasts we all are on the inside.

It's both enlightening and disheartening to realize that at the core of our beings, we're no better than animals fighting for survival.

I'm no exception. The events of this evening have taught me as much.

And now, as I stand here with the curtain peeled back, every-thing seems sharper and louder. A minute later, and everything feels like it's underwater. I'm struggling to connect who I was before this day to who I am now.

Because they are not the same person—I have been irrevocably changed.

And I don't know what to do or how to act now. How does one act after they fought for their life—and won?

I'm lost in my philosophical musings when another explosion lights up the sky. On reflex, I turn toward the noise. Rush and Sully sprint toward us, backlit by the bright-orange flames consuming another cabin.

"Anyone else?" Wolf yells.

"No. The rest of our boys have pulled out. Let's move," Rush yells as he closes the distance to us.

My gaze bounces from Rush to Sully, and my heart pounds in anticipation. I'm relieved to see them both relatively unharmed. My gaze finds Sully's and I can't look away. His lips part and he mutters what sounds like a curse.

They reach us and Sully pauses in front of me. I don't realize that I'm reaching toward him until he takes a step closer to me, and my hand brushes against his shoulder. I smooth my hand up and curl it over his shoulder, using it as leverage to bring him closer to me. With one hand still holding onto Wolf's hand, I lean into Sully. My face still fits perfectly in the space between his neck and his shoulder.

"James." A hitch in my breath interrupts his name, and he wraps both arms around me.

His kevlar vest presses into me, his shoulder holster and gun dig into my shoulder. But I don't let go. I don't think I'll ever let go of him.

Of any of them.

Sully pulls back and smooths some of my hair off my face. His gaze bounces around my face as he cups my cheeks. Tears well in my eyes as I finally—*finally*—see him. A tiny crack in his armor shows me the James that I met years ago. The James that I fell in love with—the James that I'm pretty sure I'm *still* in love with.

He rests his forehead against mine, his minty breath feathering across my lips as he exhales.

"Princess." His nickname for me sounds like a tortured prayer leaving his lips.

I can't stop my body's instinct, and I tip my chin up and my lips graze his. It's the barest of touches, but it's enough.

Sully freezes at the contact, every muscle in his body going taut. His grip on my face turns to stone, but I don't stop looking into his eyes. I'm desperate to hold on to any scraps of my James before he turns back into this newer version of him—the one that despises me.

I watch the transition happen. In two blinks of his long inky lashes, all traces of the boy I knew are gone, and instead, I'm staring into the soul of one of the members of the Brotherhood.

I feel Rush's heat at my back two seconds before I hear him. "Can you walk on your own, birdie?" Although his tone is low, I feel the underlying urgency in his words. Wordlessly, I nod and I feel his hand on my lower back, encouraging me to move. "It's about a half-mile walk through the woods."

"Okay, Rush," I murmur.

"Eyes up, brothers. We still don't have the full picture," Rush commands as he takes his gun out of his shoulder holster and scans the surrounding woods.

Wolf and Sully follow his lead, each taking their guns out, fingers patiently waiting. All three of them swivel their gazes around us, but I can't take my eyes off of them.

My three white knights in shining armor.

No. That's not right.

Strapped with more weapons than I've ever seen on a single person—let alone three—they're not content to live within the restrictive lines society has drawn. They're prepared to leap over those lines—for *me*. No, they're not my white knights. They're my dark kings. Gods in their own right—all of them.

An unfamiliar thrill buzzes in my veins at the thought.

A nearby cabin sizzles and pops before the huge oak tree next to it catches on fire. The leaves go up in seconds before the branches hiss and blacken. A second later, the tree next to it goes up in flames, and even though sadness fills me at the thought of this beautiful forest burning, self-preservation kicks in —hard.

"Oh fuck," Wolf curses. "We gotta move or we're going to be trapped in here. Now!" He spins on his heel and starts to run back toward the cabin I was in—the cabin with a dead man in one of the—I shut that thought down and focus on putting one foot in front of the other.

It's ten steps until we're out of the clearing and back in the little front yard of the cabin I was in. With Rush at my back, Wolf next to me, and Sully in front of me, I feel the most protected that I've ever felt. But nothing stops the bone-chilling fear that slithers down my spine when I sprint past the window to the room I was in.

A shudder works its way over my body, starting at my head and moving all the way down to my toes. I squeeze Wolf's hand on reflex, and he turns to look at me over his shoulder.

"Okay, Red?" Wolf spares me a single glance before he returns his gaze forward. When I don't answer, he squeezes my hand.

I glance at him to answer, but before I do, I trip and fall. Before I can hit the ground, Rush's arms wrap around my waist. He holds me for a second, his face in the back of my hair, before he rights me on my feet.

"You're alright, birdie," Rush whispers against my neck.

I nod my head a few times and will my legs to move and my

mind to empty of everything except for moving my legs one in front of the other.

After the third time I trip, Rush growls and grabs me around the waist again to stop my fall. In one swift movement, he switches his hold to have one arm under my knees and the other around my back, so he's carrying me bridal style.

"Oh." The word comes out on a squeak as the blood rushes to my head. I wrap my arms around his neck and stare at his face, but he faces forward.

I feel his chest rise as he inhales, and then he barks, "Keep moving."

We follow the barely noticeable trail until we come to another clearing. It's a small gravel parking lot, and I see one black SUV parked in the middle under the lone street light.

It's only been a few minutes, but I can't keep my eyes off of Rush. His profile looks like it should be carved in some ancient Roman ruins.

His sharp jawline and proud nose. Like his brothers, he has a bump along the bridge—likely from a previous break—that my fingers itch to trace. Threads of auburn catch the light in his chestnut-brown hair, and I desperately want to feel it against my fingers.

Wolf opens the back passenger door and climbs inside, and Rush places me in the open backseat next to Wolf with more care than I might've used in such a time-sensitive situation.

My body feels liquid and pliable as he maneuvers me into the backseat, and still, I can't pull my gaze. As he buckles my seatbelt—something I normally would protest someone doing for me—I reach a hand up to brush along his jawline. It's scratchy and smooth, more than stubble but not quite a beard. I trace one finger along his jawline, and he stills and flicks his gaze to mine.

"Time to go, little bird," he murmurs.

I drop my hand to the collar of his black tee, right above his vest, and curl my fingers around the fabric.

"Don't go," I plead with him. I feel the panic unfurling low in my belly at the thought of him leaving me now.

He places one tattooed hand over mine on his collar, but doesn't remove it, just gently squeezes. "I'm not leaving you. Ever."

The conviction in his words sends spikes of relief through my bloodstream. I nod my head a few times, but I'm not ready to let go of him. I'm not sure that I'll ever be ready.

I feel a hand on my other arm, and a glance over my shoulder shows Wolf staring at me, brow furrowed.

Fuck.

I can't explain it exactly, except that I feel this need to keep him—all of them—close. It beats incessantly underneath my skin.

"C'mere, baby girl," Wolf murmurs as he tilts his head toward his side of the car.

I turn to search Rush's eyes, seeing sincerity shining in them before I nod once and uncurl my fingers from his shirt. I take a moment to smooth the fabric, and he drops his hand from mine. Rush leans in and sweeps his lips across my cheek and lingers on my lips for a moment. My eyes flutter closed without thought, and I feel myself sway toward him.

As soon as it starts, it ends. I open my eyes and blink a few times to clear my vision. Rush closes my door and rounds the front of the car to get in the driver's seat. It's then that I notice Sully's in the passenger seat talking on the phone. His voice is low enough and I'm distracted enough that I can't make out any words.

Wolf shuffles toward me and wraps his arm around my shoulders.

"You're alright, Red. We've got you," Wolf assures me. His

63

voice soothes some of the raw aching in my soul, and my eyelids droop.

I fight the hold that sleep is trying to take out on me, but after my head dips and eyelids close a few times, I lose that fight.

It's probably the only fight I don't mind losing tonight. I know that my dark kings will protect me.

I turn my head into Wolf's chest, and he places a few chaste kisses on the top of my head, murmuring something too low for me to hear.

Surrounded by them, I let myself rest.

8

RUSH

SULLY ENDS his phone call and tosses his phone in the cup holder in the middle console. He exhales, though the scowl doesn't quite leave his face. "He'll do it. But he said it'll be double our usual fee."

"Double?" My eyebrow quirks, and I flick another glance in the rearview mirror to check on my little bird. She's curled into Wolf's chest with her eyes closed. Good. She needs the rest. Tiny embers of jealousy swirl in my gut—I want to be the one to comfort her right now. It was my job to protect her, and I failed. But I did find her. That has to count for something, *right*?

I douse those embers with truth, enough that they flicker and steam out. I know that this is the plan. I just have to stick to the plan.

Now that Wolf's on board, all that stands in my way is Sully. I glance at my brother and notice his clenched jaw and curled fist as he stares out the window. Tension lines every muscle in his body, and I just know that whether or not he's ready to admit it— he loves her.

Which is good.

It is good, I tell myself, even if some parts of it feel like someone stuck a hot poker in my gut. I knew it wasn't going to be easy at first—sharing a woman like this. Sharing a woman for one night is one thing, but sharing a woman for the rest of our lives is something else altogether. We're three possessive alpha assholes, and we've been trained to be the best, so I knew that it wouldn't be as easy as dropping her in our universe and saying "play nice." But I didn't expect this—any of this.

I didn't anticipate the juxtaposition that is Alaina.

She sings in front of a crowd every week, but she took a year to walk up to me.

I didn't expect her laugh or the way she fiercely loves her cousins. I didn't expect her to charm Wolf so innocently and easily or for her to be the one that broke Sully's heart all those years ago.

I have a suspicion that she's going to surprise me at every turn.

I exhale through my nose, and any lingering jealousy leaves me. If it can't be me that offers her comfort right now, then I'm happy it's one of my brothers.

"Aye, double. He said double *and* a favor," Sully says with a growl in his voice.

"Mm, someone's getting greedy. And we're sure Doc can't meet us?" I sigh, trying to get the adrenaline to level out.

"Aye. He's caught up on vacation down the coast," Sully says as he taps his foot on the floor. "Fucker hasn't taken a vacation in ten years, and he chooses this week of all weeks to go?"

I feel my brows furrow as I slot this piece of information into the big puzzle. "Did Da okay it?"

"Dunno. Doc said he did, but since service is spotty where Da is, I can't confirm." Sully clenches his jaw, and I know he's thinking the same thing we all are. He should be home for this.

"For as much as we pay him, Doc should run when we call. I

don't give a fuck where he is," I grumble. Using a new person is always a gamble, and lately, I'm not feeling very lucky—or charitable, but I don't need to tell Sully that. I'm sure he already knows. "What's your take on the guy? Should we change our meet-up to somewhere further away from the safe house?"

"Depends. How trusting are you feeling?" Sully pauses. "Enough to risk her?" He jerks his head toward the backseat. "Because we don't really know jack shit about him."

I glance at her in the rearview mirror again. She looks like a fallen angel—covered in dirt, scratches, and blood. There's no way she realizes her own ferociousness. Not yet. But she will—one day soon.

I'd already made a silent vow to her, to my brothers, to *myself*, that I'd make her one of us.

She doesn't realize that she wears her fierceness like a soft leather jacket.

"Doc's been on our payroll for at least twenty years. If he wanted to bury us, he's had plenty of opportunity to do it before now. And if he vouches for this guy—"

"Sam," Sully interjects.

"For Sam, if you asked me last week, I'd say sure. But today? Nah, today I'm not feeling very trusting. Move it to somewhere totally random and a couple hours away."

Sully shrugs—this forced, rigid movement that looks more uncomfortable than nonchalant. "Sure. It's up to you, brother. It doesn't matter much to me either way."

"Shut the fuck up with that bullshit, man," Wolf snaps from the backseat.

Sully stiffens and whips his head to face Wolf. "Fuck you, man. This doesn't change shit between us." He gestures between himself and Alaina. "I came for you guys, because we're brothers."

"Aye, we're fucking brothers. So you best remember that next

PENELOPE BLACK

time you try that bullshit again, clear?" Wolf's tone is hard, unyielding.

He's not wrong. Despite Sully's loud protest to our little birdie, he's been amped up since her kidnapping. I decide not to bring up the fact that he had to be pulled off not one but two guys in the basement of the carriage house earlier today.

"Alright, Wolf," Sully grits out between clenched teeth. It sounds a lot more like *fuck you, Wolf.*

I glance at Wolf in the mirror, his jaw clenches, and his glare would make lesser men piss themselves. Sully weathers the glare like only a brother could. That's their shit they're going to have to sort out. No one said this would be easy. But we're brothers, and we're more than just blood.

Ten silent minutes later, I clear my throat. "Okay. So we're going to use this backup guy then. Tell him to meet us at—fuck, where are we again?"

"Fuck if I know. Some unincorporated town. I'll find some-place we can meet about eighty miles west of the safe house," Sully says as he opens his phone and pulls up the GPS app.

I nod at Sully, then quickly meet Wolf's eyes in the mirror. "How's our girl?"

Wolf sighs and softly runs his hand over her matted, blood-crusted hair. "I don't know, man—I just . . . there's a lot of blood and—"

Sully whips his head around to glare at the backseat in general. "What do you mean there's a lot of blood?"

"I mean, dickhead, that she's covered in blood, and I can't tell if it's hers or that motherfucker from the cabin," Wolf all but growls at Sully.

"We're going to have to talk about everything that went down. Get her side of things," Sully says, eyebrows pinched.

"What happened to 'it doesn't matter to me'?" Wolf mocks.

70

Sully whips around in his seat, a scowl painting his face. "Are you fucking kidding—"

"Enough," I say with a sigh. "Getting back on track. I'm willing to bet that most of it is not hers. But she still needs to get checked out. She's got some serious lacerations, and I'm sure she has a concussion."

"We're meeting Samuel at the Wolfpack Lodge," Sully says as he faces the front again and scrolls on his phone. "It's the closest hotel where we can get some privacy and still have several exit strategies in case things go sideways. Again."

"Any intel on the people who did this?" I ask as I merge into heavier traffic.

"Nah, not yet. Our boys didn't see much before the explosions started, so even if there was any evidence, it's long gone by now," Sully says as he types on his phone. "Checked-in. Now we don't have to carry her through the lobby and risk any good Samaritan calling the cops on us." He turns to face me. "Hear back from your guy yet?"

I shake my head. "Not yet. But we'll get something soon. Of that, I'm sure."

"And you're sure we can trust him?"

We've had more than our fair share of bullshit lately. If I didn't have my brothers, I don't know what I'd do. We've all been given a healthy dose of paranoia—it's a necessary evil in our lives—but ever since our brothers turned rat two years ago, it's been at an all-time high. Every waking minute.

Fuck, I'm even doubting my own da these days. Which reminds me . . . "Neither of you heard from Da?"

Sully cuts his gaze toward me, his face hard. "What do you mean? I thought he was on his way home? Didn't he call you when he landed like usual?"

I shake my head and try to control my swirling thoughts. "I'm not sure if I can add another fucking stress to this day—wait. What day is it?"

"Almost Sunday." Wolf's voice is low, but after a glance at my little bird, I doubt she'd wake up if we yelled. She's totally out.

I sigh and run a hand over my face, feeling my stubble scrape against my hands. "Fuck. I haven't slept in over twenty-four hours." I pause. "But no, I haven't spoken to Da. And I haven't forgotten everything that happened before O'Malley's." I sigh and stare at the endless road in front of me. There's not a lot of traffic here—at least not at this time of night. "But let's proceed with caution. I still don't trust him."

"We're not going to a Brotherhood safe house then?" There's no question in his tone.

"Aye. We're going to *our* safe house. We're going to Golden Oak," I confirm. We named our property Golden Oak as a nod to the way the surrounding oak trees turn in the fall.

The choice to go to the safe house that only the three of us have any knowledge about is a purposeful one. I don't know what game my da is playing at, but since he hasn't seen fit to include any of us, I'm inclined not to include him in our plans. My decision is only solidified by the fact that he hasn't reached out in days. It wouldn't be unusual if he were on a normal family reunion, but someone broke into Summer Knoll days ago. And we're at war.

There's no record of this property my brothers and I have anywhere—not a long-buried paper trail or anything electronic hidden under a shell company. We did a lot of the work ourselves over several years, and the stuff we couldn't do, we hired out and paid cash for.

After twenty minutes, I glance back at Alaina again. "She asleep?"

"Aye." She shifted during the drive, so now she's laying on

Wolf's lap and he's running the tips of his fingers along the exposed skin on her collarbone.

I nod and drum my fingers against the steering wheel.

"What the fuck is wrong with you? Pull over, and I'll drive."

I clear my throat to get their attention. "I'm fine to drive. And I'm calling the Kings. I don't know everything that we're up against, but I know it'd be smart to have them in our corner. Fuck, just having Ro help me would be reason enough." I sigh. "Buzz is good, but he's just one man. And my other contact has questionable morals on the best of days—and I'm not judging, but that means that I can't fully trust him. And I trust the Kings."

Neither of them speaks for a second.

"Fuck, we should've thought of that earlier," Wolf muses.

Sully lifts one shoulder up. "I don't see a problem with it."

I toss Sully my phone. "Call Maeve." We're in a rental car, and we plan on switching cars at least another two times before we hit our safe house, so I didn't bother pairing my phone.

The noise of the line ringing fills the interior as Sully puts the call on speakerphone.

"Rush Fitzgerald, to what do I owe the pleasure? It's been nearly a year since we last spoke. I'm crushed." Amusement colors her voice.

"Maeve." With one word, she hears the tone change. It's a tangible thing, and she's smart enough to recognize we're monsters masquerading as men.

"What do you need?" she asks, her voice low.

And that right there is why you simply can't buy loyalty. Friends for nearly fifteen years, and she's happy to jump in to help if I need it without asking for specifics.

"The boys are here too."

"Wolf, Sully. It's been a while," Maeve says.

They both murmur their hellos.

73

"We need your help." I'm too tired and wired for pleasantries.

"I heard that you lost something. Do you need help with that?"

"How the fuck did you hear that? It's been twenty-five hours!" Sully's mildly explosive disbelief hangs in the air.

Maeve chuckles. "My baby sister heard about it shortly after everything went down at O'Malley's. It was enough for me to piece together some info. If I'd known you were still looking for her, I would've hustled. I was just checking it out for fun."

"We found her, so no need to check the lost and found," I tell her as I take the exit lane to get off the highway.

"I also heard that you had a little housekeeping trouble," Maeve says.

"Aye. That's part of it." I scratch the stubble on my chin, my thoughts drift.

"I'm listening."

"There are some unknown players, and we could use some backup." I need time to reevaluate the board again—too many variables and too many pieces. "Soon. Maybe a week or two?"

"What about Papa Smurf?"

Wolf huffs a laugh and Sully smirks. "Calling the Butcher *Papa Smurf* was cute when you were eight, but I don't think you'll get the same response now."

Maeve's laughter filters through the air. "Yeah, yeah. That old man loves me." She pauses. "There's just one hiccup I have to deal with here, and then we'll be there."

"You good?" Sully asks as he looks at the phone.

"Nothing I can't handle, so don't you worry your pretty face about it, Sully. Just have to get out of the arranged marriage my father approved this morning—the old fuck."

Maeve delivers the news with such an easy tone that it takes me a moment to realize what she actually said. Before I can comment, she hangs up.

"Did she just say *arranged marriage*?" The disbelief in Sully's tone matches my own.

I rub my jaw while I try to work out if this little *hiccup* of Maeve's is going to impact us.

"At least Da didn't do that to us," Wolf grumbles.

"Aye. But that sneaky bastard hasn't returned yet, so who the fuck knows. He could be bringing us home three little Irish birdies." Sully sneers.

"Too bad we already have ourselves an Irish bird." No one says anything for a while. We're all content to sit in the silence as the dark, starry night eats up the dark-colored SUV.

9

RUSH

HOURS LATER, we're pulling up to a resort. I see a water park behind the hotel lit up like it's daytime and eyeball the crowds of people milling around. It must be a twenty-four-hour park. I follow Sully's instructions and park us around the other side of the hotel—the one furthest away from the water park—and pull into a spot right in front of what we think is our room.

There's a small balcony area with a sliding glass door facing the parking lot in every room, which is perfect. The less eyes we have on us, the better.

"Fancy meeting spot. We sure about this?" Wolf's voice is low.

"And busy."

"It was the only place remotely close to eighty miles west of the safe house. Do you really want her to get checked out in some black-light nightmare of a motel room?" I don't miss the bite in Sully's tone.

Neither of us say anything.

"Alright then. I'll go get the key." He gets out of the SUV and stretches his arms above his head.

I reach behind me to grab a zip-up black hoodie from the backseat and toss it to him. "Here."

He nods and puts it on, effectively covering up his full sleeves of tattoos. I have a feeling that we'd stand out in this family crowd, and the idea is to fly under the radar—not give everyone a hundred recognizable features. If I trusted this doc, I'd've picked a different location and spared us this bullshit.

I look over my shoulder and see Alaina still out cold on Wolf's lap.

"How is she?" I nod at her.

Wolf doesn't lift his gaze from the sleeping girl on his lap. She's been mostly out for the last few hours, and my throat constricts as worry crawls along my spine.

He doesn't answer me right away. "I don't want this to touch her ever again. Not like this, brother. Never like this," he murmurs as he sweeps a piece of hair off her forehead. "So we need to vote."

Wolf looks at me then, his gaze full of self-loathing and something else I'm not used to seeing in him—desperation. The emotion stills the words trying to come out of my mouth.

Everything inside me stops as thoughts swirl around too fast for me to grab them.

"Are you suggesting that we give her up?" I pause as I try to put into words the emotions battling inside me. I've experienced a lot of firsts in my life, but they've never been pure—not like she is. I look out the window and shake my head. "I can't do that, Con. I *won't* do it."

He scoffs, no doubt the use of his childhood nickname grating on his nerves. "You're a selfish asshole, Dec," he spits, but there's no real heat behind it.

I shrug, the movement at odds with the pounding of my heart, because I already know I'm a selfish asshole. I've never acted like I wasn't.

But this is different. It's less like I'm choosing her, more like I won't let her go. And it might be the most selfish thing I've ever done. But still, I can't stop myself from wanting to keep her.

But I have a fucking plan, goddamnit, and I'll see it through. In the end, it'll be the best thing for all of us, he'll see.

They'll all see.

We're quiet for a moment as we wait for Sully to open the sliding glass door to our room, the soft sound of Alaina's deep breaths the only noise in the car.

"I don't think I could let her go either." Wolf's voice is low, and I know it has more to do with him wrestling his demons than waking her up. "And don't think I forgot about your little bird caged in the city. There's no way I'll let you treat Red with that kind of disrespect. So, if you're serious about your little proposal from before"—he waves a hand around in the air—"all this, then we'll be having a chat soon."

Anger pricks my skin at the acid in his voice. I cut him some slack on his inability to connect the dots—it's been a long couple of days. I shift my gaze at the group of teenagers walking down the sidewalk, towels in hand. "And Sully?"

"Please," he scoffs. "He's not fooling anyone—except for maybe himself . . . and Red."

A smirk tips the corner of my mouth, but before I can respond, the man himself appears in the doorway of the room in front of us.

"There he is. Let's go—I'll grab her," I tell my brother as I turn off the car.

"Fuck off. I've got her. You just worry about getting the rest of our shit outta here," Wolf says as he holds open the door with his foot and bundles her in his arms.

I look around and grab the handful of our things. I get out of the car and leave the keys in the middle console. We have a friend of a friend coming to swap cars for us as soon as I give him the all-clear. He'll take this one and bring it to a local chop shop, and in its place will be another dark SUV.

I walk through the door to our room and close it behind me, pulling the shitty drape across it. Wolf laid Alaina on one of the two double beds, and one look at the bedspread has my lip curling.

"Are we sure that's sanitary? You know they never wash the bedspreads, and our girl has who knows how many open wounds." I cross my arms to stop them from fiddling with the stupid piece of fabric.

Sully takes two steps toward her before he stops himself. We may be at war with an unknown enemy, but he's at war with himself too.

Wolf shrugs. "For now, it's the best we got. Sully, when's the new doc coming?"

Sully checks his phone before stuffing it in his pocket again. "Ten minutes."

Seventeen minutes later, there's a knock on the door to the hallway of the hotel. I pull my gun from my shoulder holster that I never took off and move to stand just inside the bathroom. It's located to the left of the door and bathed in shadows, so whoever's at the door won't see me. It's the perfect—and only—place for any advantage.

Sully checks the peephole and Wolf stands in front of our girl, gun casually hanging from his hand.

Sully disengages the lock and opens the door, and a weaselly-looking fuck walks in the room.

"You're late, Doc." Sully's voice is unyielding.

A bead of sweat rolls down the side of his face and gets lost in his shirt collar. "Yes, well, I got caught up in traffic," he says as he walks further into the room. He pauses to stare at Wolf before looking around him to Alaina. "What happened to her?"

I step out of the shadows holding my gun aimed at him. I

walk until the barrel of my gun presses into his back. "I don't see how that's any of your business."

He stills.

Ah, so he does have some self-preservation, after all.

"And I don't appreciate having to wait," I tell him, holding the gun so it just presses into his skin. "Do you have any more questions?"

"N-no. I'll just treat what I can. But . . ."

"But what?" Wolf snaps.

"Well, it's just that I can't tell if this blood is hers, and without taking her dress—"

"Finish that sentence and it'll be the last thing you ever do," I growl in his ear as I click off the safety.

The doctor's gulp is audible. "Yes, yes, of course. I'll just look for open wounds."

He gets to work, and Wolf stands over him, watching his movements like a hawk. Tension lines every inch of his body, but he's not so wired that he's going to take the doc's head off prematurely.

I back off a little and stand next to Sully. "He's right, though. We should've brought clothes for her."

"Aye. That dress looks rough. I passed a gift shop in the lobby. I'll go see what I can get."

I lift an eyebrow. "At midnight?" I pull my attention away from Alaina long enough to see Sully shrug.

"I'll get . . . creative if I have to. But if their water park is still open, I'm betting their other shit is still open."

I nod my agreement. "Be careful, brother."

"Always," he says as he walks out the door.

I refocus on Alaina just in time to see her stir awake as the doc reaches inside his black duffle bag. Before I can even shout, Wolf has his arms wrenched behind his back.

"I was just getting her some pain medication. That's it—I swear!"

I walk toward them and pause next to him. Tilting my head, I let him see the monster inside me. Satisfaction rolls through me when he shudders.

"For a doctor, you sure are jumpy. Where do you practice again?"

Wolf tugs on his arms, and the doctor yelps. "St. Luke's Medical Center."

"Remind me never to go there," I tell my brother, quirking a smile.

"What's going on?" Alaina groans the words, stealing our attention. "Wolf? Rush?"

I walk around the bed until I'm standing next to her. I lean down and brush away some hair from her face, my gaze bouncing around her beautiful face. "We're here, baby. We're getting you checked out, okay?" My voice is low, meant only for her ears.

She holds my gaze as she nods. "You're not leaving, right?"

I hear the thread of panic in her voice, and I can't deny her this small comfort of my reassurance. Not after everything she's gone through because of us.

I slowly shake my head. "No, we're not leaving you."

She exhales, and I see some weight lifting from her shoulders. Her gaze bounces between my eyes. "Everything hurts, Rush."

I smooth back her hair with the palm of my hand. "I know, little bird, I know. Tell me where, okay? And we're going to get you taken care of."

I straighten and step back, but before I can get two steps away, she snakes her hand out and grasps mine, linking our fingers together.

I nod at her once before I turn to face the doctor—who's

arms are still pinned behind him. I'm not surprised to find Wolf staring at me, but I'm a little thrown by his knowing smirk.

I'm sure the smug dick thinks just because I showed a little compassion and humanity that I'll be all soft. Fuck that. Any softness I might've had was conditioned out of me years ago.

Until her.

She's reignited a part of me I thought I lost long ago. Unfortunately for her, it means she gets my undivided attention right now. That's a lot for anyone to handle—most don't.

I tap my fingers against my leg as Alaina details everywhere she's hurt, my blood pressure rising with every cut, injury, burn she points out. I'm itching to *do* something, but she never lets go of her grip on my hand, so I stay put.

Finally, after way too long, the good doctor peels off his blue rubber gloves and tucks them inside his duffle bag. He pulls out an orange prescription bottle and cranks off the white lid.

"Here. Take these for the pain. They're a little stronger than your average ibuprofen, but you should only need them for a few days," he says, tipping the bottle over and dumping a handful of pills in Wolf's hands.

"What the fuck kind of backwoods prescription is this?" Wolf yells, curling his fingers around the pills.

The doctor pales and his hand trembles, the pills rattling against the bottle. "I-I told you, I was running late. This was all I had with me."

"What is it?" Wolf enunciates each word, nostrils flaring.

"Just hydrocodone-acetaminophen."

"Why the fuck didn't you just say Vicodin?" Wolf flattens his lips, glare firmly fixed on the good doctor.

The doctor stumbles over his words as Sully comes back in the room with a bundle of clothes under his arm. He sets the clothes down and moves to stand next to the doc.

"Time to go, doc." Sully claps a hand on his shoulder and steers him toward the hotel door.

"Oh, okay. What about my payment?"

Sully chuckles. "It's already been wired to your account—the original amount. And if you fuck us, don't forget we know where you live, Samuel Barnes of 876 White Tail Court."

The doctor—Samuel—trips over his feet at the sound of his given name.

"Ah, did you really think we didn't know who you were, doc? C'mon, I know our reputation precedes us, so you should've known better." Cruelty drips from my words, a deadly promise in each one.

Samuel picks up the pace as he practically scuttles out of the room. Sully walks out with him to make sure he leaves without making a scene. Wolf and I help Alaina change out of her ruined dress and into the hotel-branded tee and leggings Sully bought at the gift shop.

All this time here makes me twitchy. I feel exposed and out of control—and I don't fucking like it.

"Rush?"

The sound of Alaina's drowsy voice snaps me out of my paranoia spiral. I turn to take her in. There wasn't anything I could do about her hair, but I ran a washcloth over her face. I got most of the blood and dirty smudges. I didn't want to press too hard—she was so covered in blood and scratches and dirt that it was hard to tell what was hers and what was *his*.

I want to resurrect him just so I can bring him down to the basement of the carriage house and kill him myself. Though judging by the way my brother hasn't gone more than two feet away from her, I'd have to fight my brother for the opportunity.

Like I said, though, I don't mind sharing.

10

ALAINA

I WAKE SLOWLY WITH A GROAN. My head is on something hard and scratchy, and my throat is on fire. I cough on instinct, and the hard surface moves, jostling my head. Another groan escapes me, and this one feels like it's reverberating in my head. I reach a hand up to the spot that's aching when warm fingers stop my progress.

"Open your eyes, baby girl."

I know that voice. I think I'd know that voice anywhere. My eyes feel like they're glued shut, and it takes me more than a couple of tries to open them. When I finally do, everything is fuzzy around the edges.

"Aye, there she is," Wolf murmurs as he runs his hand over my hair, smoothing it off my face. "Here, have a sip."

I turn my head to the side and see a straw poking out of a water bottle next to my face. I wrap my lips around the straw and practically inhale the entire bottle.

"It's the meds. It makes everyone thirsty."

I clear my throat and ask, "Where am I?"

Wolf's eyes are warm when he looks at me. "You're safe now

—I promise. Here, take these." He hands me two white pills. "We're taking you somewhere safe."

I swallow the pills with another drink of water before I register his words. Panic wells up inside me, swift and demanding. I clutch his t-shirt as nausea rolls through my body. "You're not leaving me, right?"

He strokes a hand down the side of my face, never taking his gaze off of me. "Never. Never again."

"Okay, good. Because I don't want you guys to leave me now . . ." My words trail off as my eyes get heavier and heavier, until finally, I don't bother opening them.

THE SOUND of crunching gravel and the repeated bounces of my head against something is enough to rouse me. I don't really remember falling asleep. Everything is kind of hazy, but I remember being in a hotel room and then Rush carried me to a car.

My head pounds and my body aches. I'm not sure how long I've been in this same position, but everything protests when I even think about moving.

Pop punk plays through the speakers, so I assume Sully is here too. That boy always did love pop punk from the aughts. The corner of my mouth ticks up when I remember how we used to share playlists.

I open my eyes with effort and use my hands to push up to a halfway sitting position, groaning when I feel something pull along my ribs. My mind races as I look around.

"Easy now, baby girl." Wolf's words come from above me, and it takes me a second to realize that I was lying on a pillow on his lap.

"Wolf?" My voice carries a thread of panic as I swipe my tangled hair out of my eyes and look around the dark car.

"Aye. I'm right here," Wolf says as he sweeps a stray lock of hair off my cheekbone.

Relief sinks into my limbs as my surroundings start to make more sense. I don't feel quite like myself—almost like I've been sleeping too long or not long enough. Everything feels foggy, and I'm struggling to stay awake even now. I look at Wolf, but the interior of the SUV snags my attention.

"Are we—are we in a different car?" My words end on a yawn that feels like it cracks my face in two.

"Aye. How are you feeling?" Wolf's hands glide down my back in long, soothing motions as I try to get my bearings.

How *am I* feeling?

Like one giant bruise. Like one giant, confused bruise.

"At least she still has her sense of humor." Rush's wry voice comes from the front seat, and I startle a little. I didn't realize I said that out loud.

"You're talking right now, Red." Amusement colors Wolf's voice as his hand makes another gentle sweep down my back.

My eyebrows pull in. "Huh."

"And so eloquent," Rush says with a chuckle.

"Oh wow. Oh, wow, wow, wow," I say. Hearing Rush laugh feels like a monumental thing—like a triple rainbow or getting your favorite latte for free. "Oh my god, an iced chai latte sounds *sooo* good right now." I lick my lips as I think about drinking my favorite drink. I'm so parched. I feel like I could drink an entire lake and *still* be thirsty.

"Red, look at me." Wolf's voice startles me out of my fantasy of having a chai latte lake in my backyard, and I open my eyes.

With one finger on my chin, he applies a little pressure and I turn my head to meet his gaze. My breath hitches when I stare into his eyes. I watch in fascination as they darken the longer he stares at me.

"Your eyes really are the color of espresso," I say with a sigh. The corners of his lips turn up and dimples wink at me. "Whoa," I breathe the word. "Your dimples are lethal," I tell Wolf as I sway a little closer.

"Well, at least we know the pain meds kicked in," Wolf says with a smirk, and Rush chuckles again.

Something about that sound settles into me, burrows into my bones. And it might be because I'm on some serious pain medication—I remember bits and pieces of some doctor patching up the worst of my injuries—or it might be because I just had a near-death experience. But I crave more of that feeling. Not the feeling of thinking I was going to die. The feeling of Wolf's voice sinking into my skin and settling into my very soul.

Sully's so quiet in the passenger seat that I didn't realize he was still in the car—not in my current state at least.

The car bounces along in silence for a few more minutes. Hamilton Leithauser's "In a Black Out" plays from the speakers. He sings about everything going away in a black out, and it feels like he's singing directly to me. My life has been forever changed. And it all started in a black out at O'Malley's.

And now, now nothing will ever be the same.

It just occurs to me that I have no idea where we are. And what's stranger is despite the last twenty-four hours, I'm not afraid to go anywhere with the three of them.

We pull up to a small guardhouse in front of a wrought-iron gate. I half expect a guard to stroll out of the small building, but everything is dark. Just as I open my mouth to ask where we are, Sully pushes open the door and jumps down from the SUV. He doesn't say anything as he rounds the hood of the car and heads toward the guardhouse. After entering some code embedded on the door, he opens it up. Thirty seconds later, and the gates unlock and roll open.

To my surprise, Sully doesn't get back in the car—he turns left and runs along the fence line. I quickly sit upright and clench and unclench my fist.

"Is Sully leaving?" My voice cracks with panic. I feel the intensity of Wolf's stare on the side of my face, but I don't look at him. I turn my head to scan the trees Sully disappeared behind as Rush slowly drives through the gate and pauses.

"He's just checking the perimeter. Once he gives us the all-clear, Rush will bring us up to the house," Wolf says.

I don't take my eyes off the trees and bushes along the fence. It's then that I notice barbed wire curling along the top of the entire fence line. I crane my neck to look for the barbed wire fence on the other side.

Where are we?

"Somewhere safe." Wolf's minty breath stirs the loose hair on my neck, and I turn my head to look at him. "You're talking out loud, baby girl."

Behind Wolf's head, I see the trees dancing and swaying, taunting me with a melody only they can hear. Before I can open the door to join them, the car moves forward. Rush drives up the rest of the bumpy gravel driveway, and I keep one eye on the dancing trees in the distance. I swear one of them smirks at me, and a sudden urge to find Sully overtakes me.

"I bet those trees would just love a night with Sully. They're trying to lure him in, but it won't work," I murmur. I don't miss the raised eyebrow and smirk that Wolf sends Rush over my head, but I'm too preoccupied to care too much.

"That's the Vicodin talking. Sully'll be right back." Wolf plants a kiss on the top of my head.

I ignore him and bite my nail, plotting a way to distract the trees. We pull into an attached garage before I can really plan out my rescue mission, and I blink in the sudden darkness.

"C'mon, Red. I'll show you around," Wolf says as he slides out of the car and holds out his hand for me.

Without hesitation, I slide my hand into his. Warm tingles shoot up my arm when he wraps those beautiful tattooed fingers of his around mine. I glance at his eyes, those endless dark windows into his soul, and I feel a little bit more like Alice falling down a rabbit hole.

And just like Alice, I welcome the adventure with open arms.

I let Wolf help me out of the car and lace our fingers together as I follow Rush into the house.

I ONLY GIVE the quick tour of the house half of my attention. The other half is mesmerized by the swirling tattoos on all three of them. It feels like they're moving—dancing—to a beat I can't hear. I idly wonder if it's the same beat the trees were dancing too outside. I feel like a snake being charmed by Rush's octopus tattoo as it slithers up his arm, swirls around his neck, and dips beneath his collar before peeking up at me with a wink.

A small part of me recognizes that this isn't normal—trees don't smirk and dance and tattoos don't swirl and wink. We're walking down a hallway, and I consider for a moment if I've had a mental break from all of the—*things* that happened earlier. But if I was actually having a total breakdown, would I be aware of it? Maddie would know—

"Oh my god! Where are my cousins?!" The words are loud in the quiet space, and everyone pauses.

Rush turns around to look at me. "They're safe."

Some clarity filters in, softening the edges of my fog a little.

"But where are they? Oh my god—they were with me! Where are they?"

Wolf pulls my attention from his brother with his arm around my shoulder. I let Wolf turn me toward him.

Wolf's uncharacteristically serious dark eyes meet mine, and he says, "They're safe. We have security on them—and men watching them. I wouldn't leave them unprotected—"

I felt hysteria burn in my belly. This awful acidic burning sloshes around, and I have no idea how to stop it.

"What do you mean, security? Why are there men watching them? Does it have to do with whoever t-t-took me?" With each question, each sentence, my hysteria grows and my voice gets louder and higher.

Visions of red-eyed demon men swarming me cloud my vision, and a hot flush of fear rolls through my body.

I don't give anyone time to answer my questions. "I need to go home. Now. I need to go! Now, Wolf!"

Cold sweat coats my body, and my knees feel weak.

"Shh, it's alright, baby girl," Wolf says as he brings his hands up to cradle my face. He leans in so our noses just barely touch. "You're safe here. We'll never let anyone touch you again."

He swipes his fingers underneath my eyes, and it takes me a moment to realize that I'm crying. Tears fill my eyes as I grab his wrists, holding him to me. Everything else disappears—the hallway, the house—everything as I slice myself open a little more to show him the fear eating its way through my gut.

"I'm scared, Conor," I whisper.

"I know, baby girl, I know." He places small, soft kisses on either side of my mouth.

With each brush of his lips on mine, I feel a little less hysterical. Each touch grounds me a little more.

Fear holds me immobile in a vast and deadly ocean, and Wolf has quickly become my life raft. I'm not sure if I should be alarmed at how quickly it happened or relieved that I'm not alone.

"Let's get you cleaned up, okay?" Wolf whispers against my mouth. I nod my head, unable to release my hold on his wrists.

As if he can read my thoughts, he nods a few times. I let go of his wrists, and he smooths his hands down my neck and shoulders, never breaking eye contact. His hands skim my sides to land on my waist, infusing his warmth. He lifts me up, and I wrap my legs around his waist.

I bury my face in his neck, placing my lips on the flower etched on his skin. Sandalwood invades my senses, and it feels like my soul takes a breath for the first time in hours—days.

Wolf carries me through a bedroom and into an en suite bathroom. I don't pay much attention to anything until he sets me down on the counter. Reluctantly, I peel my face and hands from his neck where it was safe. His hands bracket me on the counter, and he leans in until he's all that I can see.

"I don't know what to do now." The admission leaves my lips in a whisper, and I feel my eyes well up again. I curl my hands around the edge of the counter and beg Wolf with my eyes to help me. I'm in uncharted territory, and I feel like the ocean is rising up around me now again.

And I don't fucking know how to swim.

"You're going to take a shower, and I'm going to get you something to eat. And then you're going to sleep." His gaze searches mine, and I nod. A muscle in his jaw clenches when he spots the tear slowly rolling down my cheek. "Just those three things, okay? Nothing else."

I sniffle and nod. "Shower, eat, sleep."

Wolf stares at me for another moment before he spins around to turn on the shower. I take a quick look around, enough to realize that I'm sitting on a wide white-and-gray marble double-sink vanity top. The walls are so light blue they're nearly white, and the space is decorated in soft whites and grays. A double window lets the darkness of the early morning in. Three black and white photos of the beach hang on the wall next to me, and the shower is almost as big as the one at Summer Knoll.

The sound of water hitting the shower floor pulls my attention away from the spacious bathroom. I watch the muscles in Wolf's broad back flex and move as he fiddles with the temperature settings on a panel inside the shower.

Once he's satisfied with the temperature, he turns around to face me. I wonder what he sees when he stares at me. Does he see all the jagged, broken, and burned pieces of the girl I was last week?

A myriad of emotions play in his gaze, but some of them are gone before I can name them. I release a breath I didn't know I was holding when I don't see pity in his gaze.

"Get in the shower, baby girl," Wolf says as he holds out his hand to help me off the counter.

"Okay, Wolf," I murmur with my eyes locked on his. The foreign feeling of someone taking care of me hangs above me like a cloud, attempting to corrupt the gratitude I feel into something far more sinister.

I've never done this before—let my vulnerability show. Right now, it's shining like a beacon from a lighthouse. Besides my cousins, I've never had anyone to show me this kind of care before.

I can see why people crave it. And I can see myself becoming addicted to it. Specifically, from three broody men.

"I'll be right back, okay?"

I nod and turn to watch him leave the bathroom. I listen for his footsteps, but I can't hear anything over the water hitting the tile floor in the shower.

11

ALAINA

I DON'T FACE the mirror as I pull off my clothes. I vaguely remember Wolf helping me out of my ruined birthday dress and into these clothes—a bright blue tee with an unfamiliar hotel logo on it and too-big gray leggings pants. Despite the clean, new clothes, I feel like every inch of me is dirty. Contaminated. And as I unclasp my bra, I notice the dark brown stains on the cups. I can't stop the full-body shudder that rolls through me when I realize that blood has been touching me this whole time—*his* blood. With a desperate cry, I wrench it off my arms and fling it across the room. My chest heaves as I stare at the offending piece of fabric. With trembling hands, I quickly slide my ruined underwear down my legs and kick them toward the bra.

Images of Sean leering at me with blood dripping down the side of his face flash before my eyes, and I gasp. I rush into the shower, not bothering to close the door and stand underneath the showerhead. Water assaults my senses, muffling sounds and shrouding everything in front of me in a watery veil. I hold my breath and close my eyes as I tip my head back, so the water rains down directly on my face, willing myself to forget.

A sob travels up from my gut as images from my time at the cabin fire one after the other, too rapidly for me to relive but slow enough that an overwhelming feeling of helplessness and desperation weigh me down.

When I hear the noise the gun made and see Sean's eyes stare at me with retribution as his heavy body fell on mine, I can't contain it anymore.

The sob erupts from my soul, and I lurch forward, sputtering under the hot spray. I brace myself against the shower wall with one hand, gasping for breath and praying for salvation for what I did.

And once I start, I can't stop. I grieve for the girl I once was and for everything that I had to do to survive. I move until my back is against the wall and slide down until I'm sitting on the cool tile floor. I draw my feet up and wrap my arms around my knees as I stare at the wall.

My soul is splintered, and I don't know how to staunch the bleeding.

RUSH

I HEAR Wolf moving around in the kitchen, probably fixing something for Alaina to eat. I take the opportunity to swipe the clothes he set aside for her on the back of the couch and tuck them under my arm as I walk down the hallway toward the bedrooms.

I've never been more thankful for my own paranoia than I am right now. I don't know where we would've gone if we didn't have this place to hide out in. The need to solve the riddle and fix the problem itches underneath my skin. But before I can dive back in, I need to check on my girl.

Stepping inside the bedroom across from Alaina, I drop the stack of Wolf's clothes on the armchair and go to my dresser. We all keep enough clothes and staple items here to last a month.

I grab her one of my black tees and a pair of black boxer briefs. I know they'll be big on her, but I can't deny myself the chance to see her in my clothes. It feeds something primal inside of me. Something I've never really had to examine before.

I don't want to make waves with my brother—either of them —but I can't deny the need that's pounding at me to make her mine. To protect her and provide for her.

I need to stick to the fucking plan. There's a reason I haven't approached her in all the time I watched her leave her heart on the stage at O'Malley's. For everything to work, I just have to stick to the plan.

I take a deep breath to center myself. I'm finding it hard to think clearly when I know she's hurting.

With my clothes in hand, I cross the hall into the bedroom she's staying in. The shower still runs, and the door is open, so I slip inside, intending to put the clothes on the counter and leave.

But then I hear her sobs. These muffled, hiccuping sobs that tear at the very fabric of my being. I feel the empty spot where my heart should be throb, and I rub at the spot absentmindedly.

The shower door is wide open, so I take a step toward it cautiously. "Alaina?"

Her only answer is another sob, louder this time, and the spot in my chest throbs again, harder and more painful this time.

"It's me, birdie. I'm coming in," I tell her as I reach behind my head to grab my tee and pull it off. I already dropped my gear in the living room when we were done with the tour. I hesitate a second before I pull off my boots, socks, and jeans, leaving my black boxer briefs on.

I step into the shower and close the door behind me, trapping what little steam is left. The water has run cold, so I quickly bump up the temperature on the panel before I squat down in front of my beautiful, broken bird.

No, not broken.

Never broken.

Just bent.

She lifts her head when I place my hand on her arm. The look in her eyes roots me to the spot.

"Dec?" Her voice cracks and her eyes spark. I nod once, never taking my eyes off of her. She jerks out of her prone position on the floor and launches herself at me.

I have just enough time to put my hands out to catch her before she's in my arms. My ass hits the floor and my shoulder hits the bench next to me, but I'd trade all that and more just to feel her again. The water hits her back, but she doesn't falter as she wraps her arms around my neck and glues her face to my neck. Her legs land on either side of me as she sinks down on my lap.

My dick swells with the attention against my will, but as her body trembles in mine, it gets the memo that now is not the time. I cradle her to me, transfixed by the little sparks lighting everywhere our bodies touch.

I free one arm, keeping the other wrapped tightly around her, and reach behind me where I know the coconut body wash is. I squirt some in the still-dry washcloth on the bench and begin to run it over her skin slowly.

I have half a thought to ditch the washcloth so I can feel her skin on mine. I imagine it'd be soft. But I know that's not what she needs. Right now, she needs someone to take care of her— not fuck her.

Slowly, I feel her muscles relax the longer she's in my lap. I take my time, getting another refill on body wash once before I feel like the events of the cabin no longer taint her—at least not physically.

She winces when I run the washcloth along her ribs, and I make a mental note to wrap those after the shower.

Alaina pulls her head back and loosens her grip around my neck. Her face is close enough that I can't quite see her expression clearly, but she's far enough away that her lips don't brush mine when she talks.

"Thank you, Dec." She brushes a kiss on the corner of my mouth. "For this." Another kiss on the opposite side of my mouth. "And for coming for me." A third kiss against the center of my mouth. "And for being here."

I let her take the lead, never pushing to claim her like I've been aching to do for nearly a year.

She places feather-light kisses along my face, her palms resting on the top of my shoulders. It's all I can do not to push into her and give her what she's so tentatively offering. Instead, I squeeze my grip on her hip and hope she understands the silent memo I'm sending.

I stand up with her in my arms and make my way out of the shower. I'm grateful Wolf talked us into renovating the bathrooms in this place. We took a place that was passable and turned it into a true safe house that we could comfortably live in for a very long time.

I set Alaina down on the counter in between the double sinks and reach behind me to grab the towel from the floor. Someone must've accidentally bumped it, but it's strange that I didn't hear anyone. Of course, it's entirely possible that I just didn't hear over the shower. But usually my senses pick up on these sorts of things.

It's a blessing and a curse to know when someone's going to meet their maker. I'm still not sure how I'm still breathing most days, but I do know that I'm willing—begging—to put up with the curse if it means she stays safe.

Thoughts of what could've happened if we were late or if we couldn't find her plague me, and I have a feeling they're going to twist my nightmares into something unbearable for a very long time, maybe forever.

She doesn't protest when I wrap the towel around her body and snag another one for her hair. Her eyes close when I gently squeeze her hair in the towel, tugging on the strands a little. Her lashes are dark smudges against her soft skin—a juxtaposition with the purple bruising around her eye.

Fear makes my chest tight. It's not a new emotion for me, but it's one I've rarely felt. And never like this. I've never felt the soul-crushing panic and fear of loss of control like I have for the last day and a half.

"You're dripping," she says, her eyes closing.

"Don't worry about it. Let's get you to bed. Wolf's bringing you some food first, and then you can sleep."

12

ALAINA

AFTER RUSH TOWEL-DRIES my hair and helps me get dressed in borrowed clothes, I feel practically comatose. Between the soothing words he murmurs and the steamy bathroom, I'm fighting sleep.

Rush helps me into the giant bed in the middle of the bedroom. I'm too drained to appreciate the luxury of the plat-form bed. It must be an extra-long California king, and it's covered in a fluffy duvet that looks like it would feel like clouds.

As soon as I get settled in the middle of the bed, Wolf walks in the room with a plate of food. My stomach rumbles on cue, and I genuinely wonder how long it's been since I ate.

"What day is it?"

"Sunday morning," Rush answers as he bends down to brush a kiss across my forehead. "I've got a few things to take care of now that we're here, but Wolf will stay with you." He brushes a wet strand of hair behind my ear, his expression unreadable but intense nonetheless.

"Swear you're not leaving?"

"Aye. I'll be in my office."

I nod and watch as he crosses the room, looking back at me when he reaches the doorway. Wolf slides in bed next to me, holds out the aluminum-foil-covered plate to me in one hand and two white pills in the other.

"What's this?"

"I made you blueberry waffles. And you need to take these. It'll help with the pain," Wolf says.

"I love blueberry waffles," I murmur. I'm surprised that I'm feeling so pleased. Like it might be wrong somehow . . . to feel so joy after I just ended someone's life.

"I know," Wolf says with a knowing smirk.

I settle against the headboard next to Wolf and tuck into my plate of food. There's something so comforting about a big, fluffy waffle—nostalgic almost. The waffles are delicious—crisp on the outside but gooey in the middle with a hint of cinnamon and vanilla. I sigh in satisfaction.

I look at Wolf from underneath my lashes as I chew another bite. "Where did you to make this?"

He breaks a piece of waffle off and pops it into his mouth. "Sarah, mostly. I wanted to be able to make myself food if she wasn't around, so one day I asked her to show me how to make a few easy meals. Then she showed Rush and Sully too. I'm not nearly as good as her, but I can get by."

"How old were you?"

He rubs the stubble on his chin as he looks to the side. "Around twelve probably."

I nod as I eat another bite. "That's around the same time I learned too. We had just moved into a new dorm suite, and even though we had access to a dining hall, I wanted to make us chocolate chip cookies in our small kitchenette to celebrate." I smile as I remember pulling the cookie sheet out of the oven. "I burned that first batch so bad, they looked more like hockey pucks than cookies."

Wolf chuckles. "You don't strike me as the kinda girl that gives up that easy."

His words so easily given serve to remind me of what happened earlier—at the cabin. I don't want to think about what could've happened had I given up. It's a dark road that I'm not sure I'll be able to get off once I start.

I turn to face him. "I'm not. I made dozens of cookies that day until I got them just right."

He must hear the difference in my voice because he looks at me quickly, the smile dropping from his face.

"You're alright, baby girl. You're here—I'm here. And you're safe." His voice is low and measured, it's the perfect balm to my frayed nerves.

I nod a few times and turn back to my plate of comfort carbs. We're both silent as I take my time eating. It tastes sweeter some-how, knowing that Wolf made it for me.

I lick my lips, tasting the remnants of sticky-sweet syrup. "Wolf?" I ask, turning my head to look at him. His eyes are closed, hands folded on his chest, and he's reclining against the headboard.

"Hmm?"

"What's going to happen to that guy. The one from . . . you know."

Wolf's eyes pop open, and he turns his head to look at me. "You don't have to worry about that. We took care of it."

"Oh." I set my plate and fork on the nightstand beside me to buy myself some time to process.

Do I want to know what that means?

Would he even tell me?

"I . . . I'm not sure that I need to know what that means, but a small part of me wants to know. I feel—I feel like we're starting something." I pause and look at him. When he continues, so do I, "We're starting something, and I have this gut feeling that it's

PENELOPE BLACK

going to be amazing and scary and a bunch of other adjectives that I can't think of because it hurts my brain right now." I flash him an apologetic smile. "So I'm not sure if I should know so we can start this with honesty."

He nods. "I respect that. Do you remember what I said that night you ordered pineapple on your pizza?"

I tap my finger against my bottom lip. "You said a lot of things."

He reaches out, curls his hand around my shoulders, and pulls me into his side. I snuggle against him and smell sandalwood. Pretty soon, I'm going to start associating that smell with only him instead of one of my favorite candles.

"You don't have to worry about it, baby girl. It'll never blow back on you—we wouldn't let that happen. I promised to protect you, didn't I?"

I nod. "I know. I'm just . . . scared." The words come out slow as drowsiness blankets my body.

"I know, Red." He places a gentle kiss on the top of my head. "Go to sleep. I'll be here when you wake up."

I WAKE WITH A JERK, but surprisingly, I don't budge from my prone position. It takes me more than a few seconds to realize that I'm not at home—and another couple of seconds to remember that I'm at the safe house with Wolf, Rush, and Sully.

The former tightens his arm banded across my stomach, my back perfectly fitting in front of him. Lying side by side like this brings back memories of falling asleep together back at Summer Knoll.

God, it feels like years since that night—not less than two weeks.

"Penguins in the cactus . . ." Wolf exhales, his warm breath stirring the strands that fell out of the messy bun at the back of my neck.

The corners of my lips tip up at his sleep-talking gibberish. One of these days, I'm going to wake him up to ask him about his dreams. The couple of times I asked him about it, he said he never remembers his dreams in the morning.

I sigh and shift my legs to ease the pressure on my bladder. I wouldn't be surprised if that's what woke me up. Wolf had me slam a bunch of Gatorade and water when I woke up shortly after I fell asleep.

"The dolphin . . . guitar boats . . ." Wolf mumbles before burying his face into my neck.

It's strange how such new things are comforting me. I've known him less than a month, and yet, his presence soothes me in a way I've never experienced before. I feel . . . safe.

I wiggle around and slide Wolf's arm off of me. Surprisingly, he loosens his python-like grip enough that I can maneuver out of bed. I pull the blankets up to keep my spot warm and keep any draft off Wolf, but I'm not sure anything could wake him up when he's deep asleep.

I pad over to the bathroom on silent feet, thankful for the small light filtering in the room, so I can navigate around the few things furnishing this room. I could've sworn I counted four bedrooms when they showed me to this room yesterday, but I'm having a hard time recollecting a few different things, so I could've mixed it up.

Once I relieve my bladder, I stand in front of one of the sinks in the vanity and wash my hands. I'd been avoiding looking at my reflection earlier, and I'm not sure if I want to start now.

There's something so deeply personal about staring yourself in the eye and letting your insecurities blaze.

My emotions feel like they've been exfoliated—they're red and raw, and all my impurities are brought to the surface. Every horrible thing I did in that cabin in the woods plays on repeat across my vision. Every stab, assault, every opportunity I could've done something different. But I didn't.

Everyone has a choice. I had a choice in that outdated, damp room. I could've let him take me somewhere, but I didn't. Logically, I understand that if I didn't at least try to get away, then I wouldn't be here right now. I know that—I do.

It's just that yesterday I was just Alaina. Straight-A student, bar singer, tutor-to-underage kids.

And today, I'm a killer.

I roll the word murderer around on my tongue. It tastes like ash and dead things. But a part of me—and it's not nearly as small as I think it maybe should be, isn't all that broken up about that. It was a choice born out of necessity. Out of the primal human desire to *survive*.

And I'm nothing if not a survivor.

When you're basically forced to raise yourself in an unknown city full of millions of virtual strangers, you adapt to survive.

And that's exactly what I have to figure out how to do now.

It's light outside, but exhaustion weighs heavy on my shoulders. I leave the bathroom and climb into bed again. Wolf's mumbling something too low for me to hear, but he reaches out and curls his arm around me. I snuggle into his chest, and breathe him in. The tension in my body slowly slips down my limbs, leaving me feeling mellow.

I rest my head right above the swallows inked on his chest and listen to the rhythm of his breathing.

Before long, the melody lulls me to sleep.

13

ALAINA

THE AFTERNOON light streams through the drapes and swathes the bed in warm golden sunshine. It takes me a moment to realize where I am. The soft gray walls and ivory drapes help me realize that I'm still in the bedroom at the safe house.

The body behind me is warm and the scent of sandalwood fills the air.

Wolf.

I'm content enough to stay snuggled up next to Wolf, but my stomach has other ideas. A rumble followed by a hunger pang makes the decision for me. I slide out of the bed and make sure not to wake Wolf up. He looks so peaceful in his sleep—it makes him look younger. He's easily the most playful of my boys—that thought stops me in my tracks.

I feel my brow furrow as I look at Wolf without really seeing him. *My boys?* Why the hell did I think that? I mean, sure, I'm attracted to all three of them. Who wouldn't be?

And I definitely kissed all three of them—even before the whole oh-my-god-I-thought-I-was-going-to-die kisses—and I . . . I liked it. I like *them*.

Oh, *shit*.

I like them.

"Tarantulas in the garden . . ." Wolf mumbles as he rolls over onto his stomach and buries his face into my pillow.

His random sleeptalk brings me out the beginning spiral of panic I was in, and a small smile curls up the corners of my mouth. I sigh, a wistful sort of sound as I stare at the shirtless god in my bed.

If gods were covered in tattoos, etched in darkness, and brimming with violence ready to be unleashed at a moment's notice.

My stomach rumbles again, and I step forward to pull the blankets up over my boyfriend, reluctantly covering all those beautiful tattoos on his back.

Celtic designs, several birds, classic Sailor-Jerry-style tattoos, and some sinister things cover about half of his torso—front and back. He's got inked designs on most of his chest and almost two full sleeves. He's a walking masterpiece.

Honestly, all three of them are. I think Rush might have the most tattoos, but I haven't really had the opportunity to really look. And the shower together doesn't count. I wasn't in the right frame of mind for anything like that.

I can't wait to map his tattoos out though . . . with my tongue. Visions of the two of us in this shower play across my mind's eye, and then the fantasy switches to the gigantic shower at Summer Knoll. And all four of us under that practically industrial-sized shower.

Okay, so clearly, I'm feeling better today, mentally at least. My dad used to tell me that everything looked better in the morning. A glance at the window tells me it's not morning, but the same thing still applies. I think it's the sleep factor anyway.

God, I miss my dad.

Now that thoughts of my dad have cooled my libido, my body decides to remind me that I need food.

I tiptoe out of the bedroom and quietly close the door as I leave. I take a moment to look around. I didn't get much of a chance to explore this place yesterday, so I'm going to take advantage now. I'm not sure how long we'll be here, but I don't want to miss a single second of opportunity to dig for info on my guys.

The hallway is bare except for two framed photos of three little boys. I step closer for a better look, and I can't stop the smile that takes over my face. A black-haired boy smiles with his arms thrown around two other boys—a little blond-haired one with dimples and a dark-haired boy with a smirk. I see a Ferris wheel is in the background, and I wonder if they were at Coney Island.

I went there with Maddie and Mary a few different summers. It's always fun to grab a funnel cake and people watch. I wonder if we were ever there at the same time.

I note four other doors in the hallway as I move to look at the other photo. If there was any question about who the little boys were in that photo, there's no question who's in this photo. Rush, Wolf, and Sully stare back at me from this photo. They're in a similar position—Wolf in the middle and the other two on either side. But long gone are the smiles and Ferris wheel. All three of them have their arms folded across broad chests and none of them are smiling—not even a hint of a smile. They're standing in front of some kind of garage, but other than that, there's nothing else in the photo. It's an interesting photo to frame, that's for sure, and I wonder what the backstory is. Maybe one day I'll ask them.

With one final glance at the photo, I leave the hallway and walk through the living room until I reach the kitchen. It's an open floor plan, so you can easily see everything—the kitchen, the living room, the family room which is really just an extension of the living room and two hallways. One hallway, the one I just came from, leads to the bedrooms, and the other hallway leads down to an area of the house I haven't seen yet.

A built-in bookcase lines the wall directly across from the kitchen with some books, a ton of vinyl records, a few candles, and a couple of video game systems on the shelves.

Those vinyls definitely piqued my interest.

A rustic table with six chairs sits in the middle of the dining room. Some of the guys' tactical gear sits on top of the table, but otherwise, the room looks a little unused.

I make my way toward the kitchen. It's huge by anyone's standards, but it seems small compared to Summer Knoll's.

White marble countertops cover all the counter space around the kitchen, including the island. Four light-blonde wood stools with backs sit nicely underneath the island.

This looks like the place they'd spend time and eat their meals at.

A fancy coffeemaker, microwave, and an empty fruit bowl are the only things on the counter.

I spy a bottle of rum and a couple of cans of Coke on the island, three empty cups, two with a ring of condensation around the bottom. Wolf once told me that vodka is for secrets, tequila is for losing your inhibitions, and whiskey is for making shit happen. But he never told me his philosophy on rum. I wonder what occasion calls for rum.

I feel a little bit weird about just helping myself to food without asking, but my stomach growls again, reminding me that I need to eat.

Ten minutes and a sandwich later, I bring my plate to the sink and quickly wash it. It's one of those deep farm tub sinks—big enough to wash pots and pans in it. After I rinse the plate and set it in the drying rack next to the sink, I turn around and lean against the counter. The kitchen is nothing like the kitchen at Summer Knoll. This one is smaller—obviously—but it feels more like them to me.

I roll my eyes at myself. I've barely known these guys, and here I am acting like I know their style.

Though, I suppose there are certain events that can happen that might bond two people together. Or in my case, four. And I think the events of the last couple of days are enough to bring even strangers together. And we're hardly strangers, the Fitzgerald boys and I.

The bottle of rum catches my eye, and I decide that if there was ever a time to pour myself a stiff drink, it's now. Grabbing one of the glasses on the island, I toss a few ice cubes in the glass. I flinch at the sound before I can stop myself.

With a deep inhale and exhale, I pick up the bottle and bring it to my nose. One sniff and my eyes water.

Perfect.

I want something that'll hurt a little, help me bury the emotions I can feel bubbling up to the surface again. My hand is steady as I pour a splash in the glass and immediately toss it back. I wince as the liquor hits the back of my taste buds, but it quickly evens out as the rum settles in my belly. Warmth spreads through my body, starting with my fingers.

"Okay then," I murmur as I pour another generous splash in the glass, this time adding a little Coke. Setting down the bottle, I cradle the glass up by my shoulder as I spin around and take in the space.

The open floor plan really makes this space seem large but still homey. The high ceilings and floor-to-ceiling windows make the space feel a lot bigger than it actually is. I walk into the room and trail my free hand along the top of the gray leather sectional couch. The matching overstuffed chair sits in the corner of the room, both facing the TV hanging on the wall. Unlike the hallway, there are no photos here. A few game controllers on the coffee table are the only signs that this room was recently used.

A noise catches my attention, and I freeze for a moment

before I remember that no one can reach me here. And if some-how, someone got inside the house, I have no doubt that all three of them would be here in an instant.

When I hear the low hum of what sounds like the news, I decide to snoop just a little longer. If I'm lucky, I'll be able to observe them for a few minutes before they realize I'm there.

As quietly as possible, I tiptoe through the living room and kitchen, and follow the low murmur of the TV down a hallway off the kitchen. I don't remember seeing this part of the house when we got here, but that's not saying much. A lot of the last few days seems like a dream—too far-fetched to be real but too painful to be just a dream.

I take care with each step on the gray hardwood floors, careful not to make too much noise. Three more doorways branch off this hallway, and I suddenly realize that this small hideaway house is much larger than I originally thought.

Two doors are closed, but a third is halfway open. Soft light spills into the hallway, shining on my chipped pink polish on my bare feet. I peek inside and see Rush sitting at a mini command station.

14

ALAINA

"COME IN, LITTLE BIRD."

His voice startles me, and I jump a little, knocking my shoulder into the doorframe.

I slowly push open the door and take a step inside. I bump the door closed with my hip and lean against it as I glance from his broad back to everything else in the room. It's about the size of the room I'm staying in, but it's outfitted like a mini command station.

"Do you need something?" he asks without turning around, and a flush of embarrassment warms my cheeks.

Shoot. Maybe this was a bad idea. But I know that I didn't hallucinate him helping me—almost lovingly—in the shower. It was unexpected but not unwelcome. And I . . . I want to see what he'll do next. Will he kiss me again? Will he tell me to leave? Will he tell Wolf?

Shit. *Wolf.*

Shame blankets me as the realization that I left my boyfriend snuggled up in my bed to come do what—kiss Rush?

I bite my lip as I contemplate my motives. *Was I really coming here to make out with Rush? Or did I just want to see him—talk to him?*

I'm not naïve enough not to realize that if given the chance, I'll definitely kiss Rush—and more. Then an idea strikes me. It's maybe the most ludicrous thing I could've thought of, but after my time in the cabin, I think . . . I think I might be ready to step outside my carefully laid plans.

And do something daring.

Be bold.

And date both of them.

I'm not sure that I should feel so excited at the prospect of having them both. It's a lot of assumptions.

You'd date all three of them if Sully gave you even half an inclination, a voice in my mind drolls. The voice reminds me of Maddie so much it hurts. I know it hasn't been long, but I miss my cousins fiercely. I make a mental note to call her and Mary as soon as I can.

"Birdie?" There's no impatience in his tone, just curiosity.

He pulls me out of my musings and I take a moment to look around. Four computer monitors take up most of the space on his big white desk. The only other things are a keyboard and three cell phones. A navy-colored couch sits against one wall, a cream-colored plush throw tossed over one arm. It's that throw that draws me in, softens me even more toward Rush.

Two TVs are mounted on the wall I'm leaning against, the low hum of some news station telling us that we're reaching record high temperatures again today. With startling clarity, I realize I really have no concept of time.

"What day is it?" I ask him, knowing that I won't really be able to piece it all together right now. Not when I'm granted unlimited perusal of Rush. With his back still facing me, I don't have to pull my gaze away or only catch fleeting glimpses of him.

Rush is the most mysterious of all the Fitzgerald boys. I'm not sure if his mystery is intentional or if it's just part of the package that is Declan Fitzgerald. I wonder what his middle name is? It's probably something regal like Edmund. He has that air about him—importance, refinery, and old money.

I run my gaze all over his broad shoulders, the tattoos crawling up his neck. My fingers itch to trace those tattoos—to explore all of his tattoos and see just how far they go down his body. Vague memories of his tattoos dancing and winking at me surface, and I shake it off. Those hallucination dreams are the worst.

"Birdie," he says as he hits a few keystrokes. Rush spins around in his chair in one fluid motion. It would look cheesy on a lesser man, but I don't think Rush has ever looked cheesy a day in his life. Stormy gray eyes meet mine, and my breath catches. How can one look pack such a punch?

I swear those eyes of his pierce something deep inside me—something no one has breached before.

I search his face—I'm not even sure what I'm looking for exactly, but I know that I need it. And I need it from him.

"I wanted to say thank you." I pause and lick my lips. "For earlier. In the shower."

My heart pounds harder with his silence, so I push off the door and take a step toward him, clutching my bravery in both hands. My bare feet are silent on the hardwood floor, and I swear he can hear my heart beating. I stop right in front of him, close enough to touch if I reached my hand out.

"And for coming for me." I exhale as soon as the words leave my lips, the feeling of togetherness wraps around my muscles and threads into my veins.

Rush came for me—they all came for *me*. That thought loops around in my brain until my heart beats with each word.

"Why." The word is a plea ripped from my very being. Why did they come for me—what about me is so special? What about me made him come back week after week to hear us sing?

Rush scans my face for a moment as he holds himself very still in his chair. "I think you already know why."

I take another small step forward until my legs brush against his. He glances down at where our legs touch, and I watch in fascination as a shudder rolls through him. The way he looks at me afterward can only be described as hunger.

"I think I need you to spell it out for me, because I—" I shake my head, cutting myself off.

"How are you feeling?" His words are low, and his abrupt change in subject confuses me. I struggle to concentrate on them as he leans forward, his hands wrapping around the back of my calves and slowly dragging them up my leg. His tattooed, calloused fingers scrape against my skin, leaving a trail of goosebumps.

I'm still wearing the clothes Rush brought me after I showered—a shirt and a pair of boxer briefs. The shirt is big enough that the collar nearly hangs off my shoulder, and the boxer briefs are rolled a few times at the band.

My breath hitches when he reaches the back of my thigh and pauses. "I'm okay." The words leave me in a rush when he gently squeezes, and I amend my answer. "My body aches and my ribs hurt every time I twist or move too fast."

"Good girl," he murmurs.

My nipples pebble in response, and I have a half a second to wonder why I had that response before his hands continue their exploration. I take another sip of my drink before I place the glass on edge of his desk.

I lick my lips, and my heart pounds. "What, uh, what are you doing?"

"I think it's fairly obvious what I'm doing," Rush says as his hands smooth up the back of my thighs until they reach the curve of my ass. His breath caresses my thighs as he leans forward another inch. I resist the urge to run my fingers through his tousled hair as another image superimposes itself on the scene in front of me.

My breath hitches as I let the fantasy play out in my mind. Rush's strong fingers curling around the waistband of my borrowed shorts and slowly dragging them down my legs. The feel of his breath against my thigh as he drags his lips over my skin until I can't take another second of his teasing touches. I imagine curling my fingers through his locks—it's long enough that I know I could get a good grip on it—and holding him right where I want him for as long as I want.

Rush ghosts his face above my pussy, and I involuntarily hold my breath, disrupting my fantasy. I can't stop the shiver that rolls through me or the way my heart races. I mentally urge him to keep going, to stop teasing me.

In one slow, torturous movement, he slides his palms over my hips and up my ribs, mindful to not put too much pressure on them, and drags his face up the front of my body. I can feel his breath through the thin material separating his mouth from my skin, and longing surges through me.

"Why didn't you tell anyone about our kiss, little bird?" He whispers against my right nipple, drawing it to a near painful point. "Or about all those Friday nights."

I use all the restraint I didn't know I had or ever needed to have and stand still in front of him. I'm smart enough to realize that this enigmatic dark king who's bowing before me still holds the power. He's just letting me think I have some sort of control here.

"I-I don't know." My breath hitches as he grazes my nipple with his teeth. It feels like a warning. When he does it a second time, I realize that's exactly what it was. "I didn't want to," I say in a rush. "I-I feel greedy, and I—I don't want to choose." The words leave my mouth on a whisper, and I close my eyes as shame and lust war against each other.

Rush skims his lips up until they land on the exposed skin of my shoulder, his hands settling gently along my ribs. "I'm not asking you to choose, little bird."

I tilt my neck to the side to give him more room to explore. "But what about your brothers? I don't—" My words cut off on a moan as Rush sucks that spot where my neck meets my shoulder. It feels like a straight shot right down to my pussy, and my clit throbs in time with Rush's mouth.

He backs off enough to talk against my skin. "What about them, baby?"

I tilt my head back and he resumes his exploration of all the exposed skin around my shoulder and neck. I'm distantly aware of the fact that he's making me spell everything out for him.

Like Wolf.

"I don't want to be someone's dirty little secret, Rush," I say as I thread my fingers in his hair, stopping his movements.

He lifts his face to mine, and I bear witness to the smirk that spreads across his face. It's a sexy sort of smile that promises bad intentions and countless pleasure. Lust permeates the air, and it's enough to fog the entire room. I breathe it in and trap his promises in my lungs.

"Oh, baby. I'd never keep you a secret—but I'll keep you dirty. My dirty little bird." His eyes darken to the color of the sea before a storm, and I shiver in anticipation. "Tell me what you want."

His words are firm, and I hear the band of steel beneath them. He's a man used to getting his way, but he's not pushing me—he's looking out for me. I'm not sure what the hell is happening to me when I find myself yearning to nod my head, agree to anything he says so long as he keeps his lips on my skin.

"I want your words, baby."

I lick my lips and open my eyes. "I want you. All three of you." My voice is clear.

The corners of his mouth slowly curve until his dimples peek out. "Don't worry about Wolf. Or Sully. We know what we're doing."

"But what about me? What if I don't know what the hell *I'm* doing?"

"Is this what you want?" Rush punctures his words with a roll of his hips.

A whimper escapes me when I feel his hard cock right where I need him the most. "Yes." The word leaves my mouth on a hiss as everything in my body clenches.

"Good girl," he says against my lips, and I can't hold back any longer. I bridge the gap between our mouths and crash my lips against his.

15

RUSH

A SLOW CLAP cracks the air, and out of instinct, I flatten my body against Alaina's, pushing her into the wall. I snarl over my shoulder as I see my brother standing in the doorway, his smarmy little smile grating on my nerves.

"What the fuck, Sully?" I growl out.

He shrugs and crosses his arms across his chest, feigning innocence. "What?"

"What the fuck do you want?" I'm still pressed tight against Alaina, but I can't physically make myself step away yet.

My chest heaves, and it's not solely from her. I'm fucking rattled. I can't believe I didn't hear him—or fuck, at least feel him. Where the hell is that goddamn sixth sense now?

"I thought you said we'll debrief as soon as she's up?" Sully raises an eyebrow.

He's trying too hard to look unaffected, but I've known him his whole life. I clock the tic in his jaw and the clenched fists. Realizing that he's struggling actually brings a smile to my face. I knew that fucker couldn't act so unaffected forever.

I turn to rest my forehead against Alaina's shoulder—the spot between her neck and shoulder that I know just drives her wild. I exhale and mentally count the seconds.

One, two, three.

She shivers right on cue. That little movement, her reaction to me, calms me down enough that I'm able to get my shit together.

There's something about her that disarms me. I lose the constant weight of my obligations and the pressure of being the president of the junior council.

I only hope that I don't lose myself entirely. She's a siren cloaked as an innocent doe-eyed woman, and I'd willingly follow her to the depths of the ocean, if only for another taste of her lips.

"Debriefing?" Alaina asks, her hands still clutching my shoulders.

I lean back so I'm not crushing her into the wall. It takes physical effort for me to separate myself from her, but I do. Her hands slide down my shoulder and rest on my wrists—I'm still holding her against me.

Sully's right—now that she's up, we really need to figure out what happened.

"The sooner we figure out who took you, the sooner we eliminate them." My voice is low, meant only for her ears. "Okay?"

Her eyes, wide with panic, hold me captive. "We just need to hear what happened as you remember it, okay?"

She nods, but her fingers clench around my wrists.

"I need your words, baby." I search her gaze, waiting.

I know she'll get there, but I need her to do it on her own. If I push her too far too fast, she'll run, and we'll likely never see her again.

I mean, I can find just about everyone, so I'm sure I'd *see* her, but I'd never get to see her like this. Lustful one minute, vulnerable the next.

"Okay, Rush," she says on a breath.

I step back, grab her hand in mine, and head toward the sectional couch on the other side of the room. Sully's made himself comfortable on one end. I clock the way his jaw ticks and his leg bounces, and I lead us to the opposite end. So he can have a better view of our girl in my arms.

I sit down on the couch, pulling her with me by our clasped hands.

"Wow. That must be some kind of record, huh, Alaina?"

"What's that supposed to mean?"

"First Wolf, now Rush."

"Don't forget to add yourself to that list. Or did you forget that I had you once upon a time too?"

"Aye. I remember it very well," Sully says through clenched teeth.

I wonder if she realizes he's vibrating with jealousy? I suppose his tight jaw, crossed arms, and tapping foot could be confused with anger—and I'm sure he is angry, but he's also jealous as hell.

I'm curious enough to let this thing between play out without interfering too much. I'll only step in if one of them is about to make a life-changing decision. Otherwise, this might be exactly what he needs to work through his shit with Alaina.

Whether he's realized it or not yet, it doesn't change the fact that this is happening—with her. I'd never force someone into something they weren't comfortable with, and if I didn't already know that he still loves her. I'm not naïve enough not to realize the feelings he has—they both have—but I am crazy enough to push him into acting on them.

I turn to my brother. "Where's Wolf?"

"Here, I'm here," Wolf says around a yawn. He runs a hand through his hair as he walks in the room. He looks like he literally rolled out of bed and walked down the hall—shirtless and gym shorts on, hair a mess.

I notice the moment he sees Alaina sitting next to me, and the second after that when he realizes that we're holding hands.

Jealousy flashes across his face in a split second before he tamps it down. Wolf takes the seat directly in the middle of us, and I mentally file it away for later for naming.

"How did you sleep?" Wolf asks, and it's obvious he's talking to Alaina. Fucker can't keep his eyes off of her.

"Good." She flashes him this small, inside-joke smile, and I fight the urge to shout that it was *my* tongue down her throat. My own jealousy chafes, and I tell myself to chill the fuck out.

"Why didn't you wake me?" Wolf leans back against the couch, spreading his arms along the back. He flashes a glance at Sully with a smirk.

"I got hungry, so I came looking for a snack—and found one." She looks at me, her laugh lines around her eyes winking at me.

I haven't seen her laugh much with us, if at all. Perhaps we can use this time at the safe house for more than just laying low.

An idea formulates in my mind—instead of staying just a few days, we could stay for a week or two. It'll give us the time we need to get to know one another. And we can still get shit done here and figure a few things out.

"Are we doing this or what?" Sully leans forward, bracing his arms on his legs.

I stare at him for a moment, but he doesn't look up from the floor. Tension lines his shoulders, and I can imagine the turmoil rolling around inside him—he always was a moody bastard. Never wanted to talk shit out like Wolf and never gives anything away freely. He's had a chip on his shoulder since he was a toddler. The only time I've ever seen him any different was a few years ago—the summer he spent in the city where we rarely saw him.

I'm convinced there's more to Sully and Alaina's story. One look at them, and even I can read the angst and tension tethering the two of them. I didn't have time to dig deeper into her past properly, but I don't mind flying blind in this situation. Especially if it helps this situation—and them.

"Let's start with O'Malley's. Do you remember what happened?" I turn to face Alaina.

She inhales deeply. "I-uh-I thought I saw Wolf head toward the bathrooms, so I followed him. It wasn't until I was back there that he turned around and I realized my mistake."

"Do you remember what he looked like? Anything stand out?" Wolf asks, voice soft.

"It's dark back there, so I can't describe him fully. But he had red eyes—contacts—and he was tall. He didn't really say much, and then the next thing I remember is waking up inside a burning van."

I suck in a breath and slowly, carefully exhale. I make a silent promise for vengeance on everyone involved.

Alaina stares off to the side, her eyes unfocused as she recalls the events of that evening. After she finishes detailing everything she can remember or piece together, she finally looks at me.

Her gaze is probing, questioning. I'm not sure what the question is, but I pull her into my lap in response.

She sits across my legs and wraps her arms around my neck, burying her face into my shirt.

"I thought I was going to die in that cabin. I thought I was going to die, and I'd never do all these things that I had planned to do. I thought I'd never get to see my cousins or friends or family or . . . you guys."

Her anguish is palpable, and I feel ill-equipped to stop it. I can hack into the most complicated and secure systems most people can't even dream of, and I can envision possible outcomes for just about every scenario. But I don't know shit about consoling anyone—I've never needed to do it before. But the redhead slowly, quietly falling apart in my arms has me rethinking everything.

"Shh, it's alright. You're here, you're safe." I slowly run my hand up and down her back.

There's no question in my mind that I want her here—with us. But she's a variable I stupidly hadn't accounted for. Not properly. I planned to introduce her to the Brotherhood—this life—slowly. Instead, she's been thrown into the middle of shitstorm before we've all had a moment to just breathe together.

I knew better than that—I should've had more contingency plans. She's not in this life, and that's just part of the appeal. She's inexperienced, but not incapable. Her actions at the cabin proved as much.

I've been watching her on Friday nights for the last year, but that was more casual recon than anything. I still remember the first time I saw her.

"You stayin' for a pint? We've got some nice little songbirds tonight," Jack O'Malley *says from behind the bar at his pub.*

"Karaoke still going strong?"

"Aye. Been a couple years now. We've got people that come in just to see the regulars." Jack *shrugs as he dries a pint glass.*

A rejection is on the tip of my tongue when the sweetest noise hits my ears —a laugh. I can't say what about it that stood out in the crowded space, but something caught my attention.

Joy. The noise sounds like if joy could be bottled up into sound. It's such an interesting concept—joy. In theory, I should be happy. I've got my brothers and the Brotherhood, my house, my cars, my tech—I want for nothing. And yet, I'm not sure that I've ever felt the way that sound feels.

I give Jack my back as I scan the crowded bar for the source.

Wavy deep-red is the first thing I see. Then the rest of her comes into focus. Ripped Ramones tee, pleated black miniskirt, white Vans. She's a goddamn wet dream with curves in all the right places. Her head is thrown back and that joyful sound spills from her lips and settles into the crowd around her.

She's standing next to two girls who look just like her, who are both laughing, but I don't hear those sounds. Only hers.

An ember of something foreign starts in my gut. It reminds me of the warmth you feel standing in front of a fire pit, slow at first, then it grows until it's nearly scalding you and you're positive you're going to catch fire any second.

Such an innocent little thing to cause such a fierce wave of need in me. I take a step away from the bar when the lights dim.

"Oi! It's Thursday, and our songbirds are back!" Jack yells from behind the bar.

The crowd quiets and turns to face the stage. I watch right along with them as the object of my fascination and the other two who look like her climb the couple of stairs to the rectangular stag on the other side of the bar.

"Thanks, Jack! I'm Maddie, and these are my girls, Alaina, and Mary. We've got a couple new ones for you guys tonight. Hope you like 'em!"

I can't pull my gaze from the girl in the middle. I'm dying to hear what her voice sounds like wrapped around notes.

I make myself stand still and not act on my impulse to snatch her off the stage and hide her in my wing of the house. The territorial urge is enough to give me pause, but then she opens her mouth and sings.

And Jesus, fuck, she can sing.

My heart pounds and my palms sweat, and I feel like a fucking idiot. Yesterday, I watched my brother mete out justice on some motherfucker who tried to peddle underage skin on the backside of our port. I didn't even blink.

And here I am, fucking sweating because of some little bird in a holey band tee.

What the fuck is going on?

A hand claps my shoulder, and I just barely pull my urge to grab my gun in time. "Jesus, Jack. You wanna stay breathin'?" I snarl. "Then don't fucking sneak up on a man like that." I'm breathing heavy as I glare at him.

Jack throws his hands up in surrender and takes a half-step back. "You alright, Rush?"

I roll my neck and take a deep breath. I'd been so engrossed in her rendition of (Love is Like A) Heat Wave that I let my guard down, and Jack, of all people, snuck up on me. That dude is a six foot five redheaded ex-boxer— he doesn't sneak up on anyone.

"Aye. I'm fine." The words are clipped. A flush starts to creep up my neck. I see him nod from the corner of my eye.

"Those are the songbirds. They come just about every week."

I nod and keep my attention on the three redheads on stage.

"They're good, huh?" he asks as he stands next to me. The girls started singing some Taylor Swift song, and the whole bar joined in on the chorus. It's fucking weird . . . and oddly endearing.

"Aye, they're good," I murmur. "Do me a favor, Jack? Call me whenever they're here, yeah?"

I feel his eyes on me, but I don't pull my gaze from the one in the middle. He nods his agreement, and then we don't talk for the rest of their set.

I leave O'Malley's just as my little bird steps off of the stage. I can't help the smile that spreads across my face. I have some planning to do.

I offered to stop at O'Malley's again the next Friday. And the next. And before I knew it, I was counting down the days, the minutes, until I would see her again.

She piqued my curiosity that night, but every time I saw her, she pulled me in a little bit more. She captivated me, and I was singularly focused on her.

I didn't really think beyond getting her into the fold with my brothers. I couldn't think beyond that—it was my long-term goal, and admittedly, I didn't prepare for *this* part of the relationship. And I don't mean the fucking kidnapping.

"What happens now?" Her lips brush across my shirt with each word.

I keep sliding my hand along her spine, and I feel her relax. "Now we lie low for a bit. We'll stay here for two weeks—"

"Two? I thought we were only crashing here for a few days?" Sully interrupts me. I glance at him over the top of Alaina's head, but he's not giving much away.

I nod. "We were, but then I realized that we have a few different things to figure out, and this is the safest place for us to do that." I send a pointed look at both my brothers, hoping they read between the lines. We have to figure out who took Alaina, what Da is up to, and who the fuck ordered a hit on her. "Plus, I want Alaina to get some self-defense training."

"Aye. That's a good idea. I'll handle some weapons," Wolf says with a nod.

I look at my other brother. His stiff posture and scowl don't scare me though.

"Fine," Sully says through gritted teeth. "Every morning, she'll be with me for self-defense."

"And I'll explain some more . . . technical aspects to her."

"Are we really doing this then? We're just going to bring her into the fold like that?" Sully alternates his glare between Wolf and I. "What's Da gonna say about that? Fuck—what's the Brotherhood going to say?"

I raise a brow at his challenge. "That was always the plan, you know that, Sully."

"Breaking into Summer Knoll was enough to incite war, but taking our girl like that?" Wolf raises a brow as he stares at Sully. "They're begging for it. And I'm going to give it to 'em."

Wolf's maniacal grin matches my own. People often misjudge me because physical violence isn't my go-to when I'm destroying someone. Not that I'm above it—because I'm not. But I prefer to dismantle a person systematically, step by step— finances, savings, property, integrity, credibility, reputation, and so on.

The result is much sweeter than one to the chest and one to the head. Though I've done both plenty of times.

"Aye," Sully says with a nod. "But you're talking about spilling Brotherhood secrets, and I can't help but wonder what Da will think of this move."

"He's always known this was a possibility—us settling down. Besides, we should be more worried about what the fuck he's been up to. Not whether or not he approves of our girl."

Sully nods a couple of times and steeples his fingers, resting his arms on his legs. "Cross that bridge together."

Something inside my chest loosens at his words. That's as good of an olive branch that I'm going to get.

"Together," Wolf and I murmur together.

Alaina clears her throat. "That's not the first time you've called me *your girl*. And I feel like . . . maybe that's something we should all talk about. Together." She looks at Sully when she talks.

He runs a hand down his face before he looks at me with a small shake of his head.

I pinch the bridge of my nose when I feel the start of a headache forming. I haven't slept much since we got here, and it's catching up with me now.

"Let's take it one day at a time, Red, yeah?"

"Okay, Wolf. One day at a time," she says, glancing between the three of us.

Sully exhales and taps his fingertips against his lips. "And how're we going to find the fucks behind this?"

"I have a few leads. And Ro King started digging already."

"Who's Ro King?" Alaina asks me.

I look at her, my hand still curled around her thigh. "A friend who's going to help us find out who did this to you."

"How? I thought you guys didn't know who was behind this?" Her gaze darts around, connecting with all three of us.

After a moment, I decide to jump in the deep end with both feet. "A hacker. All the Kings have agreed to help us, and outside of us"—I gesture to my brothers and me—"they're the best at what they do. And more importantly, we trust them."

She searches my gaze before she nods. "Okay. What can I do to help?"

I hear Sully's soft snort, but Alaina's too busy looking at me to notice—good. It seems he'll need a bigger push. We'll have to see how training goes with Alaina.

"Nothing outside of what we already talked about, baby." I punctuate my words with a squeeze on her thigh. "We've got work to do, brothers. Reach out to your contacts too. Maybe we'll get lucky and someone squealed. Burners are on the island in the kitchen."

"Oh, god! I've gotta call my cousins."

"I thought you might want to. There are plenty of burners in the kitchen. Just grab one and call them." I tip my head toward the kitchen island.

Alaina leans in and places a soft kiss against my cheek. "Thank you."

16

ALAINA

I SNAG a burner phone from the island and walk back toward my room. Even though I had my phone with me, and I probably could've gotten their numbers from it, Rush disabled it so it can't be tracked.

I'm so grateful that I memorized both of my cousin's phone numbers back in middle school. They teased me about it since everything is saved in your phone—eliminating the need to memorize anything.

I climb into the massive bed and key in Maddie's number. I hold my breath as ringing fills my ears.

"Hello?"

Maddie's soft voice fills my ear, and my breath hitches. "Maddie?"

"Holy shit. Alaina?"

I clear my throat as tears unexpectedly fill my eyes. "It's me, Maddie."

"Oh my god, Lainey! Mary, it's Lainey! Come in here!" She forgot to pull the phone away from her mouth before she yelled for Mary. "Okay, you're on speaker now."

"Lainey! Where are you?"

"Mary, hey," I say though a watery laugh. "God, it's good to hear your voices again."

"What happened, Lainey? Some biker-looking dude came and picked us up from O'Malley's. Jack vouched for them—said Wolf sent them for our protection. What the hell do we need protection from?"

I sigh. Both Rush and Wolf coached me on what I can't or shouldn't say—either for my safety or theirs—but the weight of what happened settles into my bones, and suddenly, I want nothing more than to spill everything to them. They've been my sounding boards—my rocks—for more than half my life, and this feels a little like lying.

I know it's to keep everyone safe—and the idea of one of them being in a cabin like I was is the only thing that keeps me from telling them everything.

"It's a long story, and I don't think I can tell you most of it. Not yet. One day though."

There's silence on the other end, and I know I've just shocked them.

"I didn't think we kept secrets, Lainey."

Maddie's accusation hits its intended mark, and I flinch.

"I know, but this is for your protection—and mine. I can't bear the idea of you guys getting hurt because of me."

"Where are you?" Mary asks, her voice low.

"I'm . . . safe. I'm with Wolf and Rush . . . and Sully. Where are you guys? Are you okay?"

"Okay . . . okay. We're fine. We're back in our dorm suite for now, but we have several security guards with us twenty-four-seven," Mary says.

"Yep. Several huge, muscley, hot dudes follow us around all the time. If I didn't know they were here because something bad happened to you, it'd be my fantasy come to life."

I chuckle despite my watery eyes. Trust her to bring some humor to a serious conversation. "Oh Maddie, I've missed you."

"You too, babe." She's quiet for a moment. "But seriously, are you okay? Can you tell us what happened?"

I exhale, this noisy purge of emotion. "I . . . uh . . . I was kidnapped. Taken from the back hallway of O'Malley's."

"Oh my god, Lainey," they both say.

"I love it when you guys do your twin thing."

"Stop deflecting, babe. Tell us what happened—what you can, I mean." Maddie's voice is stern but not unkind.

"Okay." I take a breath and dive into the Cliffs Notes version of events.

I tell them about the guy I fought, but I don't tell them that I killed him—I leave the whole gun part out of it. I'm still wrestling with the events of the last however many days it's been, and I love my cousins—I do—but I'm not sure how they'll react to that sort of news.

The truth is that I don't feel like the same person, and I'm not sure how to explain that to them. I'm sure they'd be supportive and kind. That's just who they are. But I feel this divide between us now. It's small and shallow, but it has the potential to be big enough that not even the bridge of love between us can stretch across it.

Even knowing that, I don't think I can go back to who I used to be. I don't think I want to.

"Jesus, Lainey. I-I-I don't even know what to say to that," Maddie says with a sniffle.

"I know. It's a lot to process—I'm still processing." I nod even though they can't see me.

"Are you okay? I mean, physically? I can't believe you got into a fight with some guy! You could've been killed!"

"I'm okay, Mary. Some serious bumps and bruises, and it still feels like someone took an axe to my head." I gingerly touch my hairline by my temple. "Luckily, it'll all heal. They're taking good care of me."

"Mm-hmm, I just bet they are." I can hear the knowing smirk on Maddie's face just by her tone. "And how good of care are they taking exactly? Or should I ask who?"

"It's really good to talk to you guys." I laugh, the sound quiet and full of warmth.

"Stop avoiding, babe, and spill. Don't think that we forgot your little bomb you dropped on your birthday. You know, the one about your *ex-boyfriend* being your *current* boyfriend's brother and your possible *stepbrother*."

Maddie's voice is so dry that a laugh takes me by surprise. Trust Maddie to move on from the kidnapping and bring up boy drama instead. Though, is it boy drama? I mean, they all seemed weirdly okay with all the PDA.

I tap my bottom lip with the pad of my index finger. I feel like there's probably something I'm missing, but I like being able to kiss all of them whenever I want—well, that's not entirely true. I think the kiss with Sully was more of a thank-god-you're-not-dead kind of thing. Either way, I'm not too keen on making us slap labels on anything right now.

I clear my throat. "Well, about that. I kind of, sort of, kissed all of them. Recently. And, uh, maybe something more with Rush—and you already knew about Wolf."

I feel my face get warm, and I hold my breath as I wait for their judgments.

"Damn, babe." Maddie whistles. "Good for you." Rustling comes through the line, and I imagine she's settling in on the couch. "Okay, spill. Who's the best kisser?"

A smile curls up the corner of my mouth.

"Sully kisses me like he's afraid I'll disappear if he stops. He kisses me like the fate of the world rests on that one kiss—every. single. kiss. Wolf kisses me like he's trying to consume me, and he's fucking *famished*. And Rush—Rush kisses me like I'm the unexpected answer to every one of his prayers."

"Wow, Lainey, you sound like you . . . like them."

It's hard to tell, and it's probably my imagination or my insecurity about seeing three guys at the same time, but I swear I hear some judgment in Mary's tone.

I work hard to shove the shame that's slithering up my throat down. I will not be made to feel bad like my *whatever this is* with all three of them is shameful. Because it's not.

"Well." I glance to the side of the room as I fiddle with the duvet cover. "I do like them, Mary."

"Yes, babe! I knew it!" I can hear the smile in Maddie's voice.

Mary clears her throat. "That's great then. I'm just surprised is all. I mean, I remember what happened a couple years ago when Sully just dumped you out of the blue, and Maddie and I had to wipe your tears. So I don't really understand why all of a sudden you're making out or whatever."

The acid in her voice takes me by surprise. I have to take a second to respond. "That's fair, I guess—"

"No, it's not fair. Mary, what the hell? If she wants to make a mistake, it's our job to wipe up her tears. That's what best friends do. And just to be clear, Lainey, I don't think this is a mistake. I'm just proving a point."

My eyebrows hit my hairline. This feels like it's not really about me anymore, and I wonder if something else is going on.

"If you have something to say to me, sister, then say it." The sneer in Mary's voice is palpable.

"Yeah, okay. I'll say it. It's total bullshit that you've been sneaking around with some guy for *months* and haven't said anything to either one of us. I'm your *twin sister*. So either you're ashamed of this guy—which you know means you shouldn't even be with him—or you're ashamed of *me*. So which is it?"

I whistle under my breath. Okay, so it's not really about me.

That's good, I guess. I wish I could've video called them. It's quiet on the other end for a few seconds before rustling fills the line.

"Bye, Lainey. Glad you're not dead. Enjoy your three boyfriends." Mary's voice gets quieter with each word, and the final word is punctuated by the slam of a door.

"Did she—did she just leave?"

"Yes," Maddie grits out. "She's been like this for the last few days. I don't understand what's going on with her, but it's like she's not the same person!"

A swarm of hornets fills my belly, and I bite my lip. Shit, how's she going to react to the new version of me then? I stomp the flutters out. I'll deal with that when I see her next.

"I don't know, Maddie. Did she tell you if she was seeing someone? I remember you talking about her texting nonstop while you guys were in Europe, though some of those details are still kind of fuzzy."

"Shoot, Lainey, are you really okay?"

Worry bleeds from her, through the phone, and lands into my heart.

"I'm okay." I sigh. "Or, I will be."

"Okay. But you call me if you need me to come get you from wherever you are." Crinkling fills the line, and it sounds like she just popped open a bag of chips. "And to get back to my dear sister, I don't know. I mean, she didn't outright tell me, but she alluded to it, which is her version of practically screaming it from the rooftops."

I chuckle. "That's true. Okay, well, let me know if you get his name. I'll have Rush look him up or whatever. He's very tech savvy."

"Sure, sure. You have Rush look him up," she mimics me in an over-the-top tone of voice. "Rush, can you help me? I'll do whatever you want." Her voice is high-pitched and ridiculous, and she ends it with kissy noises.

"Oh my god, you're so ridiculous," I say around a laugh.

"I've been watching a lot of cheesy rom-coms." Maddie laughs. "Oh, crap. I've gotta go. I'm late for lunch with an old friend."

"Do I know this old friend?" I ask with an arched brow.

"Probably. It's been a few years since I've seen him though. I'll fill you in next time we chat!"

"Okay, have fun and be safe! Take a bodyguard with you!" The words rush out fast.

"Will do! Love you, babe! Byeeeee."

Maddie ends the call before I can say goodbye, but I don't mind. I'm just so grateful that I could talk to her and Mary, even if Mary was acting a little off.

I hope Maddie comes through with a name, because I bet Rush could find out all sorts of things about him. The guy has like a million computers and gadgets—only a fraction of which I understand.

But I imagine Rush is a good teacher—I bet they all are. And I'm looking forward to finding out firsthand.

17

ALAINA

LIGHT STREAMS IN THE WINDOW, creating patches of sunlight inside my bedroom—whoa. The thought stops me in my tracks.

How long have we been here that I started calling this bedroom *my room*? I'm not sure if I should be alarmed at how quickly that happened or comforted that I feel so at home here—subconsciously at least.

I still feel like I'm walking on eggshells around a certain Fitzpatrick brother. And one of these days, we're going to have it out. I can feel it.

There's a storm system happening inside this house, and with each day, each hour that the two of us don't talk, it gains speed. Before we know it, it'll be a category five, and I fear that neither one of us will survive it.

And if I'm honest with myself, I'm aching to have him back in my life—really back. Logically, I know that we can't go back to how it was two years ago. But the wide-eyed romantic in me still sees the chip-on-his-shoulder punk who always softened for her. And she desperately wants to help him.

But we're not those people anymore, and we're not in the New York Public Library. We're in a safe house in the middle of —I'm not even sure where—and I killed a guy days ago.

Jesus, I *killed* someone.

Sure, it was self-defense, but I never thought I'd ever do something like that. I'm still struggling with the fact that I don't feel worse about it. I think because it boils down to one question: him or me? And in the matters of life and death, I'm going to choose me over the random guy who's been stalking me and apparently planning our life together. Every time.

I stretch my arm out, surprised when the spot next to me is empty. It's still faintly warm, so Wolf couldn't have been gone too long.

For the past several days, we've had a routine of sorts, and it's been . . . honestly, nice. Really nice. This house lives up to its name, and I feel safe.

Usually, one of the guys makes breakfast—I'm still not sure where the groceries came from. I haven't seen them leave, and no one has driven up the two-mile-long driveway. Wolf teaches me how to handle weapons—primarily a gun—but yesterday, he had me get creative with a hypothetical situation in a kitchen.

One of the first days here, Rush explained some things in his mini command center. One of those things was a sophisticated security system that he made himself. As soon as someone turns on the driveway, an alert goes out to every security box—a lot like the ones at Summer Knoll. Apparently, Rush made those too. If someone gets within a half mile of the house, then the alarm blares in the whole house.

Sully offered to teach me self-defense, but so far we've only talked about what-if scenarios. Today he's finally going to teach me some moves I can use.

We've spent the afternoons together—all four of us—hanging

out in the living room, playing video games, listening to records, laughing.

But my evenings belong to Rush. He's been showing me how to navigate his command center—in an elementary way. I thought I was tech-savvy until I saw Rush do his thing. He's got a gift.

It's surreal and bittersweet. I feel a little guilty for how much I'm enjoying being in this bubble with just the three of them. It's putting these . . . thoughts in my head about the four of us. Together. In a relationship.

Which is a totally crazy idea, I know.

There haven't been too many outward displays of affection when we're all together, aside from hand-holding and chaste kisses on the top of my head. But when we're one-on-one, it's a different story.

And part of me fantasizes about what it would be like to have all of them—together.

I close my eyes and slide my hands underneath the comforter and sheets. I follow the natural curves and valleys of my body until I reach the borrowed boxer briefs I've been wearing to bed.

I tease my clit through the fabric as I imagine what that would look like.

We're all in this bedroom, but instead of the California king bed, it's a custom-made platform bed that comfortably fits all four of us.

Wolf is the most impatient, so he picks me up and drops me on the bed, coming down on top of me and kissing the breath out of me. He grinds his dick against my pussy, and I moan my approval.

Sully kicks the door closed and leans against it—he's punishing himself still. And Rush reclines against the headboard, content to wait until he can have me all to himself.

Wolf slides down my borrowed boxer briefs, his calloused

PENELOPE BLACK

fingertips digging into my skin. Once they're off, he drags his nose from my ankle all the way up, placing small kisses along the way.

His warm breath ghosts over my pussy, and—

"Holy shit, Red."

Wolf's voice startles me, and I tear my fingers off my clit with an embarrassing squeak. I open my eyes to see Wolf standing next to me, hunger in his gaze.

"Did you need something?" I curl my fingers around the top of the comforter, but I leave it pulled up to my chin.

"Aye, baby girl, I need something."

My heart beats fast at the intention behind his words. The hunger in his gaze reignites the fire that was prematurely cut off.

I lick my lips and push the comforter down to my waist. My oversized shirt shifted while I slept, and now it slipped down one shoulder.

"What do you need, Wolf?"

His smokey-gray eyes darken as he reaches behind his head with one hand and grabs the collar of his shirt. In one stupid-hot movement, he takes off his shirt, exposing all that tattooed skin. His muscles flex, and I feel warmth radiate throughout my body.

Wolf tosses his shirt somewhere behind him but leaves his gym shorts on. He places one knee on the bed and leans over me. "You," he says against my mouth.

Then he kisses me like I'm his oxygen to survive. There's something so eerily similar to my fantasy of Wolf I *just* had that my head spins. I half expect to see Rush next to me, stroking his cock while he watches, and Sully holding up the door until he's done punishing himself.

Our tongues fight for dominance as I tunnel my hands into his hair. I use my grip on his hair to bring him even closer to me. Wolf groans into my mouth as he grinds his cock against me through the blankets. But it's not enough.

I take precious seconds to shove down the rest of the blankets and spread my legs. Wolf wastes no time settling between them, groaning his pleasure when only two thin pieces of material separate us.

I want to set fire to the few layers of cotton between us, so I can feel him against me. I've fantasized about this moment more than I care to admit, and I'm practically salivating at the promise of pleasure from his hands—from his cock.

My lust quickly heats up until I can feel it throbbing like a heartbeat. I roll my hips upward, and he moans my name when I drag my hot pussy along his cotton-covered cock.

I spend half of a second wondering if I left a wet patch on my underwear—or his. But then Wolf pulls back a few inches and his fingers start their exploration. Then I don't have time to think about anything.

"So soft, Red," Wolf says against my mouth as he slides one hand up my ribs, pushing my borrowed shirt up along the way. "So sweet."

He teases my nipple with his thumb before he lowers his mouth. His tongue encircles my nipple, and when he uses his teeth to tug gently, I feel it straight in my clit.

I haven't done this a lot before, but even if I had, I don't think anything would feel like this.

My head swims when he alternates his attention between both of my nipples. His fingers, his mouth—his *teeth*.

I arch my back and attempt to keep his head there, but he has other ideas.

"I wonder if you're soft and sweet everywhere, baby girl." Wolf murmurs against my skin as he slowly descends my body. He glances at me from underneath his sooty lashes, and I swear I come a little from that look alone.

His black hair, tousled from my fingers, hangs across his forehead and his grin is the most carnal thing I've ever seen in my life. It sends a shot of lust buzzing through my veins.

Wolf's mouth leaves a trail of fire until he reaches the apex of my thighs. He teases me, brushing his pouty lips against the sensitive skin of my inner thighs. He skims his lips right over my clit, and through the fabric of my borrowed boxers, he sucks. *Hard.*

My legs tense, and my back arches as the sensation hits me like a lightning bolt. He tongues my pussy through the fabric, and I'm desperate to feel him on my skin.

Wolf lifts his face from me, and I whine my protest. I'm not sure I could form words that weren't *more* and *stay* and *please.*

"A truth for a truth, baby girl."

Wolf's grin can only be described as devious, and it tears a noise of frustration from my throat.

"Wh-what?"

With one finger, he pulls the boxer briefs to the side, enough to run the tip of his tongue just along the edge of my pussy. Before he can do anything else, he pulls back and looks at me through his lashes.

"Oh-okay." I clear my throat and look at the ceiling to sort my thoughts. Everything is scrambled and covered in a lusty haze. "I-uh-I haven't really done this before."

I swallow as I feel my cheeks warm. My muscles clench as I brace for rejection.

I should've known better though. When he doesn't respond right away, I look down at him, my eyes half open.

He lightly strokes a finger down my center. "You're telling me this pussy hasn't been eaten before?"

I bite my lip and shake my head once.

"Oh, baby girl," Wolf says through a chuckle. "It would be my pleasure and honor to eat this pretty pussy for every meal."

His blunt words flare my arousal, and I clench my thighs, squeezing his shoulders.

"Ah, my girl likes the sound of that, does she?" His taunting smirk is dirty and cocky. And now I know for sure that I've changed, because it's all I can do not to push his face down and into me.

"Yes, yes, I want that," I say with a nod.

He tugs my boxer briefs to the side, exposing my pussy to his hungry gaze. I can feel his stare on me, and instead of feeling self-conscious like I thought I would, I feel empowered.

I widen my legs, and that's all the incentive Wolf needs before he dives in. He licks and nips and sucks until I'm a sweaty, squirming mess.

Before long, my legs start to tremble and my fingers tingle. I close my eyes in anticipation.

"Wolf, I-I——" I don't finish my sentence before my orgasm rolls through me, stealing my words and my breath.

My chest heaves, and my body sighs as I slowly relax my vice-grip on Wolf's head.

Wolf gently runs his fingers up and down my legs, murmuring his praise against my skin.

"Oh my god." My words end on a disbelieving laugh. "That was amazing. C'mere."

Wolf gets close enough for me to grab his face and bring his mouth to mine. I taste myself on his lips as our tongues tangle together.

I let my fingers wander down his hard chest, over tattooed muscles that I vow to trace with my tongue, and dip into the waistband of his shorts.

He groans, this long, drawn-out noise when I wrap my fingers around his dick.

I stroke him, and a little trickle of worry spears my lusty post-orgasm daze. He's big—like really big.

How the hell am I—

I lose my train of thought when I hear a creak. Turning my

head to the side, I break the kiss and Wolf takes the opportunity to slide his lips down my neck, but that's not what makes me lose my breath.

Sully stands in the doorway, hand on the doorknob and door partially opened.

His eyes blaze with hunger as they feast on the scene before him—my knees wide, shirt above my tits, and hand down Wolf's shorts. Surprise keeps me immobile, but as the seconds tick by, something else keeps me quiet.

Sully's muscles bunch and his jaw clenches. He's waging a war on himself, and I'm not sure which side will end up victorious.

Warmth pools low in my belly as my fantasy comes to life. I decide to be brave, and I tempt him further. I slide my hand out of his shorts, over his hard muscles, and push on his shoulder. He reluctantly pulls back.

"I want to taste you."

Wolf falls to the bed on his back with a grin that lives up to his name. "Whatever you want, Red."

I slide his shorts down, freeing his dick. I don't give myself any more time to get intimidated by his size, and I lick the tip, circling my tongue around the head.

I teased him, flicking my tongue on the sensitive spot underneath until his moans got lower and longer. I slowly took more of him, glancing up at Wolf and holding his gaze.

I watch him bite his lip, hear his breath hitch, and feel his body tense—his cues giving away what he likes. I find a good rhythm, the combination of my mouth and my hand, and start working Wolf over.

His groans only ramp up my own desire, and I hollow out my cheeks. He slides his fingers through my hair, resting them against the back of my head.

"I'm going to come, baby girl," he groans out.

I suck even harder, deeper, and my eyes water, but I don't stop. I keep my gaze on him as he falls apart. Head tipped back and eyes closed tight, every muscle in his body pauses and tenses. It's one of the most beautiful things I've ever seen.

When he comes down from his orgasm high, he sits forward and pulls me up with him. His lips meet mine in an intense kiss that has tingles racing down my spine.

I wrap my arm around his neck and deepen the kiss. Wolf breaks the kiss to trail his lips down my throat. I turn my head just in time to see Sully shudder and step backward until he's out of the room. He closes the door softly, and then a second later, he pounds on the door with his fist.

"Let's go, princess. You're late."

Wolf groans into my neck before he turns his head to yell, "Fuck off, Sully."

Sully pounds on the door again. "I'm not going to wait around all day. And if you don't come now, we're going to go back to instructional lessons only."

Wolf rolls off of me, hops off the bed, and storms to the bedroom door. He flings it open and points right in Sully's face. "Stop fucking cockblocking me, you asshole."

I make sure my shirt covers my tits, but I don't move otherwise.

Sully raises a brow, but his innocent look needs some work. "How was I supposed to know you were in there? I thought she was just skipping out on me."

Wolf drops his hand and tilts his head back and laughs. It's a dry and disbelieving sound. "Oh, fuck off. Don't act like you didn't just stand in the doorway and watch Red suck my dick for five minutes."

Sully scoffs. "Five minutes? Please. It was like a second."

"Ha! So you admit it!"

Sully bares his teeth at his brother. "I admit nothing." He

looks over Wolf's shoulder at me. "You've got two minutes to get to the gym, or I'm leaving."

I bite my lip and nod. I wonder how much farther I can poke and prod at Sully before he finally snaps.

There's only one way to find out.

18

ALAINA

AFTER WOLF SLAMS the door in Sully's face, he turns to face me with his hands on his hips, but all I can focus on is his impressive dick straining against his black gym shorts.

Black gym shorts come in a close second after gray sweatpants.

Wolf runs his hands in his hair as he exhales. "I can't believe I'm the one saying this, but you gotta get up and get that sweet ass to the gym. Sully's a prick sometimes, and I know you've been itching to learn more self-defense techniques."

I focus on his face when I reach my arms above my head and stretch. His answering groan fuels my fire, and I can't stop the little smirk that tips up the corner of my mouth.

"C'mon, baby girl, don't look at me like that," Wolf says as he rearranges his dick.

I roll over and push up to a sitting position before I crawl across the bed.

"Goddamn selfish fucking asshole," Wolf mutters low, but loud enough for me to hear. His voice sounds tortured, and I do feel a little bad that I'm leaving him with blue balls.

I slip off the bed and pad toward the bathroom. When I

reach the doorway, I look over my shoulder. Wolf's gaze is glued to my ass.

"Come find me after training?"

"Aye. I'll come after training."

His words sound like a promise, and a shiver of excitement zips down my spine.

———

I WALK into the gym in the basement of the safe house. It's a huge space that runs about half the length of the house. The other half is finished with several rooms—none of which I've seen. Rush told me there's another weapons room and some storage down here, though.

Floor-to-ceiling mirrors line two of the four walls across from one another. The floor is light gray wood and the walls are a soft white, and coupled with the high ceilings and strategic bright lighting, it doesn't feel like a basement at all. It feels like I just walked into some luxury gym a few blocks away from my dorm in the city.

Standard gym equipment takes up one side of the gym—treadmill, elliptical, bench press, and squat machine. A full weight rack sits in the far corner next to a couple of exercise balls and a few sets of resistance bands.

The other half of the room is mostly empty, with just soft black foam flooring over the wood. That's where I find Sully standing, arms crossed and scowl directed my way. He tracks my movement as I walk toward him, never losing his rigid posture.

And then it's like a lightbulb goes off in my mind.

"Ah. I get it now," I murmur as I stop in front of him.

His brow raises and his cheek ticks. "What's that, princess?"

"Your name. It's because you sulk all the time, isn't it?" I lose

162

the battle with myself and the cheeky grin I was holding in slips free.

Sully uncrosses his arms and scoffs. "Really? That's why you think they call me Sully?"

"Makes sense to me. I don't remember you being this sulky a couple of years ago," I say as I give him my back. I'm pushing it —I know I am, but still, I can't stop.

I'm begging for a reaction from him. For him to lose control again.

"Really? That's it? Some bullshit about my name? You're not going to ask me what I was doing this morning?"

I twist my lips to the side and tilt my head as I go off my hunch. "Yep. That's it."

I turn to make my way to the treadmill to warm my muscles up, just like he's instructed the last few days. But today, I'll finally get to *do* something instead of just watching other people do things.

It feels like there's this itch just beneath my skin that's persistent, and the only time it's satiated is when I'm either with one of them or doing something proactive—like learning how to defend myself.

Sully takes two steps forward and reaches out to stop me with a hand on my shoulder. I wait him out, still facing forward, but I can see his reflection in the mirror across from me. Tortured heroes look less troubled than my ex-boyfriend does right now.

I almost feel bad for him—almost. Maybe if I understood why he's fighting this—me—so hard, it'd be easier. But until he's ready to tell me what really happened that night two years ago when he up and left me, I'm not really sure how to help him.

Maybe I shouldn't be pushing so hard. Maybe I'm being greedy—shit, I'm *definitely* being greedy.

Wolf and Rush are so insanely hot and kind and wonderful and they take care of me and—

"Sully is short for O'Sullivan." When I just stare at him through the mirror with a blank expression, he sighs. "As in James Edmond O'Sullivan Fitzpatrick."

I feel my eyebrows draw together as I try to piece together all the small bits of information I know.

"Cormac adopted me when I was a baby."

"So you really were raised as brothers," I muse as I turn around to face him. "Where are your parents?"

"Dead or gone, doesn't really matter either way to me." Sully shrugs, but I don't buy it. No one is that unaffected by losing your parents—either by choice or circumstance.

"I know what you're thinking, and you're wrong. Cormac is my Da—he always has been."

I raise my hands up. "I wasn't thinking that." I pause and look around before I ask, "But I was wondering why he didn't change your name when you were a baby then? Y'know, drop the O'Sullivan?"

Sully shrugs. "Dunno, I asked him once. Said there's power to a man's name, and it's up to god to take that power away, not him."

I bite my lip as I look at him. I contemplate what to ask next. He's in a surprisingly giving mood, and I want to take advantage of that.

"About that night, two years ago—"

Sully turns around, the movement interrupting my train of thought. He walks away from me, and I swallow everything I wanted to say. For now.

"Let's start with the wrist grab. Think you can handle that, princess? I'm going to put some music on while you get into position." Derision drips from his words, snuffing out the beginning stirrings of want that started when he told me to *get into position*.

I don't know what's going on with me, but I feel like ever

since we came here, I unlocked a part of myself I've never seen before—not really.

If I think back to a couple of years ago, to that summer that I shared with Sully, I might find some parallels, but I don't usually make a habit out of traveling down that memory lane. The end result is still painful for me to remember. I had more than a few dark days afterward—and I honestly thought I'd never see him again.

But fate has a funny way of working out, doesn't she?

She's given me an opportunity to explore . . . myself. Who I am when you strip away all my accolades and accomplishments. Who I am when I stop letting past relationships hold me hostage.

And who I am when I give myself permission to explore my heart . . . and my libido.

I watch Sully as he messes around with the stereo in the corner of the room. I hadn't really noticed the speakers until now, since they're built nearly seamlessly into the walls and ceiling. "Hateful" by The Clash fills the gym, and I raise a brow.

Okay, so he wants to play dirty. Well, luckily for him, I'm into pushing his buttons.

Sully walks back and stands in front of me. "Ready?"

"I'm ready."

Sully slowly grabs my wrist, giving me plenty of time to place my free hand on top of his hand. I swing my arm—the one he's holding—around and outward to grab his wrist. His arm is now twisted behind him, and the angle is purposely awkward. All I have to do is apply a little pressure, and he folds to the floor.

I release him and jump a few times, my heart beating fast and my smile widening. "Yes! I did it."

Sully gets up off the floor and turns to face me. "Good. Again. This time a little faster."

My smile wilts at his lack of praise, but I brush it off. He

165

starts off with the same movement—grabbing my wrist—but this time he's quicker and he takes a step into my space.

I complete the same movements and force him to the ground again. We run through this move dozens of times until I can do it without conscious thought.

"Good. Let's move to the next one."

My breaths are fast from exertion, and honestly, from the proximity. I haven't ever done something like this before, so I can't say for sure if I would have the same reaction to anyone teaching me this. But my gut tells me I wouldn't. It's all Sully.

There's something electric in the air, and with each touch of our bodies, it sizzles a little more. The air is thick with tension, and anticipation builds inside me.

Sully steps behind me and loops his arms around my neck as if he's going to choke me. In one movement, I grab his wrists and pull, drop down into a squat, and turn my face to the side. This next part is trickier, and I'm not as quick. I tilt my body toward him and take a step behind him, so his leg is now between my knee and my elbow, bent in what should be an uncomfortably low position. Squatting even further to keep my weight heavy and my center of balance stable, I grab behind his knees and lift. He loses his balance and immediately lets go of my neck as he falls to the mats.

"Good. Faster. This one's important, Lainey."

The use of my nickname from his lips is enough for me to pause. He only ever called me that a few times, always when we were having a serious moment.

That little slip-up of his waters the kernel of hope that's slowly growing.

I don't respond as he gets into position, and we run through the movements again. I don't pick this one up as quickly as I did the other one, but I do improve.

After a dozen more tries, we transition into another move. We spend about the same time on three more moves before we get to the final one.

I've been dreading this move the most, and not for obvious reasons. A week ago I was in this exact situation—pinned down by a man much bigger and stronger than me. I thank the universe every day that I survived relatively unscathed, and I haven't even begun to process everything yet, but I know that if I'd known about these moves, I might've never been at that cabin to begin with. I might've been able to stop the red-eyed demon man in the back of O'Malley's long enough to run and get help, at least.

No, I'm dreading this move because it places Sully in between my thighs. And I'm pretty sure that my body didn't get the memo that this is serious training.

I take a deep breath and try to center myself, but I can feel warmth coloring my neck and cheeks.

"What's wrong?" Sully asks from right in front of me.

"Hm? Nothing's wrong."

"Why are you all flushed?"

"It's . . . hot in here. I'm hot," I say as I wave my hand around to indicate the space. I swear I can see pheromones sparkling all over him.

I fix the strap on my tank top to buy myself some time to calm down. It's a black and white Ramones racerback tank top, and it's kind of perfect. I paired it with a pair of short black workout shorts. I pluck the hem and ask, "I've been meaning to ask. Is this you?"

A light flush colors his cheeks. "You can't wear our tees and boxers forever." He shrugs a shoulder. "It's just a few shirts and shit."

Warmth bubbles inside my chest when I imagine Sully picking out clothes for me.

"Okay, well, let's get into position," he says as he kneels on the floor.

"Okay, Sully." My voice is low as I lay on my back, knees bent.

Sully climbs on top of me, in between my legs, and mimes like he's going to choke me. His face is close enough that I can see the tick in his jaw and the purse of his lips.

"Walk through these motions, okay? They're more complicated than the last ones."

I nod, and when he leans forward to apply a little pressure, I wrap my legs around his waist and lock my ankles together. His cock brushes against me, and my breath hitches.

The feeling of his hard cock against me lets loose a swarm of butterflies in my belly. I blink a few times to refocus.

"You okay, Lainey?" The concern in his voice has my heart clenching.

"I'm fine." My voice is a lot more breathless than I'd like, but the feeling of him rubbing his dick against me short-circuits my brain. With effort, I focus on my next move.

I reach up with my arms crossed and grab his elbows, almost creating a bar with my forearms. Then I push down toward my chest as hard as I can. Sully murmurs his praise from closer than before, but I don't let myself get distracted by the low timbre of his voice or the way he fits so perfectly between my legs.

In one sweeping motion, I tilt my hips and bring my legs up to his shoulders, aligning us for a single moment before I apply pressure with my legs. Sully all but collapses on top of me, and I let go of him immediately.

"Good job. Again. A little faster this time," he says as he pushes off the floor, his biceps flexing on either side of my head.

We run through the move three more times before I make a mistake. My grip on his elbow slips and my hold breaks. Sully's hands are still loosely around my neck as he presses forward, like any real attacker would. His lips are centimeters away from mine and his body presses mine into the mat beneath me.

And for a single moment, I freeze. Then I remind myself to be brave.

I don't do the counter moves he taught me—no, I do something much more effective.

I arch my back and tilt my head up and seal my lips to his. I'm rewarded for my bravery by a low, long groan as he parts his lips and slips his tongue against mine.

He tastes like sweet mint, and he kisses me like it could change the fate of the world. He moves his hands from my neck and grabs my wrists, placing them on the mat next to my head.

He invades every one of my senses, and it's intoxicating. If being with Sully has me dizzy and breathless, I'll gladly live blissed-out.

He starts a slow grind, and the way his cock rubs against my clit has my toes curling in my sneakers. I stutter out a moan as he deepens the kiss, swallowing my pleasure.

My head spins, and I flex my fingers, desperate to hold on to something—anything—while he drags me further toward my orgasm. It's like he reads my mind, because in the next instant, he slides his hand into mine and laces our fingers together.

He continues his slow, torturous pace as he rolls and swivels his hips, his dick pressing and swirling against my clit in the most delicious rhythm.

I squeeze his fingers when my orgasm sneaks up on me, momentarily overtaking my senses. I open my mouth as a silent moan slips out, and Sully moves his lips to my neck.

I'm floating somewhere above the clouds where everything is soft and dreamy when Sully pushes off of me and sits back on his knees. I open my eyes to see him swipe the back of his hand across his mouth. I feel my brows scrunch up at the look of scorn painted on his beautiful face.

My dreamy smile slips from my face. "What's wrong?"

Sully scoffs. "Whatever, Alaina. You happy now?"

I scramble to sit up and scoot back, putting a couple of feet between us.

"What are you talking about?" I ask as I smooth my hair back and make sure my tank top is in place.

"You got what you wanted, didn't you?" He sneers at me, and I look behind me to make sure there isn't someone else in the room.

"I-I don't understand."

He scoffs. "Come on, princess. Even you aren't that clueless. You've been after my dick for weeks—years. So now that you got a little taste, you can leave me the fuck alone, yeah?"

To my absolute horror, tears of anger and indignation well up in my eyes. "*After your dick*? Are you fucking nuts?! And I—I didn't *get a little taste* of anything!"

He stands up and straightens his clothes, laughing at me. It's this terrible, cruel sound that wraps barbed wire around my heart. I thought we were making progress, but now, now I don't know what the hell to do.

"Ah, you said *fuck*. You fuck around with my brothers for a few weeks, and suddenly you're this tough bird now? Please. Stop pretending, *princess*. And did you or did you not just come on my dick?" He raises one stupid, perfect brow, and I feel my blood pressure rise.

I stand up to face him head on, anger licking up my spine and curling my fists. "You know what? Fuck you, Sully. I haven't been after anything."

"Nah. I'm good."

"It wasn't an offer, asshole." I'm seething, my hands tremble and the urge to knock some sense into him pounds at my temples. I spin on my heel as Taking Back Sunday's "There's No 'I' In Team" plays from the speakers, mocking me.

I reach the doorway when clarity hits me like a lightning bolt. I look over my shoulder at my ex-boyfriend. His bright-blue gaze is pinned on me and every muscle is coiled with tension.

"We both know I didn't start anything there." I tilt my head toward the mat. "And when you're done being a coward, you know where to find me."

I walk out of the gym before he can respond, not that I think he would.

19

ALAINA

TWO DAYS LATER, I wander down the hallway with two glasses of iced tea toward Rush's office in the afternoon. After that morning in the gym, I didn't see Sully for the rest of the day. The next morning, I made sure to show up early to the gym, ready to hash it out—maybe even talk about what happened a couple of years ago. But he acted like nothing was amiss.

Like he didn't just make me come from rubbing his dick against me.

He went back to his hands-off approach of teaching me self-defense, but it's even worse now. He only talks to me when it's absolutely necessary, and he's otherwise ignoring me. It's not as easy for me to learn the movements, but I'm going to ask Wolf or Rush to come down there tomorrow, so I can practice on them.

I seriously doubt either one—especially Wolf—will object to me running my hands all over them for a couple of hours. In fact, I can see it ending with us tangled up and making out.

I'll ask them both at dinner tonight, and they can decide between themselves. Or maybe they both come down and I get to relive another one of my fantasies.

I'm not sure if it's the near-death experience or something that would've happened regardless, but being surrounded by them nonstop for the last week has my imagination running wild.

I stand in the doorway and take a moment to watch Rush in his element. Much like every other time I'm in here, the TV in front of the couch is on, some national news channel playing quietly.

He's at his desk, wearing a black tee and black gym shorts. All of his monitors are on, displaying various screens—most of which I still don't understand.

I lean my shoulder against the doorframe and watch his muscles flex as he types and two screens change to security footage of the house.

"Are you gonna stand there all day?" he asks, and I hear the wry smile in his voice.

I push off the door and walk to his desk, placing a frosty glass in front of his face. Without turning around, he wraps his fingers around the glass, brushing against mine.

"What's this?"

I shrug, even though he's not looking at me yet. "I wanted to see you, but I don't want to interrupt."

"You're never interrupting, birdie." He hits a few keys on his keyboard and spins around, taking the glass from me. He gently clinks his glass with mine. "And to what do I owe the pleasure?"

I shrug and look to the side, apparently trying to find my courage.

"It's just . . . I'm curious."

"About?"

"You, mostly." I hesitate and bite my lip. "Wolf's already shared a lot with me, and Sully and I . . . have history. And I want to know more about you."

Rush holds my gaze as he tilts his head and repeats my words. "You want to know more about me."

"Yes?" I hitch a shoulder up when my statement sounds more like a question. "Don't you think we should? I mean, I don't even know what your favorite color is. Or band. Or type of food. Or TV show."

"Black. Too many. Italian. *The Walking Dead*."

He answers so quickly that it takes me a moment to remember what I asked him.

"Wait. *The Walking Dead* is your favorite show? I expected something less . . . zombielike." My nose scrunches as I add this piece to the puzzle that is Rush in my mind.

"Right now it is." Rush nods and runs the tip of his finger around the top of the glass. "I like the idea of being prepared if our world ever devolves into something similar."

I feel my eyebrows hit my hairline, and I take a step closer to him. "That actually makes some sense. But you don't really think that could happen to us, right? Like in this day and age."

Even with him sitting down in an office chair, I'm only about a head taller than him—and I'm still standing.

He stares at me from underneath those inky lashes of his, and I decide it must be a genetic thing, because all three boys have the darkest, longest lashes I've seen. Though Sully isn't technically blood-related, so maybe they're just lucky. I know plenty of girls at my old school that would pay good money for falsies that nice. The thought makes me smile.

"I think, theoretically, our world as we know it could collapse. Either from a targeted attack or from something else."

"Something else?" My interest is piqued. I do love a good theoretical end-of-the-world discussion.

"Sure. Maybe something like those horror films happens— rabies makes a resurgence and turns everyone into zombies. Or maybe it's a tech attack."

"Oh! Like a fire sale from *Die Hard*!" I exclaim.

He chuckles as he takes another sip. "How much rum did you put in this iced tea, little bird?"

I lift a shoulder up in a half-hearted attempt at nonchalance. "A splash . . . or so."

Rush's whole face lights up when he laughs. His eyes downright twinkle as his smile spreads across his face. I don't even care if it's at my benefit—I'd do it all over again and more just to see him laugh like that.

"Oh," I breathe the word out.

His chuckles die down but his smile remains. He regards me with a raised eyebrow, and I just know without him even saying a word that he wants me to elaborate.

I'm not sure when it happened, but somehow I've learned some of his cues. The thought is enough to send a bolt of pleasure through my veins.

"I've never seen you laugh like that. It's . . . nice. Really nice."

"Mm-hmm."

I stare at him a moment longer, letting myself get tangled up in his gray eyes. They look clear today, like the sky in winter.

"So, is it like *Die Hard* then? I thought that was all fiction." I ask before I take a sip of my own rum iced tea.

"Yes and no. Theoretically, a three-part cyber attack could happen on any country's computer infrastructure."

"Transportation, financial, and public systems, right?"

His smile widens. "A fan of *Die Hard*, huh?"

My smile matches his as I curl my fingers around the glass, rubbing the condensation with my thumb. "I like action movies. And I was curious about the logistics of a fire sale, since I live in New York City."

"How interesting," he murmurs. "And yes, banking and stocks, traffic lights and airports, electricity and gas and telecommunications would all be hit. But the likelihood of it happening here—successfully—is slim."

"How come?" I ask as I take another sip. The smoothness of the rum and the fruitiness of the black iced tea really do pair so nicely—thankfully. It was all I could find in the pantry upstairs, so it was my only option.

"Well, the movie did get one thing right. You'd need a team to not only create the compromised systems, but then you'd need a team to implement it at very specific times. And maybe the most likely reason—they'd all have to keep the secret. And some people cannot keep a secret to save their lives. So they don't." He pauses and looks directly at me, face carefully blank. "Can you keep a secret, little bird?"

There's something about the way he says the question that feels like it's loaded. Like maybe there's another meaning behind his seemingly innocent question.

I find myself nodding before I even gave it conscious thought.

Rush's gaze roams all over me, and it feels like a physical caress. Awareness sizzles in the air between us, and I sway toward him.

"I know you can. C'mere." He tilts his head to the side. "I wanna show you something."

I cross the room in a few strides, drinking the last few sips of iced tea from my glass. The rum warms my veins, giving me just enough bravery to sit in his lap.

"Good girl," he murmurs in my ear as he spins the chair around so we're facing the bank of monitors.

"You remember what I told you about the security cameras around here?"

"Yes. How to access them and how to switch angles."

He sweeps my hair to one side, his warm breath caressing the sensitive skin behind my ear.

"Hands on the desk, eyes on the screens. Show me."

I swallow and stare at the blank monitors. Everything I've

ever known flies out of my brain as the feel of him leaves a life-long impression.

I type a few things and navigate the computer with more ease than the first day, but I've got a long way to go to become anywhere as good as Rush.

Security feeds pop up on all four monitors, each split into four screens. Sixteen cameras located around the property is not as crazy as I once thought it was.

The safe house sits on a big piece of land in the middle of the woods somewhere. I still don't really know where we are, and I haven't asked. I trust them to keep me safe.

"What do you see?" Rush's fingertips tiptoe along my outer thighs, and my breath hitches.

"Wh-what are you doing?"

"Shh. Focus. Tell me what you see." His breath stirs the hair on the back of my neck, and shivers tingle down my back.

I lick my lips and give the four screens my attention. Two of the four screens are all outside, so I start there.

"Eight cameras point at possible entry points, the guard gate, and the back end of the property." I stare at the screens a second longer, looking for movement, before typing in a command that pulls up movement history. "No movement detected in the last ten hours."

I switch back to the live feed and watch it for a couple more minutes, trying to ignore the way his fingertips drag along my skin. My attention shifts to him, and like the intuitive man I've come to know he is, he knows it.

So he stops touching me, because like I've also come to realize, he can be a stubborn bastard.

"The screens, birdie. Tell me what you see."

I sigh, exhaling mounting frustration and lust, and focus on the live feed of the backyard again.

"Okay. There"—I point at the screen—"those leaves are not moving in a looped pattern."

"And what does that mean?" He drags his lips along my neck, stopping at the curve of my shoulder.

My breath stutters.

"Um, it means that we haven't been compromised."

"That's right."

I glance down and see his tattooed hands spread across the tops of my thighs. A sliver of lust slowly swirls in my lower belly.

Rush drags those warm, tattooed fingers up and down the tops of my thighs, inching my hot pink skirt up with each pass. His movements are light, slow—deliberate.

"Now do the others."

I blame the hormones leaking out of my pores for the dirty image that pops into my brain—me *doing* Wolf. And Sully. And Rush.

Before I can get too carried away, and with Herculean effort, I focus back on the remaining security feeds. There aren't cameras in the actual bedrooms, but they cover pretty much everything else.

"Wolf's in the living room playing video games."

He's so animated when he plays, and by the way he's throwing his arms up in the air and gesturing wildly, I'd say he's losing whatever game he's playing.

That thought ticks up the corner of my mouth. It's good for him to be knocked down a peg or two once in a while. An attempt at keeping him humble, at least.

Rush fingers the hem of my skirt, his fingers sliding against my skin in the most delicious way, and my muscles tense in anticipation.

This one is hot pink, short, and bouncy. I found it in my dresser with a handful of new clothes yesterday. I paired it with an off-the-shoulder distressed white tee.

"And Sully?"

I arch my back at the feel of Rush's mouth against my neck, pressing my ass into his lap. His answering groan is low and long, and it rumbles against my back.

I flick my gaze around the screens until I find my missing dark king. I hit the commands to enlarge one screen, and then my breath stops while my heart pounds double time.

"Did you know these cameras have sound?"

I shake my head, transfixed on the sight of my ex-boyfriend turned *something* in the gym.

Rush takes his hands off my thighs to type something on the keyboard. I'm sure I should be paying attention, but I can't tear my gaze away from Sully.

He's in gym shorts only, sitting on the bench press machine. I hungrily gaze at all that exposed tattooed skin—and all those goddamn muscles. I'm not sure that I'll ever get used to being able to look at *and touch* any of these men freely.

My gaze flicks around his body, unable to focus on any one thing. Until sound filters in, then I can't take my eyes away from one specific part of his body.

A low groan filters through the speakers as Sully drags his hand down his stomach and into his gym shorts.

I'd forgotten about Rush behind me, so engrossed in the show Sully's inadvertently putting on, that I startle when he places his palms on my thighs again.

A breath leaves me in a whoosh when he drags his palms along the inside of my thighs.

"Should we—uh—should we be watching him like this?"

His fingers trace the edge of my thong, teasing the sensitive skin there.

"He does this every day after your training sessions with him. He punishes himself in more ways than one. But he knows you're in here." He slides his fingers over the triangle of fabric separating our skin. "With me." He applies pressure to my clit. "Working on security today." He begins slow, tortuous circles on my clit, and I curse the cotton between us.

I'm desperate to feel his skin. I lick my lips and tilt my head back, keeping Sully in my line of sight.

"So he knew we'd be watching?"

"Aye, he knew." Rush pulls my thong to the side and softly swirls his finger along my clit. A moan slips past my lips before I even realize it.

Sully's head snaps to the camera, and I freeze, startled that he's looking right at us.

"Didn't I mention that this system can tap into the speakers in several rooms?" Rush murmurs against my skin, his lips never leaving my neck.

"No," I breathe out. "You hadn't."

My lust spikes at the idea of Sully listening to me come from Rush's fingers while watching him.

Sully's arm flexes with each stroke, and my gaze stays glued to his cock in his hand. I can't quite see it in the detail I'd like to, but I use my imagination to fill in the details I can't see.

Rush widens my legs, pushing my ass against his cock. My thong stretches to accommodate his hand, but apparently, it's not enough, because the next thing I hear the tearing of fabric. And then cool air greets my exposed pussy.

"Did you hear that, Sully? I just ripped her thong off her body," Rush taunts. He swirls a finger around my clit before he dips it inside of me and then brings his finger back up to tease me. Over and over and over again.

"You motherfucker," Sully grits out, but he doesn't sound all that broken up about it. In fact, I'd say he sounds turned on knowing that Rush and I are in here doing things he can only hear.

I tilt my head back to rest on Rush's shoulders, never taking my gaze from the screen where Sully strokes his cock with fast, angry movements.

Rush pushes one finger, then two inside me, timing it with Sully's strokes.

And I'm fucking panting.

Rush's other hand drifts up to cup my throat, gentle but firm. I tear my gaze off Sully to look at our reflection in the dark, blank screen in front of us. The sight of Rush's tattooed fingers wrapped around my throat, my head thrown back in ecstasy, is enough to have me barreling toward an orgasm.

"Rush—I—" I groan, cutting myself off when pleasure spikes.

"That's it, baby. Give it to me." He gently tilts my head back with his grip on my neck, and I look down my nose at Sully working his cock faster, grunting and groaning with pleasure.

Rush keeps two fingers inside my pussy and grinds the palm of his hand against my clit, and I see stars.

Everything clenches, and I fight to keep my eyes open, desperate to see Sully when he comes, but Rush is relentless in his quest for my orgasm.

I give into my body's demands and close my eyes, letting out a moan loud enough to be heard in every room of the house.

After a few moments, I open my eyes in time to see Sully lazily stroke his dick, eyes on me and a smirk on his stupidly handsome face.

"You okay, birdie?"

I nod, too wrung out to use words.

Rush leans forward, grabs a napkin from the desk, and says, "See you at dinner, man." He turns off the security feed and leans back in the chair. "Okay, baby, scoot forward for me. I have to do some clean-up."

My muscles feel like jelly, but I do as he asks and move off his lap, turning to lean my butt against the desk so I can face him. "Clean-up?"

"Aye. It's never happened before, but you made me come in my pants like some guy who saw his first pair of tits." He winks. "It'll be our little secret, yeah?"

Something warm unfurls inside me—and I don't mean another orgasm, though that would be fun.

"I like giving you a first, Dec." I lean forward and whisper the words against his mouth before placing a soft kiss against his lips.

His eyes shine as he looks at me. "I'll give you everything, birdie. Everything."

20

ALAINA

"MMM. So good, like usual. Thank you, Wolf."

I'm at the sink, washing and rinsing the dishes we used for dinner. Wolf made spaghetti Bolognese, and it was some of the best pasta I've ever had. I still don't really understand how they've gotten food here these last couple weeks—I haven't seen them leave, and no one's breached the perimeter.

"Dreams" from Fleetwood Mac's Rumors album plays in the speakers from the living room. I discovered their record player tucked in a drawer a few days ago when I was snooping around.

To my credit, all three of them were sitting on the couch playing a video game, so I wasn't really spying too much. More like perusing their shelves, checking out book titles, generally looking for more insight on my three mysterious men.

All three of them are their own little mysteries, freely giving me bits and pieces, but like most things in life, I have to figure most of it out myself.

I'm still waiting on answers about what the Brotherhood is— and what that means for them.

I rinse the last dish and pass it to Rush to dry.

"Xbox or PS4 tonight?" Wolf asks as he jumps over the back of the couch, landing on the middle cushion with a thump.

"Depends. Which game do you want to get your ass kicked in?" Rush delivers the taunt with a wry smirk, and I bite my lip to smother my giggle at the last second.

Rush leans over and places his mouth right by my ear. "Something funny, birdie?"

I tilt my head and look at him over my shoulder, but Wolf explodes off the couch in faux outrage, stopping me from saying anything.

"Bring it, brother. I'll wipe the floor with you!" Wolf points his index finger at me. "And I call Red on my team."

I turn around completely, my arm brushing Rush's chest. I let the small smile spread across my face, content to let this play out. I'm not sure if I'd ever admit it, but I kind of like it when they play fight over me like this. The kind of teasing that tells me I'm wanted. But not the kind of arguing where one wants to over-throw the other two—not that this has happened, and honestly, I don't think it would. I mean, I already told Rush that I wanted all three of them. But maybe it's worth a conversation with all of them?

"You can have her. She's the worst teammate," Sully grumbles as he puts the dishes back in the cabinet.

"Birdie, you really aren't very good." Rush sounds apologetic about it, like he's afraid he's going to hurt my feelings with his assessment. It almost makes me feel bad for what I did—almost.

Wolf chuckles, and the smile I was containing spreads.

"What? She is. She fucking killed my guy more than the enemy did!" Sully scowls and crosses his arms. "So I'm going solo tonight."

Rush nods. "It's true. I checked the stats last night after we played. She's done more friendly fire when she's teamed with us than any of us have combined. In years."

"Of course, you would check the stats." Wolf scoffs. "Man, she fucking played you guys," Wolf says through a laugh.

Sully steps back and cocks his head to the side, looking at me. "Is that true, Alaina?"

I mimic his stance and shrug a shoulder. "Yes, and no." I see Rush cover his smile with his palm out of the corner of my eye. I'm sure he's replaying those very same words he said to me a few days ago.

"What's that supposed to mean?" Sully asks as he pushes off the counter he was leaning on and stalks toward me.

I take a few steps to the side, so the island is firmly between us. What started out as a joke quickly morphed into a game of cat and mouse. Only Sully doesn't realize that I'm a cat in a mouse's disguise. But he will. And soon.

The air in the kitchen thickens with tension, and I hear Wolf and Rush talking, but I don't take my eyes off my opponent, or my prize, depending on how you look at it. And I'd very much like to look at Sully as a prize. In fact, I'd like to have a repeat of what happened in the gym, but maybe with fewer clothes and less hostility.

Something on my face must betray my thoughts, because Sully stops moving and braces his hands on the island in front of him.

My heart pounds when I see lust swirling in his ocean-blue eyes.

Instinctively, I back up, a devious smile on my face. Instead of heading toward the living room, I make a snap decision and speedwalk to Rush. He's still standing by the sink, arms crossed, muscles bulging under his signature black tee. He's closer to Sully, but the wry grin on his face tells me he knows what I'm planning to do.

And that's where I realize my mistake. I'd focused too much on Sully, and I forgot that Rush was just as much of a threat.

He's just a quieter predator, the kind that will sneak in unde-tected. You'll only know he's there if he wants you too.

Sully stalks toward me as soon as he realizes my intention, determination and possession etched in every feature.

I step into the space between Rush and the sink two seconds before Sully reaches us.

The boys stare at one another for a second, and I bite my lip in anticipation.

"Brother?" Sully's voice is light with amusement. I peek around Rush's shoulder and see Sully with a cocky smile on his face.

Oh shit.

That smile is fucking lethal.

I'm about to step out from behind Rush to put a stop to what-ever's about to happen when Rush takes two steps away from me and stands next to Sully.

The matching smirks that slowly spread across their faces can only be described as carnal and devious. I'm not sure that I've ever thought those two words together before, but it's the best description for them.

They're backlit from the dining room lights, casting shadows across their faces. As if it was coordinated, they both fold their arms across their impressive chests, and I have to remind myself to breathe.

They leave me breathless so often I'm starting to wonder if I developed asthma and didn't realize it.

"Brother. It seems you need something here from our little bird." Rush nods toward me, but Sully doesn't take his gaze off of me.

"You playin' me, Lainey?"

My breath catches at his use of my nickname, and my heart pounds when they both step into me, each one placing an arm on either side of me, palms flat against the countertop. I tilt my head back to maintain eye contact, but it's impossible to look at both of them at the same time.

"I wouldn't say *playing* exactly," I hedge. "More like . . . beginner's luck?"

Rush tilts his head toward me, close enough for his lips to brush mine with his next words. "Explain. Now."

A shiver rolls down my spine at his command, and I open my mouth to comply without too much thought. At the last second, I bite my lip instead. Rush is always so in control, I wonder what will happen if I challenge him a little.

I push up to my tiptoes and say against his lips, "Make me."

Judging by the chuckles floating around, I'm not the only one amused right now.

Rush's jaw clenches, and his body is rigid with tension. I can feel every delicious, tense line of his muscles pressed against me, and my veins start buzzing in anticipation.

My lips part, certain that he's going to kiss me, when Wolf's voice cuts through the air, cutting the tension like a knife.

"Oi! As much as I love watching you two . . . do whatever it is that you're doing, I'm ready to kick some ass. So are we playing or what?"

Rush sighs, hanging his head forward for a second before he pushes off the counter. He spins on his heel and stalks toward the living room.

He rounds the end of the couch and sits heavily on the end. Wolf tosses him a controller, and the two of them start playing some game, acting like Rush wasn't a hair's breadth away from kissing me two seconds ago. In front of both of them.

"C'mon, birdie," Rush calls from the living room. "You're with me tonight."

Sully nudges me with his shoulder.

I startle a little, and I feel my cheeks warm. "Sorry. I didn't see you there."

"It's fine. Let's go kick some ass. You're with me next game."
Sully tips his head toward the living room, a signal to follow
behind him.

"You know it really was just beginner's luck, right? I'm not
good at those kinds of games," I say through a laugh as we walk
toward the living room.

"Oh, I picked up on that after the fifth time you killed my guy
last night."

I laugh but don't deny it.

"And somewhere around the tenth time, I know that you
figured out what you were doing, and you kept doing it," Rush
says as we round the couch. He snags my hand and laces our
fingers together, pulling me down on top of his lap.

I'm starting to think that Rush has a thing for me sitting in his
lap. I'd be lying if I said I didn't like it.

I shrug a shoulder and bat my lashes at him. "I'll never tell."

21

ALAINA

I SUGGESTED that we do something different after dinner tonight. I don't mind playing video games, but I thought a little vinyl karaoke would be fun. Not surprisingly, Wolf was all for it and volunteered to go first. He pulled out a guitar from somewhere and played along and sang "Here Comes Your Man" from Doolittle by the Pixies.

I kept the same record on and sang along to "Hey" next. And then Rush surprised me by jumping off the couch to pick a song to sing next. I knew he likes to hear me sing—there's no way he'd come to watch me every week if he didn't like to listen to me too —but I didn't know that he likes to sing too.

Pretty soon after that, we all just took turns to pick a new song or record, but we all sang along. Sometimes one of us didn't join in, and Wolf routinely messed up the words on purpose, but it was fun. A lot of fun.

I smile, looking at the three smiling faces around me. They're laughing and singing to Arcade Fire's "My Body Is a Cage"— Sully's pick—and they've never looked more at home than they do right now.

The thread of darkness is still woven inside each of them, binding them together even further, but tonight it's not as present at other times. Tonight they're just three best friends hanging out with their girl, laughing and eating pizza on the couch.

It's perfect.

Rush stares at me from over Sully's head, and rolls his eyes, a smirk pulling up the side of his mouth.

I feel my own smile spread as I envision the next day, week, month—even year—spent like this. With them.

Warmth spreads from my chest, and I do something I trained myself not to do a long time ago.

I hope.

I hope that this feeling right here will last. I hope that I get to keep them—that they'll *want* to keep *me*.

Wolf interrupts my musings when he drags me into him, throwing an arm around my shoulders and pulling me in close.

"I've got a song for you to sing, Red. I'm pretty sure you know it."

I bundle up this feeling right now, wrap yards and yards of Bubble Wrap around it to preserve it always.

I lay my head on his shoulder. "Hit me with it, Wolf."

"Oi! Red's gonna sing for us now," Wolf yells, and Sully and Rush stop singing abruptly. "Get it set up, Sully."

All three of them share a conspiratorial grin, and I feel like I may be walking into a trap of some kind.

The first few slow notes of The Weeknd's "Earned It" sounds through the speakers, and I definitely know the three of them set me up. I decide to have a little fun with them.

I slide out from under Wolf's arms, stand up, and cross the room to the sound system. I turn the volume up and restart the song.

I sing along with The Weeknd and sway my hips. By the time I hit the chorus, I've found the sultry rhythm the song demands, swaying and swiveling. I drag my index finger along their shoulders as they sit on the couch like three little ducks all in a row.

Lips parted and gazes hungry, they're quickly realizing their little prank backfired.

I sing the third verse, staring right at Rush as each word slips past my lips. And before I can sing the final chorus, all three of their phones vibrate on the coffee table with an incoming text.

I stop mid word, startled at the coincidence. Only when I look back at Rush, he's acting normal. Well, normal for him.

He unlocks his phone and says, "Call me, son. It's important. We have a fox."

All three of them share a look, faces blank. It's such a sudden difference from the smiling a minute earlier, that it takes my brain a moment to catch up and realize that it's something bad.

Sully cuts the record with a scratch, and Wolf gets a burner from the drawer in the kitchen. He dials a number and sets the phone on the coffee table before sitting down on the couch. Rush reaches up and grabs my hand, gently tugging me to sit between him and Wolf.

RUSH

THE PHONE RINGS twice as I try to control the swirling mess in my head.

Is the fox related to whoever broke in?

Or whoever took Alaina?

Are they both related?

There are too many questions and too many variables. I've been looking into that—and the hit put out on her which may or may not be related to the kidnapping itself—but I haven't been looking hard enough.

Shame coats my gut, oily and sour. I'd been fucking enjoying my time here, spending more time with my girl and my brothers than doing my fucking job. I'm supposed to protect her—protect the Brotherhood. Instead, I've been playing Xbox and fuckin' around.

These last couple of weeks have been better than anything I could've hoped for. When I started planning what life would look like with one woman, it was abstract. Then I found Alaina, and it started to take shape in my mind. I knew my brothers would need time to be carefully guided along this path, at first at least. And this time together has given us just that.

The phone rings twice before someone answers.

"Da."

"Come home, boyo. We need to talk," Da says. His voice sounds resigned, and I share a look with my brothers.

"What's this about?" Wolf leans forward, keeping one hand wrapped around Alaina's thigh.

Da sighs, the noise audible through the phone. "Aidan Gallagher."

Alaina goes stock-still, but Wolf's too busy staring daggers at the phone in the middle of the coffee table. Her reaction triggers some primal instinct inside me, and I feel myself unconsciously shutting everything else out so I can focus on the threat and eliminate it.

"Is that name supposed to mean something to us?" Sully asks as he stares at the ceiling, head resting on the back of the over-stuffed chair.

He was noticeably relaxed tonight, even smiled and joked around with us. It was the most himself he'd been in weeks.

But before that, he hadn't so much as looked at Alaina longer than two seconds since the security camera show. My brother's a lot of things, but a coward isn't one of them. He's also obvious as fuck right now—he spends so much energy *not* looking at her that even if we weren't in a house with only four people, I could feel his angst and awkwardness from the next state.

"Aye. Aidan was my best friend." He pauses. "And Alaina's father."

There's a feeling that the absence of movement creates—this weight that settles on everyone and everything in the room. For ten seconds, no one says a single thing, then Sully and Wolf talk over one another.

"What the fuck, Da?"

"How the fuck do you know Alaina's da?"

But I only have eyes for my girl, and she's not talking or moving or doing much of anything but stare at the phone like it holds national secrets.

To be fair, I do know some national secrets, but I'd never be careless enough to leave them on my phone.

And I suppose this little bomb Da dropped would feel like a national secret to her.

The ramifications of this truth swirl around in my brain.

How long has Da known about Alaina?

Does he know Lana?

This, more than anything, lends more weight to our theory that Lana's and Da's engagement is a sham. No way my da, who's instilled loyalty in all three of his sons, ups and marries his childhood best friend's wife.

Then it hits me like a freight train.

Was—Aidan *was* my *best friend.*

"Where's Aidan now, Da?" My voice is low, but it cuts through the bickering like a clap of thunder.

Alaina pulls her attention off the phone and gives it to me. She stares at me, her gaze unflinching and carefully blank.

"Dead. Aidan's dead, boyo. And you need to get home. Bring your girlie."

The sharp inhale from Alaina is the only noise she makes.

"Red?"

"I'm fine." Her response is too quick.

The phone call ends, and still, Alaina doesn't tear her gaze off of me. In my peripheral, I see Wolf and Sully staring at her, but she hasn't moved an inch.

So I make a decision. It's maybe the biggest decision of my life, but it's one that comes easily but not lightly. I know deep in my blackened soul that she's the one for me—for us. But it wouldn't be fair to her to tie her to us for life without at least giving her a little more.

"I think it's time we tell Alaina about the Brotherhood."

Silence greets me as both of my brothers look at me with matching blank faces. Wolf's the first to come to the same conclusion. I see it in his eyes before he says anything.

"Aye. It's time," Wolf says with a nod.

"Sully?"

He looks at me then, and he lets me see the vulnerability underneath his hardened exterior. It takes me back to when we were kids. Sully always looked to me when he was scared. And because he was the youngest, I always took the responsibility of looking out for him.

I nod once, tell him with my gaze that he can still trust me.

Sully sighs and looks at Alaina. "Alright. Let's tell her the cliff's notes version. I'll get the booze."

I exhale, and something inside my chest loosens. I hadn't realized how worried I was about Sully getting onboard.

Alaina turns to watch Sully go to the kitchen before she faces me. "We need booze for this conversation?"

"Aye, birdie. This conversation is better had over vodka."

Alaina nods. "Spilling secrets, right, Wolf?"

"Aye, baby girl. It's time to spill some secrets." He leans back and readjusts his hand on her bare thigh.

I never realized how alluring a woman could be in my boxer briefs—no, not any woman, Alaina. She's gorgeous and tempting everyday, but when she's in my clothes? She's goddamn irresistible.

Sully comes back with four vodka tonics and passes them out. He holds his glass in the air and says, "To spilling secrets."

We clink our glasses together and each take a sip. Alaina cradles her glass to her chest, and I take another healthy sip before I set my glass on the table.

I clear my throat and look at her, her whiskey-brown eyes kind and inviting.

"So I'm going to give you an overview, yeah? You already know that there are two councils in the Brotherhood chapters—junior council, like me and Wolf and Sully, and regular council. We're part of a bigger network that's based out of Ireland."

"Like the IRA?" she interjects.

"Kind of. More like cousins with the IRA," I explain. "We have a sort of . . . arrangement with various families in this area of the country."

She takes a sip of her drink and licks her lips. "What, like the Italian mafia?" When I stare at her, she shrugs. "I've been watching *Sopranos*."

"Actually, yes. We have ties with some Italian families in the city, among others. But we also have various elected officials and people in power in our pockets," Wolf explains.

"In your pocket?" Alaina tilts her head.

"Aye. An agreement of sorts. We help keep the ports clean*er*, and they look the other way for our"—I tap my finger against my lips as I think of how to phrase this part—"other unsavory business arrangements."

"I don't understand, like illegal things?"

"Aye, baby girl, illegal things." I wait for her to react. If she's going to split, it would be now when I just told her we deal in illegal shit.

Pride warms my chest when she just stares at me expectantly, taking the news in stride.

"This life, being part of the Brotherhood, it comes with risks. And we"—I gesture to my brothers and I—"thought it wouldn't be fair to ask you to stay with us without knowing that." I run my palm up her thigh and lean toward her, our faces an inch apart. "Make no mistake, baby girl, I wouldn't let you go even if you got spooked."

"I don't want to be let go," she whispers against my lips.

"Aye, I know." I plant a kiss on her pouty lips, wishing I could deepen it, but we're on borrowed time now. Reluctantly, I pull back and look at her. "What we do can be dangerous. That's why we've been training you in a few things these last couple of weeks."

"To protect me from your enemies?"

"Aye, and so you can protect yourself in any situation," Sully says.

"The Brotherhood has collected our fair share of enemies over the years. Which is why we don't know who's behind your kidnapping yet—"

"Or the break-in," she interrupts me.

"Aye, or the break-in. That's why you'll need to continue training when we get back to Summer Knoll."

"Do we really have to go back?" She exhales. "I kind of love it here—wherever here is. It's nice, peaceful. It feels like our own safe little bubble. And I . . . I'm scared to go back."

"It's alright, Red. We'll be with you the whole time." Wolf leans forward to kiss her exposed shoulder. "Nothing's goin' to happen to you now that you have us."

22

ALAINA

RUSH DRIVES the car in front of the garage at Summer Knoll and parks. The air in the car feels ripe with something I can't quite name. A sliver of trepidation rolls down my spine as the clouds cover the sun, casting the house in shadow. All we need is a crow to cry in the distance, and we'd be in the beginning of a horror film.

I've had enough of those horror film situations to last me a lifetime, though.

"Let's do this." Sully pushes open his door and hops out of the SUV.

"Whatever happens, we'll handle it, yeah?" Wolf says as he laces our fingers together. Rush drove most of the way home today, and Wolf sat in the back with me.

I look from our clasped hands to his face, the sight of our fingers intertwined still gives me shivers.

"Alright, Wolf."

I let him tug me out of the car by his hold around my hand. He doesn't release my hand as we follow Rush and Sully into the house.

With each step I take, I feel the walls shrink inch by inch. By the time we reach the kitchen, I feel like Alice in Wonderland where she grows too big for the room she's in. Wolf's hand in mine anchors me, and I squeeze it in gratitude before I let it go.

I walk the last few steps to the breakfast nook at the end of the massive kitchen, each footfall sounding like a chant.

Dead. Dead. Dead.

It was easy for me to shove this truth bomb aside last night and focus instead on what they were telling me about the Brotherhood. These were some of the answers I'd been looking for.

And I just couldn't bring myself to think of my father as dead. Not yet. I don't know if I'll ever be able to think about it.

I keep my head high as I walk toward them, trying to channel my cousin Maddie. She's great at those sort of power moves that get her what she wants.

I stop at the end of the table. Cormac sits across from me at the head of the table, and my mom sits just to his right on the bench seat. The seating arrangement is similar to the first night I was here, and I idly wonder if that was accidental or not.

"Have a seat," Cormac says, nodding to the chairs around the table.

"No thank you." I fold my arms across my chest and mentally fortify my armor.

I spent the entire four-hour drive here adding layer after layer of bricks around my heart. I know that whatever comes out of this conversation isn't going to be good. And I know that I just have to be strong enough to sit and listen.

Yep, just sit and listen to whatever garbage comes out of Mom's mouth, because nothing excuses her withholding that kind of information about Dad. Nothing, the voice that suspiciously sounds like Maddie says.

Cormac stares at me, but I don't waver. I feel rather than see the guys step up behind me, fanning out. None of them touch me, but I feel their protectiveness just the same.

Cormac nods. "Very well. I'm sure you have questions—"

"I do," I interrupt him. "But first, I want to know everything."

Cormac chuckles without humor. "Ah, I get it now. I see why my boy is so infatuated with you."

I nod a few times. "Mm-hmm. From the beginning, then?"

He smooths his beard with one hand while he stares at me. Again. Though I'm starting to see where Rush gets his attentiveness to detail.

"Alright, girlie, from the beginning then." Cormac sighs. "I met Aidan when we were lads. Our das were in the Brotherhood, and while we were too young to join the ranks, we still wanted to be part of something. Fast-forward a few years, and we're both members of the Brotherhood. For a while, it was as if nothing had changed. We were thick as thieves, but then our paths started leading us down two different directions."

"You became the Butcher," Wolf interjects.

Cormac nods at him. "Aye. I became the Butcher. And Aidan, well, he became the Traveling Salesman."

I can only imagine the face I'm pulling right now—eyes wide, brows in my hairline, shaking my head to make sense of it.

"What does that mean?" I ask him.

Cormac looks at his boys—I'm not sure which one since I haven't turned around yet. Turning my back to Cormac feels a lot like turning my back on a rattlesnake. And no thank you, I do not want to get bit today—or any day.

"You boys didn't tell her who I was—who you are?" Cormac's eyebrows hit his hairline.

"She knows enough," Rush says from directly behind me.

Cormac stares at Rush from over my shoulder for a moment before he shifts his attention to me. "Your dad was a hitman."

My gaze flies to my mom, and I'm absolutely floored to see her reaction—or non-reaction.

"A hitman?" My eyes are wide and my head feels light. "Why now? Why are you telling me this now?"

"I-I—" Mom shrugs her shoulders with her arms up in the classic I don't know pose.

"What? You finally decided after ten years to care?" I scoff. "Please." I roll my eyes. "I'm sure you've been fucking guys that are not my father—since he's dead—for years. No need to—"

Cormac slams his hand, palm flat, on the table, and the noise sounds like thunder in the kitchen. "Don't you talk to your mother that way."

I cross my arms over my chest and let a smirk I just know is sarcastic spread across my face. I'm a little impressed with myself —I just dropped an f bomb like it was no big deal.

"What? You gonna be my new daddy now?"

Mom shoves to her feet, anger practically steaming from her ears. "Alaina Murphy McElroy!"

"Ah, ah, ah," I tsk. "Don't you mean Gallagher, Mom?" Her name tastes like acid on my tongue. "Besides, if I want a new daddy, I know where he sleeps." I tip my head back toward the three boys standing sentinel at my back.

Wolf snickers and doesn't even bother to cover it up with a fake laugh.

"Yes, well, about that. I think it's time we have a little chat. Don't you?" Mom asks, totally brushing me off.

"About what exactly?"

Mom straightens and runs her hands over her hair, smoothing any flyaways back into place in her tight, low ponytail. "You. And your relationship with your stepbrother."

My heart skips a beat, and my sneer falters for a moment. There's no way she can know about all of them, right? I look at Wolf out of the corner of my eye, but he doesn't give anything away.

The beginning prickles of panic creep up, starting in my

fingers. My knee-jerk reaction is to comply with anything Mom says to get her approval, her attention—her love . . . but I don't think I can do that anymore.

I shouldn't have to work *so fucking hard* for her love. They say mothers are born with it—a maternal instinct that supersedes everything else in their lives to protect their babies.

I don't think my mom has that instinct. I'm not even sure she has the capability.

And that is the part that cracks my heart, the fissure so deep that I don't know if it'll ever mend.

So I do what any girl in my position would do—I stand up to my mother for the first time in my life.

"No."

She jerks her head back and stares at me like I've grown a third eye. Then again, I went through an awakening of sorts in those woods. So maybe I do have a third eye.

"Did you know I was kidnapped?" I'm proud of how even my voice is, and I feel all three of them step closer to me.

Mom gasps and looks at Cormac. "Is this true?"

The fact that my mother looks to some random guy she's allegedly engaged to instead of me when I tell her *my* truth feels like a cosmic joke. I can't stop the laugh that slips from my lips. It's bitter-tasting and sounds like disbelief.

Cormac looks at me when he answers her. "Aye."

Mom's hands flutter in the air for a few seconds before I visibly see her demeanor change. She reflexively smooths back her hair *again* and fiddles with the necklace at her throat.

She clears her throat before she meets my gaze. "Okay. Well, we can talk about that later—"

She's cut off by a trio of growls and scoffs from behind me. Their indignation on my behalf makes me feel gooey inside.

"Your daughter tells you she was kidnapped and you want to

talk about it *later?*" Rush says. His words are pleasant enough, but his tone is a menacing growl.

"Well, I-I—" Mom looks to Cormac, but he doesn't rescue her. Instead, he watches his boys as they close in around me. I watch as she throws her shoulders back and meets my gaze once more. "We were talking about your relationship with your step-brother. You know I don't like it when you deflect, Alaina."

"Again, I say *no.*"

"What do you mean, *no?*" Mom jerks her head to the side.

I lean forward, bracing myself on the table and say, "I mean, no, we're not talking about that." I stare at her for a moment, letting some of the angst and heartbreak bleed through my gaze. I'd been thinking about what I would say to my mother since Cormac called last night. I contemplate telling her that it's not one of them but all of them, but I decide against it. "Besides, it's a nonissue."

"So you'll break it off then. Good, good." Her shoulders sink and she exhales.

I laugh, a sarcastic, snide sound. "What? no. I meant it's a nonissue because it's obvious to me now—what this"—I gesture between her and Cormac—"is. You two aren't in love, and I doubt you're getting married."

"People get married for all kinds of reasons, Alaina," Mom snaps at me.

I quirk an eyebrow. "And what reason are you getting married for?"

She bristles and compulsively smooths her hair back again. "That's none of your business."

I scoff, and she cuts me a hard glare. Maybe if she parented me for a single day or a week or any amount of time, it might've had more impact. But she didn't, so I can easily ignore it.

"But we are getting married. And it's not right—you being

with your stepbrother. Think of what Page Six would say!" she yells, desperate, cheeks red.

A tiny part of me acknowledges that her reaction will be the norm—and that's not even the whole story. I fear her head will actually explode when she finds out that I'm with all three brothers.

Well, I mean, I think I'm with all three of them. Dating feels like too juvenile of a word for this bond we're forging. Definitely Rush and Wolf. And if you asked me yesterday, I would've said yes about Sully too. But that was in the protection of our safe house. We didn't have to worry about this kind of stuff—or maybe we did worry about it, but it was shoved to the side anyway.

"I'm only looking out for you," she says, and I almost believe her. Almost.

The tears in her eyes and the pleading in her gaze are good enough that it might sway Cormac, but it doesn't work on me.

"C'mon, Mom. We both know you're doing this for you—not me. Don't start trying to parent me now on my account. You haven't been around for ten years! Where were you when I gave my valedictorian speech?" I yell as I slam my hand on the table.

She crosses her arms over her chest tight, her mouth pinches. "I already told you what happened, Alaina. I'm not going to repeat myself."

"And during junior year when I won the state dance competition? Or parent-teacher conferences EVER?" I raise my eyebrow in a taunt.

She uncrosses her arms, clenches her fists, and yells, "I stayed away to protect you. I was trying to protect you!"

I laugh. The sound caustic and grating to my ears. "Protect me?" I scoff. "I didn't need you to protect me! I just needed you to be there! And you—you—you weren't there. You were never there." My chest heaves as I stare at the woman who is a mother in name only. I don't realize that I'm crying until I feel the wetness drip from my trembling chin.

I look at her and let her see all the heartbreak that's festered for a decade. "I wanted my mother."

"I was protecting you, Alaina. You have no idea what really happened to your father." She purses her lips, but I don't miss the slight wobble in her voice.

"Tell me. Tell me what happened to Dad," I plead.

Mom sinks into the chair underneath her, and there's something about that action that has a few of my walls sinking too. I'm terrified that whatever answers she gives me won't be enough to exonerate her—and then where will I go from here?

She nods a few times as she clasps her hands together on the table. She stares at her hands when she speaks. "Okay. He was part of the Brotherhood for as long as I knew him—but he never let it touch us. He used to say that you were the best thing to happen to him—not me, just *you*—and he didn't want to tempt fate by having another baby. So I was content to live my life as a mom of one, married to a man who had this—this other life that I had no part in." She pauses for a minute, and I find myself sinking down into the chair in front of me without really thinking about it.

I think I might hate her a little bit in this moment—for waiting this long to tell me about dad and for the resentment I can hear in her voice.

"Sometimes he would leave and come back the same day, and other times, he'd be gone for a couple of days. Only a handful of times over the decade we were together did he leave for a week or longer, but those times, he always told me not to expect him for a while." Mom glances at me as she asks, "Do you remember when he left that last time?"

I shake my head. "No, not really. I have these vague memories of Dad being gone and then going on one of your adventures. I remember being scared that he wouldn't be able to find us. And then I was at St. Rita's."

"Your dad could find a needle in a haystack. He'd find us anywhere. But he never found us."

"Why? What happened?"

"I remember the day like it was yesterday. It'd been two weeks since he left, and he told me he'd be back in a day, two tops. I knew that I'd have to do what we practiced—what he drilled into me to do." She shrugs. "But I was in denial. If I followed his plan, it meant he wasn't here anymore. And I . . . I wasn't ready to face that yet. So, I waited, and then I waited some more." She exhales and stares at her hands again. "But then you brought home a school project of our family tree with. Our names were clearly written, and I knew god was giving me the push I needed to listen to Aidan."

"I don't understand. Why would Dad want you to send me to a boarding school in the middle of New York City?" My brow furrows.

She shakes her head. "That wasn't the plan. I was to first go to my parents for two weeks, then buy plane tickets to Florida but really drive us to Canada. He had a safe house up there just for this reason."

"But then grandma and grandpa died." The pieces of the puzzle are changing shape and swirling around in my mind. I'm still not sure what it's going to reveal, but I'm not sure it'll be the answers I've been looking for.

She nods. "Yes. Then they died in a freak accident on the way to pick us up from the airport. And I panicked." She blows out a breath, and the action is so small, but it may be the most human thing I've ever seen her do. "I didn't know what to do or who to trust, so I changed our last names and I separated us. I thought . . . I thought that if they found me, at least you'd be safe."

Flabbergasted isn't a word I usually associate with myself, but it's the best word for what I'm feeling right now.

"I don't know what to say to that. It's"—I swallow—"a lot of information. Why that school?"

"I thought I'd hide you in plain sight but still keep you protected, and St. Rita's offered that. Plus, I pulled some strings and got your cousins there."

"Okay." I nod. "Okay. But that still doesn't explain how you and Cormac hooked up."

"I did meet him randomly one day, and we really did hit it off. We really are getting married, Alaina, that much is true." She inhales deeply and wipes under her eyes for any smudges. "Which is why I need you to break up with your boyfriend right now. I will not be made a fool of by my daughter dating her step-brother."

I lean back in the chair and look at her. It's almost amazing how she can jump from one emotion to the next so quickly like that. I'm a little bit impressed.

I'm emotionally and mentally exhausted, but I won't be pushed around on this. Not by her or anyone.

So I drum up some classic teenage angst and prepare to launch at her.

"Which one?" I smirk.

Mom sputters and Cormac's head snaps to the men behind me. I can't see them, but I imagine their cocky shit-eating-grins plastered across their faces, and my smile widens.

"It doesn't matter, the answer is still no." I push off the table to stand up. "Thanks for the info, Mom." I turn on my heel and walk out of the kitchen, intent on heading straight for the shower to wash away this day.

23

RUSH

"RUSH."

My brothers and I stop in our tracks, halfway down the hallway after our little bird. As one, we turn around and walk toward Da. Lana visibly pales at the sight of us marching toward her, and I smirk for good measure. I don't care what her reasoning is, I don't like her.

"Have a seat, boyo. We need to have a little chat." He tips his head toward three chairs. "Give us a minute, Lana?"

She nods and gets up from the table without a word.

"What's with the bird?" Da levels us with his signature no-bullshit look.

"Which one?" Wolf taunts. "Ours or yours? Because I have a few choice words about your bird, Da."

"Watch your tone, boyo. Don't forget who's your president." He points his finger at Wolf in warning.

"Oh, is that who I'm talking to now? Because I thought I was talking to my da—not my president." Wolf sneers and da raises an eyebrow in warning.

"Reel in the disrespect, yeah? I'm asking as both."

215

"What about her?" I ask. I don't need these two facing off right now. Wolf's operating on a short fuse—we all are.

Da shifts his attention to me. His intensity is well-documented, almost whispered in reverence. It's rumored that a guy shit himself from Da's stare alone. Of course, he's earned his stripes as the Butcher of the Brotherhood.

But it's hard to marry those rumors with the man I saw in fuzzy Chewbacca slippers last Christmas. He'd claimed he didn't want to hurt Sarah's feelings by not wearing her Christmas present, but I caught him wearing them long into the new year.

"You serious about her?" He steeples his fingers in front of his face.

"When have I ever claimed someone?"

He strokes his beard as he looks us over. "It's official, then? You claimed her?"

"We've been a little busy, but unofficially, yes. We'll make it official soon enough."

"Ah. And how's that going to work for you three? I'm assuming by your little power display here"—he gestures to the three of us sitting—"that you're all involved with the bird?"

"You leave that to us. We're not worried, so you shouldn't be either," Wolf says as he leans back against his chair, widening his stance.

Da raises his brows at the derision in Wolf's voice. "But I do worry about you. As your da and as your president." He looks at Sully. "You're awfully quiet, boyo."

Sully stares at da and shrugs. The movement forced. "Alaina's ours, Da, what more do you need to hear?"

"Ah, so you're with the bird too. Interesting. I don't see you hover around her quite like your brothers." Da glances at all three of us, but I'm too keyed up to take the time to decipher his practically blank look.

"That's just your perception of one interaction with the four

216

of us. Alaina was mine long before you knew her, Da, so with all due respect, you don't know shit about this."

Da leans back and folds his arms across his chest. "That's not entirely true."

I lean forward. "Explain."

"I met your little bird as a baby. Aidan brought her around a few times. But Lana was never with him, and he never talked about her. He was so goddamn proud of Alaina, though. She was a little thing, just babbled words and toddled around. We would put her in the playpen with you boys in the backyard."

Shock holds me immobile for a moment. "Why are you telling us this?"

Da looks at me, the lines along his face deepening in thought. "Part of me feels . . . responsible for the girl. Aidan was my friend for a long, long time. And the Brotherhood, they weren't as kind to him as they were to me, as they are to others." He sighs and stares out into the backyard. "What they asked of him . . . it wasn't right. And they didn't take too kindly to his refusal. Shit was never the same. He met Lana not too long after, and he started to pull away from the Brotherhood. He still showed up to the council meetings, but the camaraderie was gone."

I nod, mentally filing away that information to look into Aidan and what he did within the Brotherhood.

"Is that why you're marrying Lana? As some misplaced honor to your dead friend?"

Da's eyes flash at Wolf, but, as usual, he doesn't flinch. He gives it right back to Da. And also like usual, I wade in to break their shit up.

"Tell us about your family reunion across the pond," I interrupt their pissing contest.

"Cillian Kelly announced his successor—his nephew, Quinn Kelley."

The three of us nod as one. Quinn's just as crazy as his uncle. I suppose you'd have to be in his position.

People often talk about the one time Cillian beheaded half a room. I'd heard a dozen rumors on why he did it, but he never confirmed. Regardless, it pales in comparison to the time we saw Quinn systematically torch the house of every person who was in a pub the night before. Apparently, someone took a crack at Quinn's ma, something about her warming more than Cillian's bed, and a bunch of people laughed. That was their fatal mistake.

Quinn wasn't even at the pub when this alleged joke happened. He's conniving and cunning, and a total wild card. He'd be a great ally for us when I ascend, but he's just as likely to massacre us as he is to congratulate us.

"So soon? Cillian's not much older than you."

Da looks at Sully. "Aye. Who knows about these things. Perhaps Cill just wanted the word to spread that he's got a successor lined up. Or he's planning something, and he wants a failsafe for the Brotherhood. It's hard to tell with Cill, you know that."

"Aye. At least you came back whole."

The four of us are all silent at the reminder of Cillian's happy trigger finger.

"Retaliation."

Da lifts a brow and turns to face me. "What about it?"

"The fuck you mean, *what about it?* They stormed into our house in the middle of the night like common burglars—"

"And they snatched our fucking girl at our pub!" Wolf interrupts me, his tone hard.

"Looks like you got her back alright though," Da says, eyeing all of us.

I feel my brows furrow and my gut clenches. "Are you suggesting we let an attack like that go unchecked?"

He shakes his head and pulls at his beard, smoothing it out. "No. Just give it some time."

"Time." Wolf slams his fist on the table and stands up in one explosive movement. "Time could get her killed."

"I thought this was about Summer Knoll?" Da taunts.

"You know goddamn well this is about her too." Wolf's jaw ticks.

"If not more," I add, voice hard. "It's more about her than Summer Knoll, for me."

"While you boys were off doing god-knows-what with your bird, I made a few calls, got a few things lined up. Now I'm waiting for them to pan out before we make a move."

I look at Wolf, then Sully, and I know with just that one look that none of us are satisfied with that response. I nod a few times, more to myself than anything. I've had my suspicions for weeks, but Da's proposed *plan* tells me everything he didn't—he either knows who's behind it and he's not planning to retaliate, or he knows who's behind it and he can't retaliate. There are only a handful of reasons why he wouldn't be able to retaliate though—alliances, protected people, the select untouchables in the city, orders from Cillian.

"I'm surprised you don't already have someone strung up at the carriage house for this," Da muses, interrupting my spiraling thoughts.

"We had some people. Not the right people. We ran into some . . . unexpected roadblocks. Whoever planned it had help. It was staged and multifaceted. The power to O'Malley's was cut but not the surrounding buildings, the public cameras within 20 miles were on a sixty-minute loop but the private residences were jammed—which means they left someone behind to make sure they stayed jammed, and the crashed, burned-out van was unidentifiable, left on some back road in the middle of nowhere. No cameras. No witnesses."

"So you gave up? That doesn't sound like my son."

The rage that always flows inside of me bubbles up at his insinuation. "I'm not a fucking *quitter*."

He smiles, this slow curl of his mouth as if to say *Gotcha!* He always did like to press that particular button of mine. I clench my jaw, frustrated that I fell for his shit again.

Everyone fucking knows I get shit done, and I don't need to prove shit.

"I've earned my spot within the Brotherhood. We all have"—I gesture to my brothers—"so unless there's anything else, this conversation's over." My words are low, just barely containing the growl I feel trapped in my chest.

I give him the courtesy of five seconds to answer, and when he doesn't, I push my chair back and stand. My brothers follow suit, and we all turn and walk out of the kitchen.

"One more thing."

We stop at the threshold to the kitchen, but none of us turn around.

"I'll be heading out for a few days. Lana too. Working on something for Cillian."

I nod and walk away. Wolf and Sully follow me up to my command center, as Alaina likes to call it, and I shut the door behind them.

Sully's already sweeping the room for bugs, and Wolf's checking the obvious places for a camera. We've been gone for weeks, and I don't have any idea who was in Summer Knoll—let alone in this part of the house.

When we're sure it's safe, we all start talking at once.

"I'm calling the Kings."

"We have to leave."

"He's planning something."

"Okay," I yell. "Let's talk about this quickly. I don't want to leave Alaina alone right now, and someone needs to sweep her room."

"One of us should stay in her room at night. I feel fucking exposed here, and it's making me twitchy." Wolf shudders, proving his point.

"Aye, we're in agreement there, and one of us should be with her as much as possible during the day too," Sully says as he leans against the wall by the door. I'm sure his attention is split between us and straining to hear movement in Alaina's room. We're too far away for that, but I'm not going to be the one to say that to him.

"And I'm calling Maeve now. I think it's time we stop talking about gathering our own allies and start cementing them." My gut churns. This feels like it's straddling the line of betrayal, and we have to be careful not to fall to the other side. I fear there'd be no returning from it—not with Da or the Brotherhood.

"I'll reach out to Diesel and update him. I'm positive he'll agree," Wolf says as he reaches into his pocket for his phone.

"I'll check-in with Matteo. It never hurts to have the Italians in our corner," Sully offers.

"Aye. Maybe O'Malley and his boys. I've got a few other people to feel out too. This is a good start. Let's get it done while the old man is gone."

"Aye, sounds good. I'll make a call and then head in by Red," Wolf says, already dialing.

I sit down on the end of my couch and slip my phone out of my pocket. I dial Maeve, and she picks up on the first ring.

"I've been expecting your call."

"Aye. Still up for swinging by? We're moving quicker than I thought we would." I rub my jaw, my five o'clock shadow scratching my fingertips.

"We'll be there tomorrow with bells on," she says, and ends the call.

"Jesus, would it kill her to say *bye?*" I mutter as I pinch the bridge of my nose. We just got back, and I already want to leave.

I don't want to let my exhaustion take over, so I drag a laptop from my coffee table to my lap and open it to check the boards for new information.

24

ALAINA

AFTER I SPEND a ridiculous amount of time in my favorite shower, I slip into a pair of boxer briefs and an oversized tee. I swiped them from the safe house before we left. I've grown kind of fond of sleeping in the guys' clothes.

I bend over and blow dry my hair, idly scrunching up the waves and let my mind wander.

Logically, I knew the likelihood of my dad being alive was slim, at best. I *knew* that. But it didn't stop me from hoping that he was. Somehow.

When I was younger, I used to go to bed convinced he'd be there in the morning. After days, weeks, months—years, I'd go to sleep with a little less hope in my heart. And somewhere along the way, I bottled up what little hope I had left and buried it under six feet of dirt, vowing to never let it resurface.

The truth is, I don't really know that much about my dad. I have some standout memories from when I was younger and bits and pieces that I've heard over the years. But it doesn't amount to a whole lot.

I've learned more about him from one conversation than I

225

could've hoped for. Now I just need to figure out how to make sense of it all.

I wonder if it'll change anything with my mom—with our relationship. My chest stutters at the idea of being able to talk freely about my dad. Maybe Cormac will share some memories he has about my dad—what he was like growing up, how he got involved with the Brotherhood. Honestly, I'd take anything at this point.

By the time my hair is nearly dry, exhaustion weighs heavy. I tidy up the bathroom, my movements slow.

My heart hurts and my brain feels scrambled. It's early, but the big, fluffy bed in the bedroom is calling my name. I walk into the bedroom, not surprised to see Wolf lounging across my bed shirtless, intricate, swirling tattoos on display like the dark king he is.

"C'mere, baby girl." Wolf pats the spot on the mattress next to him.

I crawl across the bed and lay next to him. I feel strangely light, weightless almost, any time I'm near one of them.

"You okay, Red?"

I nod and snuggle in closer, leaning my head against his chest. "I'm . . . processing. But I'm glad you're here."

"There's nowhere else I'd rather be. Close your eyes, I'll be here when you wake up."

"Okay, Conor," I say around a yawn. Letting my eyes close, I feel the blankets being tucked around me, and I fall asleep with a small smile on my face.

I WAKE UP WITH A GROAN, burning up. It's hot enough in here that I'm sweating. With my eyes closed, I try to kick off the blankets, but I'm met with resistance. Cracking an eye open, I see

Wolf in front of me, laying on his back, eyes closed and dreaming.

If Wolf's here, who's behind me?

Looking over my shoulder, I'm pleasantly surprised to see Rush. He'd taken to sneaking in my bed at night at the safe house but only on nights that Wolf wasn't already there. I wasn't sure how this thing between all of us was going to play out once we left the safe house, and him showing up in my bed like this is a good sign.

I roll over to face him, unsurprised when his eyes pop open. He blinks, those clear gray eyes winking at me in the early morning light.

"Shh. Go back to sleep so I can watch you," I whisper with a grin.

His answering grin lights up his face, and butterflies swirl around in my belly. Without a word, he closes his eyes again, still facing me.

I take a few moments to admire him, to memorize all the lines of his face and the curve of his lips.

"I can feel your gaze on me," he murmurs without opening his eyes.

"Yeah? What does it feel like?" My words are quiet. I don't want to wake up Wolf.

"Like heaven and ecstasy." He opens his eyes and leans forward to capture my lips. I try to pull away in protest—morning breath kisses are not ideal—but he's not having it.

He tangles his tongue with mine, applying pressure, and I abandon my decision and quickly scramble to get closer.

He groans, this low noise that fans the flame of lust growing by the second. He reaches his hand up to place at the base of my throat, his tattooed fingers gently curling around my neck.

Arching my back, I press closer and lift my leg to curl over his hip. His cock presses against my pussy, and I shiver, lust skating down my spine.

Rush deepens the kiss, groaning his pleasure into my mouth. A fluttery sensation starts in my chest when I remember that Wolf is sleeping a couple of feet away from us.

Will he wake up?

If he does, will he join in?

That last thought lights a fire under my lust, and I slide a hand down Rush's chiseled chest and into his gym shorts. I wrap my fingers around his cock and squeeze.

The swarming butterflies nosedive as insecurities take center stage. I haven't been with a lot of guys before—hell, most of them are in this house—but I read enough and overheard enough to know that Rush is bigger than average. Way bigger.

I'm a little worried that he won't be able to fit inside of me—not that I'm saying I want him to try that with Wolf laying sleeping next to us.

I mean, if Wolf wants to lay next to us while he's *not sleeping*, I wouldn't say no.

I stroke Rush's cock between our bodies, swallowing his moans. Pleasure licks along my spine at the thought of bringing Rush to his knees like this. The sense of power it gives me is absurd but addicting.

Rush tries to slide his fingers into my shorts and into my pussy, but I press against his body, trapping his hand.

"I want to make you come," I whisper against his lips. "And then you can make me come."

"Aye, little bird, that's the best plan I've heard all day," Rush says into my mouth.

I stroke and squeeze and change up the pace until he's on the verge of orgasm, sweaty, eyes glazed, lips parted.

Two more strokes, and he comes. His chest heaves as he smashes our chests together, absolutely annihilating my mouth. It makes me wonder what else he'll annihilate with that beautiful mouth of his.

"Zebras only dance the Macarena," Wolf mumbles.

The lusty fog clears at his sleeptalk nonsense, and a giggle slips out.

"Aye, alright. Let's take this to the bathroom, yeah? I'll get you dirty, and then I'll get you clean."

I nod as soon as he says bathroom. We quietly get out of bed, careful not to disturb our Sleeping Beauty, and tiptoe toward the bathroom.

Well, I tiptoe, Rush somehow walks normally but doesn't make a single sound. I'd be more impressed if I wasn't so turned on right now.

Rush closes the door and hits the lock. "Get undressed and hop in the shower, baby girl."

I shiver at the command and do as he says. When he's satisfied with the water temperature, he slides down his shorts.

His impressive cock bobs with the movement, and I lick my lips.

Rush crooks a finger at me, and I lean in to plant a kiss on his lips. He takes this opportunity to deepen the kiss again. And then I'm flying high, without a single care of the world outside of his fingers on my most sensitive parts of me.

AFTER RUSH MAKES good on his promise to dirty me up before cleaning me, I shoo him out of the shower so I can do my normal routine.

I'm just finishing applying my mascara when I hear voices in the hallway.

Female voice.

Several female voices.

229

I put my makeup away and walk into my bedroom, surprised to find my bed empty. I worry my bottom lip that Wolf saw Rush and I and got . . . I don't know, angry. Or jealous. I really should have that conversation with all of them soon.

Curiosity piqued, I follow the sound of voices to the end of the hall—Rush's command center.

Pushing open the door, my breath leaves me in a whoosh when I see five gorgeous women hugging all three of my men.

Two brunettes, a blonde, and two redheads, they're all tall and slender. Each of them is dressed differently than the others, but they all have the same air about them. They seem like total badasses, and if they weren't all over my men, I'd want to be their friend.

Despite the different hair colors and clothes, there's something similar about them. I think they could be related.

One of them—a redhead—spots me in the doorway. "Oi! Is that your bird, Rush?"

All eight pairs of eyes swing my direction and I make a conscious effort to stay still under their gazes.

Rush is already moving by the time our gazes lock. He extends a hand toward me, and I lace my fingers with his.

"This is Alaina. Alaina, these are the King sisters." He points to the girl on the far left first. "Fiona, Keira, Maeve, Ava, and the loud one on the end is Roisin."

"Oi! I'm not loud, my sisters are just unusually quiet," the last one, Roisin, says.

"Oh, bullshit, Ro!"

"What a load of horseshit!"

Two of the sisters, Fiona and Keira, I think, talk at the same time, and then all five of them dissolve into friendly bickering.

I lean into Rush and whisper, "Who are they?"

He turns his head into me, brushing his lips across my temple.

"They're allies. Came to help us figure out who's behind your kidnapping."

Wolf walks over to us, throwing his arm around my shoulders.

"Where's your dad and my mom?"

Before he can answer, Maeve snaps her fingers, drawing my attention. "That's right. You're all step siblings. And hooking up," she says with glee. "How kinky."

"It's a technicality that probably won't even happen. With our parents, I mean." I don't know why, but I feel like I need to defend us.

Maeve holds her hands in the air, palms facing us. "Whoa, whoa. No judgment. I was just being cheeky."

I bite my lip and nod.

Roisin claps her hands once. "Okay. Rush, why don't you show me what you've been working on, and then I'll school you like I usually do." She delivers her shade with a smile on her face.

Rush smirks at her. "You wish, Ro. I taught you everything you know."

"Aye, you did. And now the teacher has become the student."

She's probably only a couple years younger than me, but she's got enough sass that makes me think she'd get on great with Maddie.

Rush slowly lets go of my hand. "I've got to catch Ro and Maeve up. Don't go anywhere alone, not even within this house, yeah? And before I forget, Da and your ma went out of town for a few days."

I nod and watch him cross the room to his huge desk full of computers and computer equipment.

Fiona and Keira wander over to us and start talking about various things I have virtually no knowledge about—guns, underground fighting rings, heists.

Somewhere in the conversation, Wolf takes his arm off my

shoulder to demonstrate some MMA move some guy did recently, and the three of them move to the couch and coffee table area of the room.

I look toward Ava, but she's animatedly chatting with Sully. And then that asshole laughs—like a full-on laugh, and I can't control the jealousy that surges throughout my veins.

I feel a flush creep up my chest, and suddenly, I feel very small.

Insecure and unwanted.

The feelings swirl around in my gut, and I'm desperate to get out of here.

"I'm just gonna go . . . to the kitchen." My words aren't quiet, but no one notices me as I turn on my heel and leave the room.

I head to the kitchen, intent on making myself something to eat. Maybe I'm just hangry.

Ugh, that's probably it.

I get out the ingredients to make myself an omelet when my phone vibrates with an incoming call. Grabbing my phone from the counter, I squeal as I hit the accept button.

Maddie's and Mary's smiling faces fill the screen.

"Lainey!" They say at the same time.

"And how are my favorite twins today?" I say with a laugh.

"Babe, I'm so much better knowing you're around*ish* now! When can you come back to the city? We miss you so much!" Maddie says, laying on the dramatics pretty thick.

"It's true, Lainey. We've missed you!"

"It would be wonderful to see those beautiful faces soon. I'll talk to the guys and see if any of them are planning any trips to the city soon," I tell them as I whisk my ingredients.

"Ooh! What about in two days at our favorite diner? They serve the best cheeseburgers there," Mary suggests.

"Yes!" Maddie claps. "Let's do it!"

I nod and giggle at her enthusiasm. "Sure. I'm sure I can make it work."

"Great! Text us later. We have to go," Maddie says with an exaggerated sad face. "I'm meeting a friend, and Mary's meeting someone, too. Right, Mary?"

"Yep. In fact, I gotta go. I'm going to be late. Bye Lainey! So glad you're back," Mary says before she gets up and walks out of the room they're in.

"Alright, babe. Text me later, okay?"

"Will do." I nod. "And I want you to text me details of this date you're about to go on, because I know that's what you're doing," I say with a smile. "You're not as sneaky as you think you are. But I still love you!"

"Fine, fine. Later, babe!"

Maddie ends the call, and I get back to making my omelet. Talking to them always puts me in a good mood, reminds me that I'm a *boss bitch*, as Maddie would say, and I can do anything I put my mind to.

I'm humming "Out of the Woods" by Taylor Swift with a smile on my face and eating a delicious breakfast. For this moment, everything feels okay.

25

ALAINA

THE KING SISTERS have been here for two days. And for two days, I've felt almost invisible. Rush is working tirelessly with Roisin—turns out, she really does kick ass at tech stuff like him—and Maeve, who has *a brilliant mind*, according to Wolf.

Sully's been off doing . . . whatever it is that he does and helps the girls with whatever that they need. Oh, and going back to ignoring me. His hot and cold shit is grating on my nerves.

Wolf's in heaven when he *talks shop*, as he likes to call it, with Fiona and Kiera. I overheard them talk for sixty minutes straight about two different types of guns yesterday and the likelihood of each of them in every situation they could think of.

Ava talked—at length—about what she did when she was kidnapped last year. And that spurned an entire conversation about how many times the girls had thwarted attempted kidnapping.

Mostly, it leaves entirely too much time for me to get stuck in my head. Looking at conversations I've had with my mother over the years with a different pair of glasses on—ones that know my father is . . . dead.

God. What a small word for something so monumental. Just four little letters don't seem to encompass the hole his absence has left on my soul.

I get particularly existential one morning and wonder what my purpose here is—here on Earth and here in this house.

Mary and Maddie have been busy, so I haven't talked to them much, except to push back our lunch date by a few days. I'm pretty sure they're both seeing someone, but neither one has confirmed it yet.

It's the afternoon of day three, and I think I've reached my limit. I feel so goddamn foolish that I can barely take it. Everyone's congregating in the kitchen right now, walking down memory lane. They're all laughing and joking around, and what's worse is that no one is being unkind.

It's just I . . . I don't feel like I fit in.

And it's depressing the hell out of me.

Maeve and Rush have been inseparable for the entire day. At least he still snuggles with me at night.

I sigh. Even my thoughts are bumming me today. I feel like I'm trapped in a ball of wool, and every time I try to carve my way out of it, it gets thicker and tighter.

I excused myself thirty minutes ago, and I've been standing in the hallway ever since. There's been a shift since the Kings got here. And somehow, my guys don't feel like *mine* anymore. Not wholly, at least.

I'm not ready to give up on Rush or Wolf or Sully, but I can't deny that I'm very different from the King sisters.

My chest aches with the thought of them belonging to someone else. I'm not sure how many more hours or days I can just sit back and watch it, though.

Melancholy envelops me, settling on my shoulders like a blanket. From an outside perspective, it makes sense—Rush, Sully, and Wolf with the Kings. They're in the same world, they like and know the same things—they can stop their own kidnapping attempts for goodness' sake!

I wipe my nose with the back of my sleeve and blink my eyes a few times, surprised to feel a tear roll down my cheek.

I knew it.

I fucking knew it.

I'd started to hope. I let that little seed grow and grow and grow and now look where I am. As if summoned by my negative thoughts, Rush steps out of the room.

His brow furrows as he assesses me. "What's wrong? Are you hurt?"

"I don't know if I can do this, Rush." The words feel like they're ripped from my soul.

"Do what?" He tilts his head to the side.

"This"—I gesture between us—"us. All of it."

His eyes look like the sea in the middle of a storm and his gaze is just as formidable. "No, you mean you *won't* do this. What's this really about?"

I shake my head, and a tear slides down my cheek. "I'm not —I'm not cut out for this life. I'm not like *her*—*them*." I cut my gaze to the right, where the object of my insecurity stands. She's sitting at the island cleaning her guns and sipping coffee like it's a regular morning—and she looks freaking amazing.

How can I compete with that?

Rush scoffs. "C'mon, Birdie. If you're going to try to leave, at least spit some believable lies my way. You're not the jealous type." His lips tip up in a cruel smile and he rocks back on his heels.

A flicker of anger licks up my spine. "You don't know me well enough to make that kind of assumption."

He quirks a brow, and that goddamn arrogant smirk spreads on his face. He could've been a model with cheekbones like those. "Don't I?"

I cross my arms tightly over my chest, the air from the air conditioning cooling my overheated skin, and I look away from his probing gaze. "I am, though." The words are low in the quiet of the night. "I'm so insanely jealous of her that I want to claw her fucking eyes out for even looking at you." I clench my jaw as I glance at him from under my lashes.

Self-loathing and possession battle for dominance inside me. Embarrassment dampens the back of my neck. I know it's hypo-critical—here I am with not one but two guys—three, if you count Sully.

And I always count Sully.

And I'm freaking out on Rush for having a childhood friend over—even if they've been spending most of their time together. His childhood friend who's the girl version of him—gorgeous, deadly, smart as hell. It's like the universe bundled up everything I'm not and I've been striving for and made it into her—Maeve King.

Ugh, even her name is badass.

There's nothing badass about quiet Alaina McElroy. Up until this summer, I tutored kids, worked at a coffee shop, and sang glorified karaoke on the weekends for fun. And since I moved to Boston, I don't do much of anything *but* get in the way. At least, that's how it feels.

I bet Maeve never feels like she's in the way with her gorgeous hair and perfect skin—ugh. I stop that train of thought.

I am *not* that person.

I'm not the kind of girl who's going to be catty to other girls over a guy—even if I think I might be in love with that guy.

The fact is that Maeve represents everything that I'm not—she's strong, cunning, and handles a gun like she's been doing it since birth. *Like my guys.*

And I know *she* wouldn't need to be rescued if someone

snatched her from the back of a bar. I want to slap a hand over my mouth for even *thinking* such ridiculous thoughts.

I'm grateful, so grateful, that they came for me.

He smiles, and a quiet chuckle leaves his mouth. His eyes sparkle at me, and I have a sinking suspicion that my thoughts have been playing across my face this whole time. I really need to work on my poker face.

I sigh. "I'm not her. Or any of them. I . . . I don't know if I'll ever be her, Rush."

"Aye. You're not."

His words sting, but they're the truth. He always gives me the truth. Wolf wraps his words in pretty bows for me, and Sully will flat-out ignore me if he doesn't feel like it. But Rush always gives it to me straight—regardless of the sting.

Waves of disappointment roll over me, weighing me down. I nod a couple of times. "Okay, well . . . I'm going to—" I hike a thumb over my shoulder.

I glance at him to find his gaze pinned to me, unwavering. "Are you done, little bird?" His tone is soft, but his words feel hard as they land in between us on the marble tile.

My shoulders sag at the nickname.

"I don't want her or anyone else. I want you." He steps into me and slams his mouth against mine. He wages a war on me—for me—and he's not offering mercy.

Rush grips my leg underneath my thigh and hikes it up to rest against his waist, never breaking our kiss. I moan into his mouth when he steps into me, pushing me against the wall.

We're in the middle of the hallway, and the idea of someone walking by and seeing us sends a lick of excitement straight to my clit.

The outline of his dick presses against my leg, and I groan. I feel hot, like I can't get enough air. But it would take a natural disaster for me to separate my mouth from Rush's. I curl my fingers around the back of his neck and arch my back, desperate for some friction.

"What do you need, birdie?" he says against my lips, never fully removing them.

"More," I breathe the word into his mouth. Pleasure coats my body from the tips of my hair to my toes, and I don't ever want to stop this feeling. Our hips move in tandem, rolling and grinding. The fabric of his jeans hits my clit through the scrap of lace separating us, and I can't hold back the whimper. I'm chasing euphoria, and I'm not above begging to achieve it right now. "Please, Rush."

His fingers flex on my thigh as he pulls me against him harder. He chuckles against my mouth, the motion vibrating more than just my lips, before he skims his lips down my neck. He sucks on my neck gently, and it's a straight shot to my pussy. I tip my head back and keep my eyes closed, so I can focus on the way he's making me feel.

"I want your words."

My breath hitches. "Touch me."

He nips my neck before laving the area with his tongue, and I realize my mistake.

"I want you to eat my pussy, Dec." I feel old flickers of embarrassment start to unfurl in my belly, but I light a match and set them on fire. There's no room for them here. My lust has grown to an uncontrollable size, and there's only one way to tame that beast.

"Ah, there she is. Good girl."

His praise sends another wave of pleasure through me, and I instinctively curl my fingers in response, forgetting that they're still in his hair. He groans before surging forward.

"You make me lose control, Birdie, and I don't know if I can hold back."

"So do something about it." The challenge is clear.

I feel him pull away from my neck, so I open my eyes and look at him. His hand leaves my leg and slides up to my shoulder. With one flick of his wrist, the straps are pushed off my shoulders, the fabric covering my tits relaxing. My chest heaves as he traces a pattern across my skin, and I can feel my nipples harden through my shirt.

Rush sinks to his knees. His stormy-blue eyes darken to the color of the sea at night. He hitches my leg over his shoulder and wedges his broad shoulders in between my legs. I can't take my eyes off the sight of him.

My dress has been pushed up around my waist, so Rush comes face to face with my lace-covered pussy. I'm not even a little bit ashamed of the wet patch.

He slowly skims a finger down the center of me. "Black. Interesting choice."

"I-uh—" He slides his finger underneath the lacy fabric, and the feel of his skin on mine in my most sensitive spot sends a shiver through my body. When he stops, I continue, "I didn't buy them." The words leave me on a rush, desperate for him to continue his exploration.

"Birdie?"

I didn't realize I'd closed my eyes until he called me by his nickname for me. I open my eyes and find his staring at me with an intensity I'd never seen before.

"Hm?" That was about as eloquent as I was getting right now.

"Get ready to sing, baby," Rush says with a Cheshire grin. With that as my warning, he dives in.

And he fucking feasts.

Using his thumbs, he opens me up as he swirls his tongue around my clit.

"Rush." His name sounds like a plea and a prayer on my lips. "Stop teasing, please."

He does something with his tongue and fingers that has me gasping, and my eyes fly open in pleasure.

A figure in a doorway in the hallway to our left catches my attention. I'm not scared or worried—Rush wouldn't really let just anyone see me like this. So it has to be one of my boys.

Another gasp leaves me when the man takes a step forward, so he's only partially concealed in shadow. I freeze for a moment when I see Sully's recognizable profile.

But what steals my breath is the movement below his belt. His jeans are unbuttoned, his cock in hand, and he's working it at the same rhythm that Rush plunges his fingers into me.

I can't quite see his eyes, but I feel them on me. I flick my gaze between his cock and his face, I'm desperate to see him come, but he's too shadowed.

As if he reads my mind, he takes another step out of the shadows. His face comes into the light, and the look on it is enough to melt butter. A bead of sweat rolls down my neck.

I slide my hand down into Rush's hair and get a good grip, just like I fantasized about. The tug on his locks sends him into overdrive and he doubles his efforts. I feel the wave rushing up around me, so I do the only thing I can.

I stare right into Sully's eyes, and I brace.

I've brought this dark king to his knees. No, that's not right—he went *willingly*.

This man who yields to no one got on his knees *for* me.

And he gave me stars.

26

ALAINA

THE NEXT MORNING, I wake up early and slip out of bed. Despite my little outburst yesterday, Rush didn't show up last night. I'm not sure if he was busy working or what happened.

I decide to head to the kitchen to make myself some coffee. The mornings are cool enough that drinking coffee on the porch while the sun rises is the perfect way to start the day.

I SETTLE into a lounger on the patio and place my phone face-up next to my coffee mug.

Thankfully Rush was able to work his magic and replace my screen. When we got here, he explained that when we're not at the safe house, we can use our regular phones.

My phone rings, the noise startling me.

"Mom?" I answer the call and put it on speakerphone. Breathing fills the line, but I don't hear anything else. My heart pounds and adrenaline soars through my veins. "Mom? Are you okay? Where are you?" I grip the phone tight. There's only one reason my mom would call me this early willingly.

There's some static on the other end of the phone before I hear her voice. "I'm fine, Alaina. But I have news."

"Okay. Jesus, you scared me for a second," I say with my heart in my throat. Like some real life bad omen, a crow flies through the backyard, cawing the whole way.

"Don't be so dramatic. Listen, it's not going to work out with Cormac, so—we have to leave. Well, I already left. So you should too. In fact, why don't you come stay with me here?" Her words are quick but not jumbled, and desperation bleeds into each of her words.

"What? Mom, no. That's crazy. What's going on?" My eyes are wide and I feel like I can't get enough air in.

"What's going on is that I left and you should too." Her tone is firm, and horns honk in the background.

Apprehension prickles my awareness and the hair on the back of my neck stands up. "Where are you?"

"Don't worry about that just yet. I'm on the way to my new place." She sounds distracted. "I need you to come with me."

"What? I'm not leaving. Are you in some kind of trouble? Whatever it is, Mom, they can help—"

"Oh my god, Alaina. Wake up," she snaps, interrupting me. "Those boys don't care about you, and you can't honestly believe they do. You were a passing fancy at best. Which is why I told you I didn't approve." She makes this noise in the back of her throat, and I can just imagine her face screwed up like she sucked on a lemon. "But you just had to date your stepbrother to get back at me." She scoffs.

Shame makes my skin hot, and I have to clear my throat a few times before I can speak.

"You don't know what you're talking about," I grit out through clenched teeth. "Just come back, Mom. I'm sure you can patch things up with Cormac."

"No. There's no coming back from this," she says.

I groan. "What did you do that you can't come back from?"

"Listen, Alaina, I didn't want to tell you this, I really didn't, but I think you should know. Cormac's been lying to me, Rush's been stalking you, Sully's married, and Wolf only pursued you for a bet."

I laugh. I can't help it. It's all so ridiculous, a blatant attempt to get me to do her bidding. "I don't buy it, Mom, I'm sorry, but no. None of those things are true. And I'm staying. Please tell me what's going on though. I want to help you."

She sighs, a wet noise right into the speaker. "Just remember, I didn't want to do this. This is all you, okay?"

"Okay?" My brows scrunch up as I squint at the phone, trying to make sense of what's happening.

Rush's voice fills the air, and it takes me a moment to realize that it's coming from my phone.

"What is this, Mom?"

"Shh. Just listen. I overheard them talking the night before we left. Now listen," she shushes me.

"Wanna tell me what's goin' on, boyo?" Cormac says.

"What do you mean, Da?" Rush asks.

Something slaps against a table, a notebook or stack of paper, maybe?

"What's this?" Rush asks, cool as ever.

"Receipts for the security you installed at St. Rita's All-Girls Academy and the surrounding cross streets last year. Wanna tell me about that?"

Cormac doesn't sound mad, but there's something in his voice I can't place.

"Nothin' to tell, Da. Just . . . protecting an investment."

There's a pause, and I hear something rustle down the line.

"An investment? Is that what kids these days are callin' it?"

"And so what—can't I have a girl, or is that not allowed anymore either?"

247

Something slams against a hard surface, and I picture them sitting in their kitchen having this conversation.

"You better watch your fuckin' tone with me, boyo. I'm your goddamn president, or did you forget that?"

Rush laughs—it's caustic and humorless.

"Don't worry, Da. *I haven't forgotten. But last I checked, who I fuck is none of the Brotherhood's business."*

"It is if it's Maeve King," Cormac spits.

My heart skips a beat at her name, and I don't realize that I'm holding my breath to hear what Rush says.

"It's not." Rush grits his words out.

"Sure, boyo, but I just hope for your sake it's not another Maeve."

"The world isn't ready for two Maeves. Don't worry so much, old man, she's nothing like Maeve."

She's nothing like Maeve.

She's nothing like Maeve.

She's nothing like Maeve.

Insecurity overwhelms me, but hearing Rush say I'm nothing like Maeve obliterates the jagged pieces of my heart. They were already crudely stitched back together, but with four simple words, Rush has taken a pipe bomb to them.

The thing is . . . he's not wrong.

I'm nothing like her.

She can disarm a bomb, and I can make a latte. She's strong and gorgeous and—and *nice.* And isn't that the worst part about it? She's fucking nice.

Shame warms my cheeks as I realize in this moment, I've become one of *those* girls. The kind that lets emotion overrule logic and lashes out.

But my god, I can't stop my thoughts and emotions from spiraling. This is dredging up old stuff I thought I long buried— things I haven't consciously thought about in years.

I think I might've opened Pandora's Box last night, and now I can't close it, and shit from forever ago is flaring up.

I can't even get my own mother to *see me*—to pick me. And here I am expecting not one but three of the hottest men I've ever seen in my *life* to pick me—*over them—the insanely gorgeous and talented King sisters?*! I honestly don't see that playing out.

I recognize that my insecurities are strangling me, but I can't stop the downward spiral.

Logically, I know that I have a lot of good qualities, but the truth is that Rush would be much better suited to a girl like Maeve.

And he probably wouldn't even have to share her.

There's an ache in my chest that radiates outward, and I swear I can see it rippling in the air, filling up the entire room.

What right do I have to be selfish and these men to share me when there's someone like Maeve—who they've known for ages, who literally kicks ass, who's in this life—right here? I'd be depriving them of a fulfilled life.

I just . . . can't. I can't do that to them.

"See? You see, Alaina? I told you you can't trust those boys," Mom says, shaking me from my melancholy thoughts.

I sigh, the sound of my heart cracking. "Why did you play that for me?"

She tsks. "I told you—you can't trust them, and they don't care about you. I spared you the rest of the conversation where Rush tells Cormac that you were something to pass the time with." She sniffs. "I did that because you're my daughter, and I care about you. And no one cares about you like I do."

"I . . . I don't even know what to say to that, Mom." My words feel hollow. How can a mother say things like that to her child?

I'm not sure that I'll ever understand my mother, but I'm

fairly certain that she'll never understand me. Not the old me—the me before I was kidnapped—and definitely not the new me.

If we were having this conversation a year ago—or even six months ago—I might have just blindly believed her. Picked up my broken spirit and dripping heart and left without a word to anyone. I would've nursed my broken heart alone.

But something changed inside me that night in the cabin. The old me is gone—she went up in flames, and I was remade.

"Well, I've done my part. I can't make you leave, but I really think you should. Call me when you do." She ends the call before I can say anything else.

I place my phone face-down on the table, tapping the case with my index finger a few times.

I exhale and stare at the swirls in the marble, debating on my next move.

After another moment, I know what I have to do.

I look over my shoulder and see three figures in the archway leading to the hallway. Rush's arms are crossed over his chest, his biceps bulging with tension. Sully's standing too still, his hands shoved in the pockets of his jeans. And Wolf's leaning against the wall in a faux semblance of calm, one foot flat against the wall behind him.

All three have varying looks of determination on their faces. With their matching scowls and furrowed brows, the resemblance is clear. I work to hide my smile at the pretty picture they make all lined up like that. They look like they're at a photo shoot for bad boys who smell like trouble. All tousled hair, ripped jeans, and dangerous expressions.

They're a goddamn wet dream.

After I've looked my fill—for now, I don't think I'll ever have enough of them—I ask, "Did you hear all that?"

Rush is the first to speak. He takes a step toward me, and

says, "I can explain." His expression is unreadable as usual, but we don't have time for this.

I hold my hand up to stop his forward progress. "We have more important things to deal with right now—like what's going on with my mother."

All three of them walk toward me, and I spin around in my seat to face them. It's overwhelming when one of them sets his sights on me like this, but when it's all three of them, it steals my breath.

With the way they're looking at me, I'm not sure that I need to breathe ever again.

"We'll get to that, Red, but first, we need to make sure you're still with us," Wolf drawls, gaze intense.

Rush steps up to me and the other two flank him. I tip my head back to hold his gaze, and a shiver skates down my back. I straighten up and gain a couple of inches, but he still towers over me—they all do.

And I like it.

Rush settles in between my legs as he slides his hand up in between my breasts until it settles at the base of my throat. His tattooed fingers gently encircle my neck, and my pulse kicks up a notch.

"I don't know what game she's playing, but that's not how that conversation went down." Rush brushes his thumb over my pulse point, and I have to concentrate on not closing my eyes at the feeling of his hands on me.

"Aye, I was there. That's not exactly how it went," Sully agrees.

I glance at him and hold his gaze as I ask, "Then how did it go, Sully?"

"It doesn't matter," Rush says, pulling my attention away from my first love. "All that matters is that there's no one else."

"There will never be anyone else," Wolf says, far closer than he was moments ago.

"Ever," Sully whispers.

It's enough to grab my attention in surprise. That sounded an awful lot like a promise. But that can't be right—my ex-boyfriend turned stepbrother turned tortured hero once swore he'd never forgive me. That tiny kernel of hope that I'd been secretly harboring flares. Just a little—enough to rekindle the embers.

"We want you. Not Maeve or anyone else," Rush says, his hand tightening briefly on my neck.

My eyes flare in jealousy. "Don't," I snap.

"Ah, my little bird is still jealous I see," Rush breathes the words against my lips as he slides his hand up my neck. "Was yesterday in the hallway outside where she was sitting not enough for you?"

My lips part, and I tilt my head back even further. Denial is on the tip of my tongue, but it's barely worth trying. They'll see right through the lie before the words even leave my mouth.

So I try something different—I embrace it.

"You're goddamn right I am," I grit the words out. "I'm going to hang out with other guys half-dressed and by the pool, and we'll see how well you weather jealousy." The smile I give him feels foreign on my face. And yet, the conniving twist of my lips feels perfect.

It's painful for me to go against my nature—I've always been a people pleaser—but the sense of satisfaction I feel when I witness Rush lose his grip on his control is worth every uncomfortable feeling caused from a few sentences.

My back arches as he presses his body into mine, one hand on my hip, the other still on my neck. My heart speeds up and I have to work to control my breathing.

His slips in control always get me so hot.

"Our little bird wants to spread her wings, brothers. What do we think about that?" His words seem simple enough, but the sinister edge lies just underneath the surface.

"I say we remind her who's cage she's in," Sully murmurs. I can see him out of the corner of my eye. His pupils are blown as he adjusts his dick through his pants.

"Green's your color, baby girl," Wolf says from right next to me before he turns my head and claims my mouth in an earth-shattering kiss.

Wolf turns me so my back hits something hard, and when a hand snakes up my chest to rest against the hollow of my throat, I know it's Rush.

I curl my fingers around the fabric of Wolf's tee, anchoring him to me as I fall into his kiss. Rush drags his lips down my neck as his other hand curls possessively around my hip.

There's barely any air between the three of us, we're pressed so tight. And just when I'm about to break the kiss to look for Sully, I feel his heat against my side. Rush and Wolf both shift toward each other, neither breaking their hold on me—lips or hands—to make room for Sully. He steps into the space they created. In one move, Wolf backs off and Sully steps in, claiming my lips as his own.

Rush never loosens his hold, and it seems I'm not the only one comfortable to let him play puppeteer.

Wolf's hands start their exploration on every inch of available skin, and I tighten my grip on his shirt to keep him close.

Sully slides his hands up my ribs as he tilts his head to get the perfect angle. Our tongues dance together, and I'm two seconds away from demanding they shed some clothes.

Someone clears their throat, and it's like a shot was fired. All three of them turn as one to protect me from the perceived threat, shielding my body with theirs, and pulling a gun from somewhere. Rush takes one from the back of his pants, Sully drops to grab one from underneath the coffee table before he quickly stands up, and Wolf grabs one from the drawer in the side table.

Warmth spreads throughout my body, different from the potent feeling of lust. This feels softer, less dense. I feel protected and safe.

It takes them a second to realize that it's not a threat, but once they do, they lower their weapons. Dave, their head of security at Summer Knoll, stands at the edge of the patio, arms behind his back. For just having three guns drawn on you, he's surprisingly calm.

I wonder if this sort of thing happens a lot around here. I make a mental note to ask about it later.

"Sorry to interrupt, but Rossi and the Blue Knights arrived."

"Fuck," Rush growls out. He turns to face me, muscles taut and intensity rolling off him in waves. "We're not done, baby."

My lips part and all I can do is nod my agreement. No, no, we are not done. Not by a long shot.

27

ALAINA

I FOLLOW my guys into the house and down into the basement in a conference-style room. The King sisters are already there, taking up one corner of the room. Wolf stretches his arm out behind him to snag my hand, lacing our fingers together, and pulling me beside him. We follow Rush to the front of the room by the head of the long table. I stand in between Rush and Wolf, and Sully stands on the other side of Rush.

All three of them wear severe expressions, a vast contrast to five minutes ago when they had their hands and mouths all over me.

I shiver just thinking about what would've happened had Dave not shown up. With how often I get interrupted, I'm starting to think the universe is trying to tell me something. I'm just not sure what.

"Pay attention, baby girl. You're about to be a part of Brotherhood business," Wolf murmurs in my ear.

My eyes snap up, and I startle at all the people now filling the room. I notice one or two familiar faces, but most of them are new to me.

Rush waits until everyone is inside before he nods, and Dave closes the door from the hallway.

"Thank you all for coming here. I know it's a bit of a drive for some of you. As I'm sure you're aware, my brothers and I are the junior council of the Brotherhood, which means we'll be ascending soon. It might even be sooner than any of us realizes." He pauses to look around the room. "You're here because you're a friend or an ally or both. And it seems we have a mutual enemy. Whoever broke into Summer Knoll, torched Mama Rosa's, ordered a drive-by on *wives*, tipped off the cops to meet-up locations—whoever kidnapped *our girl*—is likely the same person."

Murmurs of agreement float around the room, and I feel the shift—anticipation and expectation hang in the air.

"As of right now, the Brotherhood has decided not to pursue this . . . mutual enemy of ours. But I, for one, won't sit idly by while some motherfuckers take what we've earned by blood and by right."

Goosebumps sprout along my skin when cheers erupt. I taste the promise of violence in the air and marvel at the dark king next to me. He's ignited these people, and he's going to set them loose.

A smirk tips the corner of my lips at the idea of getting my pound of flesh from the people who orchestrated my kidnapping.

Six months ago, that thought never would've crossed my mind. So I guess if I needed further proof that I'm changing—evolving—I just gave it to myself.

Rush wraps it up after that, coordinating who's doing what and when. The room clears out quickly until it's just the Kings and us.

I reluctantly untangle my hand from Wolf's and walk over by them. All five of them eye me with varying expressions of curiosity.

I push my shoulders back and keep my chin up even though

the intensity they aim my way is enough to make me want to turn tail.

"I need a favor."

"For the queen? Sure." Maeve raises a brow and shrugs a shoulder.

I tilt my head as I regard her. She's the oldest sister, and the most vocal, so I shift my attention to her. She's the one I need to convince. "Queen?"

"Aye. Aren't you banging all three brothers?" Roisin asks with a smirk.

My first instinct is to clarify that we haven't had sex yet, but I stop myself in time. I don't owe them anything, and it's no one's business but ours, anyway.

I scan all five of these gorgeous girls, looking for jealousy or indignation. When I don't find a shred of either, I shrug my shoulders. "I don't kiss and tell."

Roisin tips her head back and laughs. Ava and Keira join in and the other two smirk their amusement.

"I was wondering how long it would take you to break out of that shell you wrap so tightly around yourself," Maeve says, her gaze assessing.

"Yeah, well . . . I'm going through some stuff."

"I heard about your kidnapping. Heard you killed one of your attackers," Ava says with raised brows.

"I did." I nod and fight to keep my stance casual. "That's part of my favor. I need you to teach me what you guys know."

Silence greets my request, and I shift my weight to the other foot.

"You have them"—Keira nods behind me—"why don't they teach you?"

"They are. But Sully spent nearly a week making me watch instructional videos on self-defense before he let me actually do anything—and that lasted a day. And with the other two . . .

well, they tend to get distracted." I feel a flush warm my cheeks.

Keira snickers. "Can't you just tell 'em to wait until after they teach you some shit?"

I fold my arms across my chest and tilt my head. "Not really. Would you if you were me?"

I look over my shoulder at the subjects of our conversation, unsurprised to find all three of them standing next to each other, murmuring and staring at me. A flush works its way over my body under their gaze.

"Yeah, I can see what you mean," Keira says.

I shift my attention back to the girls in front of me. "So, will you help me?"

"Aye, we'll help. We're here for a couple more days. Let's see what we can do. Meet us in the gym in twenty minutes," Maeve says.

"Thank you." I catch her gaze and hold it. She nods once before she stands up from her chair and leaves the room. Her sisters follow one by one.

I cross the room and stand in front of the three of them, my skin warming under their collective gaze.

"What was that about?" Wolf tips his head toward the last King sister leaving the room.

I shrug. "They're going to teach me everything they know for the next two days. Starting now."

I can't stifle my giggle at their matching expressions of shock.

Rush recovers first, his face smoothing into an easy grin as he leans forward and places a chaste kiss on my lips. "That's good, baby."

Wolf laughs. "Oh man, I can't wait to see what kind of shit they teach you. Be sure to come find me first, Red. I wanna see if they show you any grappling moves. You can demonstrate them on me." He waggles his eyebrows.

"Alright. I'm going to go change into something I can move in. I'll see you guys later." I walk out of the room and head up to the third floor where my bedroom is.

I know Sully's trailing me, and it's not because I have some sixth sense like Rush. His energy—frustration and lust tinged in desperation—rolls off of him, bouncing off the walls and taking up every available inch of space in the hallway.

I make it inside my bedroom before he makes his move. He grips my arm right above my elbow, kicks the door closed, and spins me around to put my back against it.

"What're you thinking, princess? Befriending the Kings like that?"

"They're going to teach me a few things—things I'll need to survive in this world. And they're not going to shove video tutorials down my throat for days, they're *actually going to* teach me," I say, leaning in his face and meeting his challenge.

"You have no idea what kind of people they are. They're not like the Betty Crockers you're used to. These girls don't think twice about double-tapping when the mood suits them."

"They're your friends, aren't they?" I ask with a raised brow.

"Aye. But you have no idea what you're getting yourself into. This isn't the place for you, princess." His tone is sincere, but his words strike a chord within me.

I lean into his face, eyes hard. "You don't know me anymore, James. And even if you did, that girl from two years ago? She's gone. She left this world on the dirty floor of a rundown cabin in the woods." I lick my lips, heart pounding, and stare into his eyes. "I've been remade, James."

"So, you're going to—what? Start hacking into government programs for fun or steal shit and sell it on the black market or infiltrate secret societies or become a sharpshooter now? Because that's the kind of things they do." He's breathing heavy.

I tip my chin up. "Maybe. Maybe I will do those things."

"This isn't a game, Lainey!" he says as he slams his hands against the door on either side of my head. "This is the real world where our actions have dire consequences."

Indignation rises within me, swift and hot, and I see red. I push off the wall, my chest heaving and my fists clenching. "I know that, Sully."

We're an inch apart, maybe less, close enough to share the same breath.

He exhales, and I inhale.

His eyes go wild and he tips his head down to rest his forehead against mine. The gentle action at odds with his clenched muscles.

"What are you doing to me, princess?" His words sound tortured, but I can't even think about that yet because this is the first time he's called me princess without sarcasm or scorn coating every syllable.

He pushes me into the door, and I have to tip my head back to hold his gaze.

But I do. I hold the hell out of his gaze.

All dark promises and barely leashed rage.

Or is it hate?

Maddie once told me that love and hate were two sides of the same coin. And that there's a thin line between the two. I've never really understood that until now.

Until Sully.

He keeps his emotions bottled up so tight it's hard to tell how he's really feeling. He makes you work for it.

I tip my chin up even further and let the cruel smirk I learned from him spread across my face when I deliver my truth. "Whatever I want."

"That so?" He leans back to give me a slow once-over. "Think you can just snap your little fingers and I'll do your bidding? Hmm, princess?" His smile is too wide and conde-scending.

I press my back against the door, pushing my chest out. The neckline of my tank top stretches tight across my chest. Then, I slowly, deliberately bring my hand up in between the both of us.

And I snap my fingers.

I watch with barely restrained glee as Sully's fuse goes up in smoke.

"You're." He takes the single step separating us, grabbing my wrist and pressing our chests together. "A." He pushes my wrists against the door above my head. "Spoiled." He leans in as close as he can without actually touching me, our noses a hair's breadth apart. "Princess."

Our breaths come in fast, and my heart feels like it's going to explode.

We're on the precipice, Sully and I. We're physically standing in my room, but we might as well be on the cliff's edge of the Grand Canyon.

It's thrilling and terrifying, but I'm not scared—not really.

I'm exhilarated. I feel alive in a way I haven't felt before the Fitzgerald brothers barged into my life.

I'm about to jump off that cliff, and I'm taking Sully with me.

I bridge the gap, bringing our lips together, and free-fall.

"And you love me anyway."

Before the last syllable leaves my mouth, I crush my lips to his. He doesn't hesitate for a second. He grabs me under my thighs and lifts me up to press me against the door, slamming his lips against mine.

Our tongues fight for dominance. I thread my fingers through his hair, loving how much he's let it grow. If he doesn't cut it soon, he'll be able to tie it back, and then I'll really have something to hold onto.

Something to anchor him to me.

He growls when I tug his hair, and I swear to god, I get wetter from just that tortured sound leaving those perfect lips.

I could spend the rest of my life kissing Sully, and it would never be enough.

I'll never have enough of him—or Rush or Wolf. I'm slowly figuring out what that means—for me, for each of them, for us.

His hands flex on my thighs, no doubt leaving fingertip-shaped bruises. Without tearing his mouth away from mine, he shifts his hold on me. One hand is still on my leg, but the other slides up the inside of my thigh, exactly how I like it. He's following the map of my sensitive erogenous zones with familiarity, but I'm not all that surprised. He's the one who originally mapped it out on my skin.

All those stolen moments in the New York Public Library and those long afternoons sneaking kisses in the park.

But I'm not the same girl I was two years ago—I'm not the same girl I was two weeks ago. I've got new places on that map with his name on them, and I'm aching for him to explore.

I moan into his mouth and arch my body against his, loving the way his cock presses against my clit with each roll of his hips.

He rips his mouth off mine, our chests heaving in tandem. And if I were a betting woman, I'd say our hearts were too.

Abruptly, he lets go of me and runs the back of his hand across his mouth as he takes a single step backward. Something akin to self-loathing shines in his eyes as he stares at me. "This was a mistake."

My head feels light and I shake it to clear it. "A mistake?"

"You don't belong here, princess, and it doesn't matter how many times you suck face—or dick—that's not gonna change."

I try to let his words roll off me, but they sink into the little fissures of my broken and newly mended soul.

And they start to fester.

"I knew you were a lot of things, James, but I didn't think you were a liar."

"You don't know me at all."

"Your hot-and-cold routine wears thin. Let me know when you're ready to act like the man I thought you were," I snap, walking toward my bathroom.

"Don't hold your breath, princess."

Those are the last words I hear before he storms out of my room, slamming the door behind him. I echo his frustration and slam my bathroom door.

I strip off my clothes and jump into a hot shower, hoping to scrub off my disappointment.

28

ALAINA

TWO DAYS LATER, Rush volunteers Sully to take me back to the city to meet Maddie and Mary for lunch. He has to check-in with someone from the impromptu meeting a few days ago. I popped my headphones in and listened to an audiobook on the drive, and the only words exchanged were when he asked for my order at a coffee shop.

I'm not even sure what I'm doing, but all I know is that he's gotta be the one to come to his decision to do this thing with me —with us. I can't keep baiting him, no matter how fun it is. So for now, I'm content to let him battle his demons inside his head alone. And when he's ready, I'm going to make him beg for it.

The King sisters left this morning too. They were surprisingly fun to be around the last two days. As promised, they gave me a crash course in all the things they do—basically lessons in being badass. I exchanged numbers with all of them, and even though I don't think we'll ever be as tight as I am with my cousins, I think we could be friends.

I arrive to the diner Mary picked out for lunch a few minutes early. Sully parked down the block and walked me to the diner. After a quick chat with a guy behind the counter I've never seen before, he nods at me and taps his wrist twice.

He'll be back in thirty minutes, just like we planned.

I'm not surprised at his radio silence, but I am disappointed. I had thought we were turning a corner in our . . . relationship of sorts. But then he pulls a stunt like he did in my bedroom, and it's like we're back at square one again.

I spy Mary's recognizable hair in the booth in the back and make a beeline for her.

Before my butt even hits the cracked leather seat in the booth in the back of the pizza place, Mary starts talking.

"I did something really stupid. Like really, really dumb. I wasn't thinking, and now I'm so screwed." Her voice cracks, and she sniffles.

In one movement, I slide in the booth, my legs sticking to the seat from the humidity. Summer in New York City can be a real pain. I slip my purse strap over my head, letting it rest on the seat beside me. It's then I take a good look at my cousin.

Her hair is dirty and thrown in a ponytail which is unusual— not the ponytail, the dirty hair part. She's never been a fan of dry shampoo like Maddie and I have, so she washes her hair every day, no matter what. Her clothes are rumpled, and she's wearing sunglasses.

"Okay. Whatever it is, we can fix it. Maddie's amazing at fixing stuff." I pull out my phone to check for missed messages from her. "Where is she, by the way? She's not usually late."

Mary sobs, it's this awful, broken sound that has the tiny hair on my arm standing.

"She's going to be so mad at me, Lainey. S-so mad."

"Whoa." I shake my head. "Start over. What's going on?"

Mary nods a few times as she swipes away tears from underneath her eyes.

"I thought he was sweet, ya know?" She looks off to the side of the restaurant. "But"—she shakes her head and turns to face me again—"it was all a lie. Everything was a lie. I don't even know how old he is or where he really went to college. Shit, I don't even know if that's his real name or not!"

"Who, Mary?" Her panic is starting to seep into me.

She looks me in the eye and says, "My boyfriend."

My eyebrows hit my hairline. "Boyfriend?"

She nods. "Max. We met online in a chatroom for the private schools. You know the fliers that are posted all over the cafeteria at St. Rita's?"

I shake my head. I don't remember seeing fliers for anything like that, but then again, I don't really look at those boards too often.

"Okay, well, it starts out simple. Kind of like a Facebook, but for the private school network—and it's only a profile with the option to chat." She sighs. "So, one day, this guy sends me a chat, says I'm cute or whatever. He said he went to St. Joseph's, and since Pam's cousin went there last year, I asked her to ask her cousin about him. I wanted to make sure he was legit before anything, you know?" Her eyes well up as she looks right at me. "I wanted to make sure I wasn't doing something stupid."

"Okay. So what happened?"

Mary clears her throat. "Well, Pam's cousin said he remembers this guy, said he's a nice guy. So I messaged him back."

"When was this?" I sit back in the booth, trying to figure out where this story is headed.

"Back in March." She looks at the table, her words low.

"Then what?"

She shrugs a shoulder, and glances at me, pain and guilt painted all over her face.

"Then we started chatting. At first it was random stuff. Like favorite movies and hobbies. Then it got a little deeper, and

269

before I knew it, we were talking all the time. Every time I asked him to video chat or meet for dinner, he was busy or had plans. I thought it was weird, but then he'd send me flowers or have lunch delivered or send me a sweet message." She pauses to pour more water in her glass from the carafe on the table and takes a drink. "But then, uh, then he asked for some photos. You know, sexy photos." She stares at me with her eyebrows raised.

"You sent some guy you've never met nudes?" I feel both brows hit my hairline. "I'm not judging. I'm just surprised."

Her cheeks pink, and she stares at the tabletop again. "I feel so stupid, but at the time, I . . . I don't know what I thought. I felt sexy, more mature, more—it doesn't matter."

"Hey." I reach out and grab her hand. "I promise I'm not judging. I'm sure I've done some things recently that you'd be surprised at too. So, no worries, okay?"

She sniffs and nods a few times. "Okay."

"What happened next?"

She looks at me, her lips tremble. "He started asking questions. At first, it was little things, like usual. But then—then he started asking questions about Maddie . . . and you. Asking for photos of all of us, just stupid ones like selfies. I just thought that he wanted to get to know me, since you guys are the most important people in my life. But then he started getting forceful in his questions. Demanding to know where I was . . . and where you and Maddie were. So, I, uh, I told him I needed some space."

"What kind of questions?"

She shrugs one shoulder, and another tear rolls down her cheek. "Little things at first, like your favorite bands, then bigger things like . . . your schedule."

My jaw drops, and I'm speechless. "Mary, that's . . ."

"I know, I know," she says through a cry.

"Why did you give it to him, though? The information, the photos."

Her mouth trembles as she says, "I don't know. He was so charming and cool and nice—god, he *doted* on me, Lainey. And he made me feel beautiful and important and *wanted*. And I was so—so desperate for affection that was solely mine, that I was afraid of what would happen if I stopped giving it to him."

I pull my hand back from hers and run it through my hair with a deep exhale. My brain feels like it's running circles around the information, unable to settle enough to make sense of what's really going on.

"I've been a twin my entire life—second always to Maddie. And I love my sister—I do—but this one thing was just mine. And I didn't want to lose that."

"So you told him stuff about Maddie—about me." I pull my phone out of my pocket and pull up a text message with Wolf. "Okay. So, I'll just tell Wolf. He's probably the best one to bring this too. He can be the most . . . persuasive. He'll make sure this Max guy forgets everything he knows about us."

"Wait," she says, the words snapping into the air like a whip.

I pause with my thumb over the keypad.

"There's more," she says as she looks away. "After some time, it was just too much, and I told him I needed space."

"And let me guess, he threatened to post your photos?"

Mary nods, her face drawn in grief.

"Fucking asshole."

"I panicked. I didn't know what to do, so I went to O'Malley's to find Jack to ask for help."

"You did *what?*! Why didn't you call me?"

Mary sits back and folds her arms tightly across her chest. "It was my problem, Lainey. I was tired of having you and Maddie always cleaning everything up for me. I wanted to be the one to take care of my mess this time."

"I can see that. But this was huge. And this involved more than just you. Jesus, Mary, you sent him photos of us—all of us!"

271

She nods slowly, a single tear rolling down her cheek. "I know. That's why I went to ask Jack for help. But he wasn't there, so I ended up waiting around for him for a little bit." She licks her lips and looks off to the side. "I had a drink, and it loosened my tongue." She looks back at me. "I ended up telling Benny everything, and he promised to help me."

"*Benny*? As in Benny, the bouncer of O'Malley's?"

"Yep. That's the one."

"Okay." I rub my temples.

"Well, then Benny helped me with Max. Said he roughed him up and deleted the photos from Max's phone, cloud, and backups. And I haven't heard from Max since."

"How . . . chivalrous of Benny."

"Not exactly . . . I sort of promised him a date with you," she says as she closes her eyes tight.

I blink at her, feeling anger and disbelief swirl around. "Why would you do that? You know I'm seeing someone. More than one someone."

"I know, and I told Benny that. But he said I'd have to convince you, or he'd take his date one way or another. And I figured Wolf wouldn't mind or whatever. You know, since it's helping me out."

I'm shaking my head before she even finishes talking. "Have you listened to nothing I've told you about them? They're alpha male assholes who are more inclined to shoot first, ask questions never." I scoff.

My phone vibrates with a new text message before I can say anything further. I glance at it, thinking it's Maddie with her eta. But it's from an unknown number, but there's a thumbnail in the preview.

I open the text message and notice it's a group message between the unknown number, Wolf, Sully, Rush, and me.

272

It takes me three tries to read the message because I can't stop staring at the photo.

> **Unknown Number: I thought you should know.**

My hands shake, and I fumble with the phone. It clatters to the tabletop and Mary gets a look at the message and the photo.

"Oh my god, Lainey! I-is that Maddie? Where is she? Do you think this is my fault?!" She starts to cry, these big, fat tears rolling down her cheeks and dripping onto the table. "Oh my god! We have to go to the police!" Mary shoots up.

"Sit down, Mary. I just . . . don't what to think, but I know we can't go to the cops." I stare at the photo of one of my best friends, my cousin, my sister in all the ways that matter, and my chest breaks open.

Maddie's bound and gagged, zip-tied to a metal chair. Her head's slumped forward, and red blooms around her hairline.

Rush once told me that he was willing to burn down the city to get me back, and I thought I understood what he meant by that.

But I didn't. Not really.

I couldn't have understood, no matter how many times I hypothesized or talked in theories.

But now I understand.

Because the rage that's been slowly simmering deep, deep down inside me since that fateful night I turned eighteen starts rising. Slowly at first, as if it's being awakened after hibernating for my entire life.

Then it flows easier and faster, and I just know that I'm about to erupt.

My phone rings, the vibration loud against the tabletop.

Rush.

7777777777777

Of course, he must've seen the photo.

"I've gotta take this," I murmur to Mary as I slide out of the booth and walk out of the diner. Each footstep feels like a drumbeat only I can hear. A war cry that I'm pounding into the earth.

I lean against the tree by the front window and answer his call.

29

ALAINA

"HELLO?"

"Wait for us. We'll be there in an hour," he says without a proper greeting.

"I can't wait, Rush! Someone has Maddie! She's my family, and I don't know what they're doing to her! W-we don't know what they're doing to her!" I yell, anguish and fear shredding my insides.

"We're your goddamn family!" Rush roars.

I feel the rage he works so hard to mask through the phone, and my heart aches for him. He hates the loss of control.

I nod even though he can't see me as I spin around and look at the bustling city street. People are moving around me on the sidewalk, oblivious to the state of fear and rage and panic I'm drowning in. Though I suppose that could be the case for any number of people in New York City at any given time.

"You're right. You are my family. But so is she. And I don't know why they took her, but it feels like it's my fault! Someone snapped that photo and sent it to all of us. And she—she looks so much like me"—my voice breaks, and I have to stop to clear my throat—"I can't just leave her there."

"I'm just asking you to wait for us—wait for me, baby. Please," Rush practically begs.

I sigh, the sound audible even amid the noise of the crowd around me. "Okay, but please hurry."

Rush exhales into the phone, his relief palpable. "Okay, okay. Just wait for me, yeah? Go back inside that diner. Wolf and I are already on the way. And where the fuck is Sully?"

I turn around and sidestep a few people to get back to the diner.

"I don't know. He dropped me off here about an hour ago, said he had some quick business to deal with." I pull my phone away to check the time. "But he should've been back twenty minutes ago."

Worry settles in my gut as I think back on everything he said before he dropped me off.

"Alaina, listen to me." Rush's words are harsh but not unkind, and they spike my adrenaline. I stop in the middle of the sidewalk, staring at the glass windows into the diner. "Wolf just tried to call Sully again, and he didn't answer. His Find My Phone location is off—or his phone is off—so I'm going to bypass it. But it means I have to get my laptop, okay? I want you to go inside the diner, sit at the furthest table, and don't fucking move until I get there. Got it?"

"What's going on, Rush?" My voice comes out quieter than I intended, but I can't help it. He always said he has a sixth sense for bad things about to happen, and I can't help but think this is one of those times. But I'm not sure if it's for me, them, or Sully. My chest clenches at the idea of them getting hurt.

"I'm not sure. Just do as I ask, yeah? We'll be there soon." Rush sounds distracted, and I hear Wolf in the background asking for a favor. "Be safe, Alaina."

His words sound ominous in my ear as the call ends. I pull my location settings up and make sure I'm still sharing my location with all three of my boys as I wait for the path to the diner to clear. I see an opening and take a step forward, only to come up short by a hand on my shoulder.

I look over my shoulder, expecting to see Sully. My heart races when I see my mom. My gaze darts all over her, unable to focus on just one thing. I don't know if I've ever seen her hair down like that, loose waves framing her face. Mascara coats her lashes, otherwise, her face is bare. I realize with a jolt that my mother has the same freckles as me. Or I have the same freckles as her, I guess.

The thought depresses me for more than one reason—I don't see my mother enough to realize we even have similarities like that, and she never wears less than a full face of makeup around me.

I scan my mom and take in the rest of her. Dressed in a white Blondie tee and distressed jean shorts, I realize with a jolt that she's dressed like me.

Literally.

I'm wearing a white Florence + The Machine band tee I got at her concert last year, light denim jean shorts, and Vans. I exhale as I stare at the black Chuck Taylors on her feet.

My heart pounds, and my mouth feels dry as I take my mom in.

"Mom, what the hell is going on? What are you doing here?" I ask as I turn around to face her.

She doesn't let go of my arm, and her gaze darts around wildly. "Where are those boys? The ones who follow you around like lost little puppies."

My brows crinkle at her assumption. They are far from lost little puppies. "Why? What's going on?"

Alarm races up my spine, and the hair on the back of my neck rises the longer she takes to answer me.

She takes me by surprise when she jostles me with her grip on my shoulder. "Damnit, Alaina. Can't you just do as your told for once?!"

I meet her gaze and instinctively take a step back at the crazed look in her eye. She switches her grip to my wrist, and I gain another step closer to the diner.

In true New York City fashion, the stream of people just part around us and keep walking, not a single person stopping.

"I thought you were supposed to meet your cousins at two." She practically snarls the words, accusation and derision dripping from every word.

A cold sweat coats my skin, and all my instincts are screaming at me to run. But I can't leave Mary inside.

"I never told you that." My words are calm, measured.

I don't know what the hell is going on, and I don't know who to trust—except that's not exactly true. I know I can trust Rush, Sully, and Wolf.

If nothing else, I know that much.

Okay, okay, so I just have to stall . . . whatever this is . . . for an hour until they get here. I can do that.

"Of course not. I bugged your phone." She scoffs and levels me with an insufferable look.

"You did *what*?!"

"Shhh!" She squeezes my arm and pulls me closer to hiss the noise in my face. "Stop drawing attention to yourself! It was temporary, and I took it out, obviously, or I would've known you changed plans!"

I yank on my arm, my fight or flight instinct kicking in. "Let go of me," I grit through my teeth. "What else have you been doing behind my back?"

The hot summer sun beats down on us, and I feel like I'm being cooked on the sidewalk in the middle of a crowd.

"Be quiet, Alania. Jesus. Or they'll take Mary and you too, and everything I've done will be for *nothing*," Mom hisses in my face. "Do you know how many hours I spent piecing together sound bites to make that phone call sound believable? And you still didn't leave!"

Her words freeze me more than her increasing grip on my arm.

"What are you talking about? You know who took Maddie? And you faked that recording?" My voice is harsh, and Mom raises her brows in response before she scoffs again.

"Oh, Alaina, drop the tough act. Let the adults work, okay? You're nothing more than a princess who's escaped from her gilded tower." Mom rolls her eyes. "I've made sure of that over the years, but now I realize it wasn't the right call," she murmurs, more to herself than me.

Her words cut like she intended—she's always been good at that. But there's something about what she said that sets my blood boiling.

It's so reminiscent of what Sully spat in my face that I can't tell if this is a sign from the universe to dive headfirst into my new life—and the lurking darkness—or to crawl back to my *gilded tower.*

"We don't have a lot of time. I need you to leave. And—"

"Lana. What an . . . interesting surprise," a masculine voice says from behind me. The low tenor would be almost pleasant if it wasn't for the prickle of awareness that spikes.

Dread pools low in my belly, and I just know that if I turn around, I'll see red eyes and a face cut from marble.

I don't have to turn around to realize one of my nightmares has come to life. There, casually walking around me like he's inspecting a new piece of furniture, stands the demon guy from the back of O'Malley's.

Fear licks along my nerves, sparking with every heartbeat, and I lick my suddenly dry lips.

"Now, now, Lana. This wasn't our deal." He tsks.

My mother changes—she fucking transforms right before my eyes. She stands a little taller, pushes her shoulders back, and stares at him with the perfected blank face I've come to know well.

"You got her, didn't you?"

I hold in my gasp at the confirmation that my mother had a hand in this whole thing. In Maddie being taken.

The red-eyed man wears charcoal suit pants and a bright white button-down shirt with the shirtsleeves rolled up to his elbows. Black Ray-Bans sit on top of his jet-black hair and black boots cover his feet. It's an interesting choice for the middle of a record-breaking summer.

He slowly walks around us with his arms clasped behind his back, and the surrounding flow of traffic parts without a second's hesitation.

"Interesting seeing you here, Lana. And your outfit looks drastically different from what you usually wear, no? Going"—he pointedly flicks his gaze to me—"casual today?"

"Yes. As a matter of fact, I'm running errands with my niece." Mom gestures to me. "And in case you didn't realize, there's a heat advisory today. So I dressed accordingly," she says as she gestures to her clothes.

It takes everything in me to lock down my emotions so they don't show on my face. But damn, is it hard.

I have so many questions—and accusations, honestly—that I don't know where to start. My head spins a little, and I'm not sure if it's from this conversation or the heat.

Demon guy walks around us one more time before stepping

in front of me, close enough that I can smell him—roasted coffee beans. It's a strange smell to associate with a person, but it's one I'll never forget.

"Hmm. Did you know, Lana, that your *niece* looks remarkably like you?" His gaze roams all over my face, assessing.

"What's your point, Liam? You know I have a twin." Mom scoffs, but I hear the waiver in her voice. "You have my daughter, so leave my niece alone. We have places to be." Mom wraps her arm around me, pulling me to her side and out of his direct gaze.

Shock and disbelief make me pliable, and my shoulder slams into my mother. My lips part as the implication of what she just said sinks in.

Mom had a hand in Maddie's disappearance?

Demon guy—Liam—tsks and takes a step toward me. He reaches his hand out and traces my cheekbone with his index finger. A second later, I swat his hand away and jerk my head to the side.

"Feisty. I like it." Liam's grin looks like mania personified. He turns his entire body to face my mother.

"Oh, Lana. You know what we do to liars, don't you?"

Mom visibly pales, but she keeps her shoulders back, and her head held high. I don't know what to do here—I don't have enough information to make the best decision.

But I know that I need to get Maddie back.

"I didn't—"

Liam holds up a hand. "Save it. He won't believe you once he gets a look at her," he says with a tilt of his head in my direction. "See, Lana, you forgot one very important thing. She's got the Gallagher eyes."

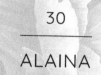

30

ALAINA

"I SEE you realize the severity of your mistake now," Liam says with a smile that's just a bit too wide. "Good. It'll make the rest of this so much more pleasant."

Liam turns to face me, handing me a business card. "Come to this address in one hour. Alone. I don't wanna see your little boyfriends around, or it won't end so well for anyone. And your ma can come too. Boss'll want to see her, anyway." He delivers the last line to my mom with a sneer. "And Lana? Don't make me come find you. I won't be as nice."

He leans forward and bops her on the nose. And if that isn't the most sinister thing about him, I don't know what is.

What the hell kind of monster delivers threats like that and then bops you on the nose like a cute kitten?

I shudder in the blazing hot sun, the sweat on my neck turning cold.

As one, Mom and I turn to watch him walk away from us, whistling as he blends in with the crowd, until finally, I can't see him anymore. Only then do I turn back to face my mother.

"What the fuck have you done?"

"Alaina Murphy McElroy, you watch your mouth," Mom says, but it's half-hearted at best.

"It's Gallagher, remember?" The response is automatic, but I don't pack a lot of heat behind it. I'm too lost in my thoughts, scrambling to catch up.

"You'll always be a McElroy. But we don't have time for your tantrum now, anyway. Now, I have to think of a way out of this mess. If you only would've done as your told——"

I whirl around on her. "*Do as I'm told?* How about you clue me the hell in now? The only thing I knew was that I was meeting my cousins for brunch while Sully took care of a few things. That's it." I rake my hand through my hair, my fingers tangling in a few loose waves. "I've gotta call Rush back—he needs to know what's really going on——"

"No. Absolutely not. What's the address?"

"What?" I throw my hands up.

"On the card, Alaina. Honestly, keep up!" Mom snaps, throwing her hand out toward me.

I'd forgotten about the small rectangular card in my hand. It's matte black on both sides with an address printed in gold.

768 West High Street.

"Here. I don't know where this is," I tell her as I hand her the card.

She blows out a breath, her cheeks puffing out with the motion. "Okay. We're going going to go in that diner for ten minutes, and I'm going to figure out a new plan." She walks toward the diner, and I follow her. "It should take us about forty minutes to get there . . . we'll need an Uber . . . and probably two exit strategies."

I follow behind my mother as she weaves through tables and heads toward the back booth—right where Mary still sits.

"Shit. I forgot you were still in here."

"Wow. Thanks a lot, Lainey." Mary's voice trembles, but I don't really have time to worry about that right now.

Mom snaps her fingers and points in Mary's face. "You can be quiet or leave." Mary's mouth shuts with an audible click. "Good. Now move over. Alaina, sit next to your cousin," Mom directs as she raises her arm to flag down a waitress and slides into the booth—all in one motion.

I stare at this woman, startled that I barely recognize her. "Who are you?" My words are breathless and full of wonder.

"I'm your mother." Her tone is biting, and it's actually comforting—which is so fucked up to think about. "Great. I'll have your largest coffee, black, please. And a danish. Thanks."

I physically feel my jaw drop. "I thought you didn't eat donuts?!"

"Alaina, I cannot hold your hand through this mess you made—"

"I didn't do anything! You stabbed everyone in the back, and she"—I hook my thumb at Mary—"told some random guy all about us. In fact, I'm the only one who hasn't been keeping secrets—except Maddie."

The waitress returns with my mom's order, and she wastes no time in digging in.

Ten minutes later, she licks the crumbs from her fingertips and polishes off the last of her coffee. Mary and I continue to sit in silence.

I glance at the clock in the corner of the diner and mentally calculate how much time until Rush and Wolf arrive. I bite my lip, because I know it won't be soon enough.

Mom drops a twenty on the table and stands. "Mary, you go back to the dorm. Keep your phone on you, but do not answer for anyone but me or Alaina. Anyone. I mean it."

Mary nods and stands up, her face pale and her hands shaking. "Okay, Auntie Lana. Okay." She turns to face me as I stand. "I'm really sorry, Lainey." She's pale, and she's biting her lips hard enough that it's starting to bleed.

I sigh. I'm pretty sure she's in shock, and I wish I could help her, but Maddie's the priority now. "I know, Mary. Let's just . . . let's just get Maddie home, and then we'll talk, okay?"

Mary nods several times, but when no one says anything else, she spins on her heel and practically sprints out of the diner.

I turn to face my mother with a raised brow.

"I ordered us an Uber. It's outside." She gathers her purse, slings it over her shoulder, and heads outside, waving to the waitress on the way out.

"You wanna fill me in on the plan?" I ask from behind her.

We slide into the backseat of the Uber, and she leans forward to talk to the driver. He's an older man, graying hair tucked under a Mets hat.

"Two stops, okay?"

"Yeah, lady, I saw the order."

Mom settles back into the seat, and the driver turns up the volume on his radio. Some jazz singer croons through the speakers as he pulls into traffic, cutting off at least three cars by my estimation.

"Mom. The plan?" I prompt her, but she still won't meet my gaze.

She exhales, this big release that has her body sagging forward. "You were bait, Alaina."

I blink several times, as if that will help me understand what she's saying.

"I spent so many years hiding you away from them. And then, somehow, they found you." She pauses. "Probably those asshole Fitzgeralds. I knew trusting Cormac was a mistake," she mumbles as she glances at me once before turning her attention back to the window.

"So Cormac really was lying to you? I know that other stuff you said about Sully, Rush, and Wolf isn't true though."

She shrugs a shoulder. "I made it up."

"I don't understand."

"A few months after your father left, and I knew he wasn't coming back, someone from the estate tracked me down. I still don't know how—special PI or trained seal or something—because I thought I'd covered our tracks pretty well." She shrugs. "Anyway, he informed me you'd be next in line for Gallagher Industries."

"Gallagher Industries? I've never heard of it."

"You wouldn't. They're a multibillion dollar technology company based in Ireland. They mostly deal with various government jobs from around the world and the very wealthy who have too much time and money." She sighs and continues to look out the window. "Well, your father was first in line for the company. It'd been passed down from father to son for many, many generations. But Aidan never wanted it. He was happy with his life here—with us. And the Brotherhood. So he gave it to his younger brother."

"I have an uncle?"

Mom ignores my question and continues with her trip down memory lane. "Unfortunately for him, it wasn't that easy. You can't just hand it over like that. It's been written into the fabric of the company the specific ways in which it passes to the next successor. And the board requires an heir at all times."

"How very archaic," I murmur.

"Yes, well, your uncle had no children. So your father was listed as an heir. They'd swapped roles. And you were listed as a secondary heir. But they assured us it would never come to that. Your uncle said he'd adopt if he had to."

"So, what happened?" I prompted when she paused for longer than normal. I was on the edge of my seat listening to her recollection of events that possibly led to my father's disappearance. And ultimately, death.

"Your father died. Your uncle died. I fled. And then my parents died. So I changed our names and paid someone an exorbitant amount of money to erase you from every database known. I still had a few friends left in the Gallagher family tree, and since they're all so technologically inclined, one of them helped us."

My head spins with this information she's just casually dropping like it doesn't change everything I'd ever thought about my life. I was still grappling with the idea that I'm a Gallagher and my father's actually dead. And now I find out that I'm the heir to some company I've never heard of? Oh, and more people want to kidnap me—kill me?

"Okay." I lick my lips and try to work through some of this information dump she just tossed on my lap. "Did you tell Cormac about this?"

She shakes her head before I'm even done speaking. "No. I love him, but I don't trust him." She looks me in the eye. "Don't trust anyone, Alaina. Anyone."

"Even you?"

"Yes, even me."

I lick my lips and try to figure out how to process that. "So if no one is left in the heir list or whatever, then who's running the company?"

She turns to look at me. "I really don't know. When I erased you—"

I flinch at her words, I can't help it. That's exactly how it's felt all these years, and to hear her so casually mention it pierces something inside of me I thought I got over a long time ago.

Mom clears her throat and looks out the window again. "When I erased you, I essentially cut all ties with that part of my life. With that part of my family. Whoever it is, they need you alive. That much I know."

"How do you know that though?"

"There's a year-long trial period. It starts the moment you're eighteen. If something happens to you during that year, then the company's assets freeze until the board dissolves it. It's how they stopped murder of the heirs. Or so Aidan told me. Most of this is from what he told me."

The car slows down on a residential street. I double-check my GPS, and we're not on West High.

Before I can question it, Mom turns to face me. She tucks a strand of hair behind my ear and stares at me with so much love in her gaze, my breath freezes.

"He loved you so much, you know. And so do I. I'd break both our hearts and send you away again if I thought it would save your life. I spent so much time filling the hole you left in my life with ice that I'd forgotten how to be your mother. And for that, I'm sorry."

Tears prick my eyes, and my sinuses burn. "Mom . . ."

"Shh, it's alright. I just wanted you to know, okay? Now I have to go in here for something, but I'll meet you on West High. Okay?"

Panic grips me, swift and hard. I grab Mom's wrist and hold her in the car. Why does it sound like she's saying goodbye?

"No. We go together, remember? Some guy wanted to see you—that Liam guy said so."

"I know. I need to get something from an old friend first. I'll meet you there, I swear it."

Mom leans forward and kisses me on my forehead before turning away and getting out of the car. I watch her climb the stairs to a multi-level home and ring the doorbell. The door opens, but whoever answered stays hidden in the shadows. My mother walks inside the house, and my gut churns.

Was that the last time I'll ever see her?

31

WOLF

DÉJÀ VU HITS me like a set of bricks, and I grunt. I pinch the bridge of my nose, trying to alleviate the free fall sensation spiraling in my veins.

"What is it?"

I spare my brother a single glance. That's all I can afford to do when I'm driving this fast down backroads. One mistake, and it's lights out.

His fingers fly across the keyboard of his laptop. We give him shit about it, but the truth is, we'd be lost if he didn't have that brick of a laptop. He made it so it's virtually indestructible—impervious to hacking, malware, viruses—and can get into just about anything. If you ask him, he'll tell you it's *not his best work* because it can't crack the high government servers. His other computers can, though. But those aren't as car friendly as his laptop.

Neither of us were willing to wait at home while Rush looked for our brother—and for who snatched Maddie.

"Nothing. Just a little déjà vu is all." I shake my head a little as the vertigo starts to fade.

"What do you mean?"

"It's just that on Red's birthday, I was in this car, driving with Sully on the way to O'Malley's to fucking win her back, ya know? And then a couple hours after that, she was gone."

I keep my eyes on the road, but I see Rush turn to look at me from the corner of my eye. "She's not gone though. She's at that diner a few blocks from O'Malley's. We'll be there in thirty minutes."

"I know," I say as I shift in my seat and adjust my grip on the steering wheel. "But what if she's not?"

Rush looks out the front windshield with me. No doubt, he's looking without really seeing, just like me.

"She will be, brother. She's learned a lot since that night."

"But not enough," I murmur. "We should've taught her more."

"Aye. Maybe we should have." Rush's voice is quiet, and I'm sure he's recalling everything we taught her over the last few weeks.

Neither one of us say anymore as we drive

"Did you track Sully yet?"

"Mm. He went to O'Malley's a little before one, which times up with what Alaina said. He left after fifteen minutes, but I was able to track his phone and corroborate it with local traffic and security cams. Looks like he went into some coffee shop, and then ten minutes later, he walks out with two coffees."

"My money's on one of those being for Red. No way he went to meet up with some random bird in the city *while* he was technically with her for the day," I interject.

"Aye. That's what I think too. Then, this is where it gets fucked up. He's walking back to the diner, I think, but about a block away, in a dark zone by a driveway, he just . . . disappears."

My brows furrow. "How can he disappear?"

"I don't know, brother. His phone stops tracking, and he

never reappears on any of the surrounding cameras. It's possible he got hurt somehow or jumped and he's still sitting in that driveway. I'm looking around the city architect plans for the surrounding buildings."

I whistle under my breath. "You can find that shit?"

He shrugs. "Everyone leaves some kind of trail. Plus, I knew the city needed to have the plans on record for permits and shit. I'm hoping we can figure out who's driveway that is."

"Aye. And Alaina? She still at the diner?" I tap my finger on the steering wheel along with the beat to Jimmy Eat World's "Sweetness."

"Fuck," Rush swears under his breath before he starts typing at double speed.

"What? What's going on?" I feel more jittery than normal, and that foreboding sense of déjà vu comes back.

"Call her. She's not at the diner." Rush's voice is low, the noise of keys clicking filling the car.

"Where the fuck is she?"

"Just call her!" The panic is palpable, and I spare another glance at my brother. His jaw is clenched and his body is so tense, I fear one move and he'll snap.

I hit her number on my favorites list and listen as ringing fills the car. My heart beats so hard, I feel like I just ran a goddamn marathon. "Pick up, pick up," I chant, begging her to answer.

"Wolf?"

"Oh thank fuck, baby. Where are you? I thought I told you to stay at the goddamn diner!" Rush yells before I can even get a word in.

"Are you okay, Red? Talk to me." I don't yell at her, even if my fear makes it hard not to.

"I . . . I don't know anything anymore."

"Where are you?" Rush all but begs. His leg bounces, jostling the computer on his lap.

"I'm in an Uber. I shared my location with you so you knew I had to leave. Something strange happened. Mom's here—or she was here. The red-eyed demon guy—Liam's his name—was here, and I think he's the one who took Maddie. Oh, and Rush, you need to look into Gallagher Industries, okay? Mom said something about me being the heir or something. And Mary sent nudes to some random guy, but then Benny helped her. So now I'm supposed to go out on a date with him. I told him that my alpha male asshole boyfriends wouldn't like that, so you'll probably have to deal with that."

"Whoa, whoa. Slow down, you're not making sense. What are you talking about, little bird?"

She exhales into the phone. The sound is noisy and strangely comforting.

"I'm in the back of an Uber on the way to where Maddie is. Liam, the guy who took me from O'Malley's, showed up outside the diner when I was waiting for you. He implied he had Maddie and told me to come to this address alone and he'd let her go."

Both of our phones vibrate at the same time. Rush holds his up and says, "This is your destination? West High Street?"

"Yes. I know I can do this, Rush. I know it. I can get Maddie —save her. Then I'll really be able to be one of you guys, ya know?"

"Baby girl, you're already one of us. Please just wait," I beg her. "I don't know where you got the idea that you're not already one of us, because you are."

"You're perfect just as you are, birdie. And I'm asking you, as your man, to wait for us. We're flying blind—and that always spells trouble." Rush's eyes are wild as he alternates staring at her name on the touch screen and the laptop in front of him.

Alaina sighs. "I'll try, okay? But if I see an opening to get her out, I'm going to take it. I trust you guys to have my back. I'm asking you to trust me to do this."

"Listen, listen to me, Alaina." I hear her intake of breath, and I know I have her attention. I made a calculated move to use her real name since I rarely do. "I love you, baby girl, but you're not ready for this yet. Not solo."

I hear another intake of breath, this one deeper than before. "You love me?"

"That's all you got from that? Of course he loves you, we all do," Rush snaps, his patience nonexistent.

I've never seen my brother completely lose control before. He's come close many times, but I don't think he's ever reached the bottom of his well of control. I have a hunch we're going to see the monster at the bottom of that well soon. And I'm afraid that I won't be able to tame him—I'll be there egging him on.

"Y-you all love me?" The disbelief in her voice is painful. "But it—it's only been a few weeks. I don't—I don't understand."

This girl hasn't had nearly enough love in her life, and though that breaks what little part of my heart is left, a sadistic part of me relishes in the fact that we get to be the ones to show her what love really means.

"I can't believe I'm going to say something as cliche as this, but it's true, and I don't have enough time to find something more fitting, so listen to me, Alaina. When you know, you know. And believe me, we all know," Rush says, staring at her name on my screen as if he can actually see her.

"I—uh—I think I might love you too. All of you. I just—"

"Alright, here we are," a masculine voice says in the background. It must be the Uber driver. Fuck—she's already there.

"Oh, okay. Thank you." Her words are muffled, and I imagine her covering the speaker of the phone for a moment.

"What's our ETA, Rush?"

"Thirty minutes," he murmurs, typing on his laptop in a flurry of movement.

"Come for me, Wolf."

"Always, Red. We'll always come for you," I promise, and she ends the call without saying anything else.

"Fuck. Just got confirmation from Matteo that Sully never showed today. And six more places were torched. Some his— some others. Almost all of them belonged to people at our meeting the other day." He pauses. "Goddamnit," Rush roars.

"Do we have another fucking rat?" The words come out on a growl, and fear grips my heart, squeezing what's left in its tight fist.

Rush drags both hands through his hair, pushing it back. "I don't know. I just don't fucking know." He turns to face me. "We can't get to them both. West High is forty minutes away from the diner and where we last saw Sully. We might be able to take a few shortcuts, but it's not enough time to look for him and get to her."

I nod, knowing that it might come to this. "So we have to choose."

"Aye. But is it much of a choice? We both know what Sully would say."

Without a word, I nod, press down on the accelerator, and focus all of my energy on getting to my girl.

32

ALAINA

"I—UH—I think I might love you too. All of you. I just—"

"Alright, here we are," the Uber driver says, interrupting my awkward declaration.

I guess we're here already. Nerves line my belly at the thought of what I'll find inside the rundown building.

"Oh, okay. Thank you," I cover the speaker to tell him.

I hear Wolf ask Rush their eta, and I think he replies twenty minutes, but I'm distracted by the Uber driver riddling off news headlines to me.

I uncover the speaker. "Come for me, Wolf."

His answer is swift, without pause. "Always. We'll always come for you," he promises.

I end the call after that. What more is there to say right now? Melancholy drapes around me as I stare at the dilapidated building.

"You sure this is the place? I heard on the radio this morning that this block of buildings is scheduled for demo."

"Demo?" I look around outside. I'm not sure what I was expecting to see, but whatever it is, I don't find it.

"Y'know, like demolition? The city's going to start fresh from the ground up, apparently. Though if you ask me, I bet they're going to put some fancy condos here and sell 'em for a pretty penny. Heard they're going to start putting in green space all over the boroughs too. What—like Central Park isn't enough green space?"

I make a noncommittal noise, mostly just to buy myself another moment or two before I get out of this car. Because I have a feeling that once I do, the hands of fate will take over. And I'm not sure that I'm ready to give up the reins to my life.

I bite my cheek as I stare at the building, imagining Maddie tied up somewhere inside, scared and alone.

I shake my head to rid it of that image, and to remind myself that this is the right thing to do.

"You okay, kid?"

I turn to look at him. He's a nice enough Uber driver—mellow music, didn't take corners at 100 mph like the taxi drivers in the city, and clean car—but I'm not feeling particularly trusting lately. Another reason I have the Share My Location option always turned on.

"Yeah. Thanks for the ride." I pull the door handle and push the door open. Smog greets me, the blanket of filth fitting for how I feel right now.

The whole situation makes my skin crawl, and I'm not sure if it's because I let my mom get into my head or if it's because I'm staring at a building that looks straight out of a bad horror film.

I walk a few steps before I pull my phone out. I send my mom a text letting her know I'm here—and I make sure my location link is still active.

I bounce on the balls of my feet and look around. The street is quiet, which isn't surprising. Most of these buildings don't look like they're inhabited.

"C'mon, Mom."

I check the time on my phone again. She said she'd be here by now. She knew what time Liam said, and she promised she'd be here.

"Shit." I realize with depressing clarity that I've been waiting my whole life for my mother to show up for me—and the one time someone's life depends on it, she can't do it. She can't even fucking do it.

My phone vibrates in my hand, and I see an unknown number. I hit accept and bring it to my ear.

"Come inside, top floor," an unfamiliar voice says before the line goes dead.

I pocket my phone and look around me, expecting to see someone behind me. Satisfied that no one will sneak up on me, I walk to the entrance. The door creaks when I pull it open, and after I step inside, it closes behind me with a bang.

The loud sound reverberates in the mostly empty building. It looks like once upon a time it was once some sort of warehouse. I walk around garbage and old cardboard packaging littering the floor to the staircase on the left side of the building.

I walk up the stairs slowly, constantly turning my head to see as much of my surroundings as possible. Ava taught me that little bit of knowledge.

I strain my ears for any noise, but all I hear is the distant cooing of mourning doves. I look up and notice a few holes in the ceiling.

They don't make these style buildings like this anymore. I bet the raw wood and metal materials in here are original, and I bet they'd sell for a ton of money.

The random theories about this building distract me from what I'm about to do, if only momentarily. My gut churns and nausea climbs up my throat as the full weight of what I'm doing hits me.

I'm walking inside an abandoned building, intending to rescue my cousin, by myself and without any weapons.

What the fuck was I thinking?

I take a deep breath and remind myself that Rush and Wolf are on the way. They have the address, and they'll be here. I know they will. They'd never let me down.

Maddie's life is on the line. And when it's put into that perspective, I'm not sure that there's anything I wouldn't do.

I exhale quickly through my mouth and school my face into a carefully blank expression.

I reach the landing on the top floor and quietly walk around, peering in each room. Most of the walls are partially broken, so I can see inside pretty easily.

In the furthest room from the stairway, I find Maddie. She's hunched over and zip-tied to a chair, dried blood coating her forehead.

"Oh my god, Maddie!" I cry and run toward her.

Before I reach her, an arm comes out strong and swift and blocks my path. I look up into the red eyes of Liam.

He looks me over, an evil smile lighting his features. "Alaina. You're here. Where's your mother?"

I lick my lips. "I—uh—"

"I'm right here," Mom says as she walks inside the room from the corner. I didn't even see stairs over there, so I'm not sure how she got in here. Maybe she climbed through one of those half-done walls.

Liam spins around and claps. "Perfect. Let's get started. Now, since you so rudely double-crossed us, Boss isn't going to be here today." Liam curls his lip and snarls at us. "It makes me look incompetent, and I don't appreciate being made to look a fool, Lana."

"Apologies, Liam. I was only trying to protect my daughter.

Surely you can understand that," Mom says, taking another step forward with her arms in the air, palms out.

Liam cocks his head to the side as he assesses Mom. "By sacrificing your niece? Even to me, that seems cold."

I slowly step toward Maddie's side, and with one eye on the storm brewing between my mom and Liam, I pat her cheeks. "Wake up, Maddie."

"That wasn't the plan," Mom grits out between clenched teeth.

"Wait." He holds up his palm, a crazed, wide smile spreading across his face. "Did you—did you think my guys would take *you* instead?" He scans my mom from head to toe and then tips his head back and laughs—a real laugh—and I decide that it's the scariest thing I've ever seen and heard.

Violence crackles in the air, and I shiver as it races down my spine. I keep expecting to see other people or hear footsteps or something. This seems strange that it's only him and Maddie in this big place. Something feels off to me, but I'm not sure if it's because I've never been in this situation before.

Liam mimes wiping a tear from his bloodred eye. "Oh, Lana. That's a good one, truly. In fact, telling the Boss that joke when I bring in your severed heads for comparison might even get me back in his good graces." He sighs with a wistful smile on his face. "He does love a good joke."

My heart races and a cold sweat breaks out across my body. I drop into a squat behind Maddie and rummage through my small purse, looking for something to use to cut the zip tie.

"Let the girls go, and I'll go with you to see the Gallaghers." Mom steps to the side and away from us.

"Oh, sweet Lana. The Gallaghers aren't after Alaina." He spins on his heel to face me. "Well—I shouldn't say that—"

Whatever he was about to say is cut off by a low rumble. At

first, I think it's motorcycles or cars without exhaust pipes, but then I hear it again. And this time I feel the ground shake a little. The cardboard pile in the corner shifts, the noise drawing my attention.

"What the hell is that?" Panic spikes my adrenaline even further, and my skin feels too tight over my body. I squash the urge to flee.

Not until I have Maddie.

No one answers me, and I double my efforts to search my purse while still keeping an eye on the standoff. My fingers touch something cool and metal, and I pull out a pair of nail clippers.

"You got a choice to make, Liam. Me or the girls? Your life or your death?" Mom delivers the ultimatum with cool indifference, but I catch the way her hands tremble as she clenches them at her sides.

"Death, Lana? Really?" Liam reaches behind his back and pulls out a gun. "You're in no position to negotiate."

I open the clippers and wedge them between the ties and Maddie's skin. And I squeeze the handles like the grim reaper himself is standing over my shoulder. Another glance at Liam in his all-black outfit and red eyes, and I'm not so sure he isn't.

Maddie groans and moves her head to the side.

"Shh, try not to move too much, okay?" I hiss, flashing a glance at Liam and my mom.

"Lainey? Is that you?" Her voice is thick, and her head hangs low.

"It's me. I'm trying to get you free, so just hang tight."

"Am I dreaming or is that Auntie Lana?" Maddie asks as she lifts her head.

I shift my gaze to my mom again, she's staring down Liam's gun when another rumble cracks through the air. This one louder and closer than the previous two. The floor shakes, and I hear things crashing on the floors below us.

"Mom, we have to get out of here," I hiss, squeezing frantically. I'm only halfway through the plastic, and sweat rolls down my temple.

"See, Liam, fortune dealt me a bit of luck today when you picked this building. It's on a block scheduled to be demolished later today, which means there is C4 stashed all over the place." Mom's smile is too wide, too triumphant for a woman facing the barrel of a gun.

Liam looks around before he takes three steps toward Mom, jamming the gun at the center of her forehead. Her head jerks back with the force, but the smile doesn't leave her face.

"I only gave a couple a little nudge," Mom says with a casual shrug.

"Mom." That one word is packed with so much desperation that it instantly takes me back to when I was younger—when I still had both parents around and they were superheroes in my eyes.

"Mom. What did you do?" I whisper-yell, fear leaking from my pores and swirling around, choking me.

"You remember what I told you in the car, Alaina," Mom says as she turns to look at me. "You remember what I said."

Liam's staring at her, brows raised and head cocked. And I'm so preoccupied with what she's saying that I almost miss the movement. I squeeze the clippers one more time, and the zip tie slides off Maddie's hand in the same instant that Mom untucks a gun from the back of her jean shorts.

In one movement, she brings the gun up and steps back, aiming it at Liam's chest with two hands.

For a second, it feels like the world pauses. Tingles race up my body and my breaths come in fast.

Then another rumbling noise cracks the air, and the building moves. Windows break somewhere downstairs, things crash to the ground, and still, Mom and Liam don't move.

"Lainey, get your cousin out of here."

"I don't think so—" Liam starts, but Mom levels her gun at his head and he stops talking.

"Mom, come with us," I beg.

The rumbling continues, and I have to shift my hold on Maddie when the wall connecting this room to another one cracks and starts to fall.

"Now, Lainey!" Mom yells. And for the first time, maybe the only time, I hear the desperation in her voice.

I haul Maddie up and start half dragging her out the door. Her eyes are wide and her pupils are blown, etched in fear. We make it down the first set of staircases when part of the ceiling falls, both of us screaming.

"Let's go, Lainey!" Maddie yells, and we maneuver around some broken stairs.

I look behind me, hoping to see Mom, but all that greets me is more things crashing.

Maddie laces her fingers with mine, and we run down to the next flight of stairs, skidding to a stop at the destruction around us below. Concrete, wood beams, and metal piping is everywhere. I scan the area, mentally trying to map out our escape route before I tug on Maddie's hand.

"Follow me and stay close."

I don't wait for her to respond before I jog down the stairs, climb over debris, and get within sight of the door. I stop, and Maddie slams into my back.

"What's wrong? Let's go!" Maddie yells.

I look around at the destruction, then flick my gaze to the staircase that leads to the third floor, and then back to Maddie.

"No. No, no, no, Lainey. You cannot go back," Maddie yells, fear twisting her face.

"I have to at least try. She's my mom." My voice breaks at the end, and I have to clear my throat before I can speak. "I have to at least try. I can be quick, and the walls stopped shaking

310

already." Maddie's shaking her head fiercely, tears falling from her eyes. "I'll be right back. Go outside and wait for Wolf. He'll be here soon."

I push her toward the exit, and with one last look at me, she runs toward the door.

I don't stay to watch her leave. I turn around and run like I've never run before, dodging garbage and jumping over fallen beams.

It's a foolish plan, I know it is. But the thought of my mother upstairs and hurt while I sit outside safe and sound eats me up inside.

I'd never forgive myself if I didn't at least try.

33

RUSH

"TWO MINUTES OUT," I tell my brother without taking my eyes off of her dot on my screen.

"She still there?"

"Aye. She hasn't moved."

"That's good, right? That she's still there." Wolf runs a hand through his hair. His face is like stone, jaw clenched, eyes narrowed. He fiddles with the buttons on the steering wheel, and the album starts over again. It's the Hans Zimmer soundtrack to Interstellar. He always plays it when he needs to center himself. "Cornfield Chase" sounds through the speakers.

"Tell me we did the right thing. That we made the right choice. Tell me we didn't just condemn our brother," Wolf says without looking at me.

I rub my hand across my chin and sigh. The weight of the burden of guilt sits heavy on both of us.

"It was the best choice, given the circumstances. Sully would never forgive us if we didn't go to her."

"Aye. He never would, even if that asshole pretends otherwise." Wolf stretches his neck from side to side and releases a breath.

Still, guilt rides me hard, and fear scrambles my senses. I don't need to see my brother's face to know he's feeling the same way.

My temples pound in time with my heartbeat. Dread coils around my black heart, squeezing barbed-wire tips into the barely beating organ.

Something's wrong.

I check my phone again—her dot hasn't moved. I try Sully's phone again—still nothing.

"Anything from Matteo?" Wolf asks.

I check my phone again, even though I know there's nothing new. "No. He's got some of his boys looking for Sully—the ones he can spare."

Wolf nods—this staccato movement that belies his trepidation.

A bead of sweat rolls down my neck, and I roll down the windows.

"Air's on."

"Aye, but I need some air."

The air that flows inside the car is thick with pollution and heavy with humidity. Unsurprising given we're in the industrial district. I think there are a few factories still working somewhere around here, though you wouldn't know it by this neighborhood. It's a ghost town.

There are cracked sidewalks, overgrown weeds, crater-sized potholes, and litter on every block. And with each broken window and each graffiti-tagged building we pass, my heart beats harder, faster.

Wolf cuts me a look, and I know he's trying to decide if he should ask me again about Alaina's location. I open my mouth to tell him anyway, just to alleviate a little anxiety when sirens pierce the air. Wolf looks in the rearview, and I turn around to look out the windows behind me.

Red-and-blue lights flash in the distance as the sirens get louder.

They're getting closer.

Wolf and I share a look, and without any prompting, he steps on the accelerator, pushing me back into the seat with the force.

Wolf drums his fingers on the steering wheel, obsessively glancing in the rearview mirror every other second. "I think I can outrun them."

I tap my fingers against my leg, weighing the options.

"If you can't, and we end up arrested, you know what we'll have to do, right? We can't leave Alaina like that."

"We won't. Trust me," Wolf says as he glances at me.

"Aye. Get us to our girl, brother."

Sixty seconds later, Wolf slams on the breaks, and the car skids to a stop. I don't wait for Wolf to throw it into park. I toss my computer to the floor and rip open the door, my heart in my throat.

768 West High is shaking.

The three-story building looks like a war zone with its blown-out windows, missing exterior walls, and concrete dust hanging in the air like fog.

A boom cuts the air, and another piece of the exterior explodes, sending shards of concrete and metal into the air.

Are we too late?

"Red!" Wolf yells as he rounds his car. The word sounds like it's ripped from his soul, battered and bleeding.

The sound is enough to kick-start my heart, and I sprint toward what's left of the building, my brother by my side.

Everything else fades away until only one thing remains —Alaina.

Out of the corner of my eye, I see her cousin, Maddie. I

spare her a single glance, but I don't stop. She's kneeling in the middle of the street, bleeding from the head, and sobbing.

"She went back in! She went back in there, and I-I couldn't stop her!"

We're five feet away from the door when something shifts. Energy fills the air, pulsating outward a second before half the building collapses. Broken pipes, pieces of twisted metal, wooden beams, and chunks of concrete go flying—some inside the building, some into the street.

Wolf grabs me by the arm and wrenches me to the side two seconds before a metal beam pierces the concrete where I was standing.

A boom wrenches the air, the noise loud enough to pop an eardrum, and I know what's coming next. A second later, we see it. Part of the collapsed building goes up in flames.

My black heart clenches, reminding me she's the reason it even beats.

I look at my brother, and I know my pain mirrors his own. His brows scrunch and lips purse, but it's his eyes that give him away. Despair shines back at me through his brown eyes.

Devastation threatens to drown me, but I wrestle it into submission. I've never given up a day in my life, and I sure as hell won't stop now.

"Brother."

With that one word, he knows what I'm asking.

"We always come for our girl," Wolf says through a clenched jaw.

I nod and wrench open the door. It falls off the hinges and crashes to the ground. I don't give it a second thought as I sprint through the wreckage inside. Piles of garbage, broken concrete, wooden boards, and a few small fires litter the floor like a fucked-up obstacle course.

The whole back right of the building is covered in flames,

and I hear another siren pierce the air, but we don't have time to wait for them to find Alaina. I'm on borrowed time.

I scan the area for my favorite redhead as I figure out how to get to the upper floors.

I won't stop until I find her.

She's ours, and no one will take her from us. Not even death himself.

TO BE CONTINUED . . .

A Note To Readers

THANK you so much for reading Rush! I hope you're not too angry with me for leaving you on that cliff like that, but rest assured the next book, Sully, is already out! You can grab it on Kindle Unlimited today! Keep reading for an excerpt!

I can't thank you enough for taking a chance on Alaina, Sully, Wolf, and Rush—and me! And I can't wait for you to read what happens next!

Read Sully, book three in the Brotherhood series here: book s2read.com/brotherhood3

I would be honored if you had the time to leave a brief review of this book! Reviews are the lifeblood of a book, and I would appreciate it so much.

xoxo

—pen

. . .

STAY IN THE LOOP!
Join my newsletter
Join my Facebook group, Penelope's Black Hearts
Follow me on Instagram @authorpenelopeblack

Continue reading for an excerpt from
Sully:
The Brotherhood book 3
Available now on Kindle Unlimited

CHAPTER ONE—SULLY

"KISS ME, James, and tell me you love me."

The sun shines down on us as we stroll through Central Park. The trees form a sort of tunnel overhead, providing shade from the unforgiving summer sun.

I stop walking and tug on our interlaced fingers to bring her closer. The teasing smirk on her face taunts me, and like the enchantress she is, she lures me in with a quirk of her lips.

I can't deny her—I don't *want* to.

I unlace our fingers and curve an arm around her lower back. A nearby bird whistles a light melody, and a soft breeze carries the sweet scent of nearby peonies. I slide my other hand along the curve of her neck and into her hair at her nape.

She winds her arms around me and tugs me closer. She's addictive, my princess, and the shriveled-up organ that should be a heart throbs at her affection.

It's only ever beat for her. And after her betrayal and absence, it's all but ceased to exist.

"You know I love you, princess," I say against her perfect, plump lips. Her bottom lip is just the slightest bit bigger than her top lip, and I can't resist pulling it into my mouth with my teeth.

Alaina pulls away to press her promise against my lips. "And I love you. Always."

Adrenaline flies through my veins at those simple words delivered with ease from those perfect lips. I used to think love was for fools, and then she crashed into my life, and everything I thought was bullshit was true.

Unfortunately, she left just as spectacularly, and I came full circle. I was the fool then.

Urgency pounds at my temple, demanding I make it so she can never leave me again. I won't survive a second time.

"This could be our life, you know. Walking through Central Park, holding hands, and bringing home our favorite pizza."

"And don't forget sneaking off behind that patch of bushes over there, bro."

I press my hand into Alaina's lower back on instinct. Once I realize it's just my brother, I relax. She twists her head around, and Wolf strolls toward her. When he's close enough, he snags an arm out and curls it around her neck, bringing her face to his for a kiss that's just a little too lewd for midday in the park.

"Where the hell did you come from, Wolf?"

He separates from our girl to lift an eyebrow at me and smirk. "I've always been here."

"Me too," Rush says from behind me.

My chest feels tight, and my gaze flies around us in alarm, kick-starting my adrenaline. *Why didn't I know they were with us?* I could've sworn it was just Lainey and me.

"Fuck, I need some sleep or something. I'm losin' it." I run a hand down my face as Rush leans in to greet Alaina with a kiss.

She turns to look at me, familiar mischief twinkling in her eyes.

"Wouldn't that be nice? All of us together, all the time."

I stare at my girl, the way her Ramones tank top flutters in the hot breeze. When I stare into her soulful eyes, I forget all the awful shit in my life. All the bad shit that still waits for me. I know deep in my gut that she's the only good thing in my life.

"Aye. I think that'd be nice, Lainey." I brush my lips along her jaw with each word.

Her fingers curl into my shirt, and she releases this little noise of contentment.

"Then why do you torture me, James? Why do you always leave me?"

I pull my head back, brows furrowed. Her smile fades with the sunshine. Midday rapidly turns to dusk, and sorrow replaces her playfulness.

"C'mon, Sully."

I whip my head around to look at my brothers. My chest squeezes again, and my thoughts stutter. "When did you get over there?" I ask Rush.

My brother just stares at me, his gray eyes darkening until they're pitch-black. When he doesn't answer me, I refocus on Alaina.

"Princess? What do you mean?"

Her beautiful whiskey-colored eyes fill with tears as she takes a step away from me, her fingers trailing down my arm.

"Come back to me, James." She takes another step back, and her fingertips just barely touch my own.

I take a step toward her, confusion furrowing my brow. I reach out for her, but there's an invisible force holding me back.

"Alaina! Wait. Come back. I'm right here."

I push against the invisible wall, panic tightening every muscle in my body and fear wrapping around my heart. She's walking away from me—no, that's not right. It looks like someone is dragging her! There, someone in a dark hoodie and dark jeans has her upper arms in a tight grip, and he's pulling her away. His features are unclear, almost like he's somehow being blurred.

Alaina's eyes widen with fear, and she screams my name. Rage erupts in my gut, burning hot and fast.

"Get your fucking hands off her, motherfucker, or it'll be the last thing you ever do!" I pound my fists against the wall, putting every ounce of strength I have behind each swing.

And still. It's not enough.

I watch as someone drags the only girl I ever loved—fuck it, the girl I *still* love—away while some fucked-up invisible barrier traps me in some kind of purgatory hell.

"Alaina! I'm coming for you!" The words are ripped from my throat, born out of desperation and sealed with determination. I'm not sure how the fuck I'm going to get out of here, but I will.

Something jerks my shoulder, hard and to the right. I spin around, expecting to see the blurred-out guy, but there's no one there. The same thing happens on my other side, and I whirl to the left. No one.

I lift my hands to drag them through my hair, but something's holding them against my side, squeezing me tight. I try to thrash my way out of this hold, but it's strong. My breath stutters in my chest as the pressure increases until my vision dims.

And then I don't feel or see anything. I'm trapped in an endless black, alone.

I'm always alone.

Abandoned by those who claim to love me.

I succumb to the darkness, letting it roll over me.

CONTINUE READING SULLY, the final book in The Brotherhood series here: books2read.com/brotherhood3

A NOTE TO READERS

Thank you so, so much for picking up Rush!

And I hope you're not too angry with me for that ending. I know I left you dangling on that cliff, but rest assured that the final book, Sully, is available now!

I can't thank you enough to taking a chance on Alaina, Wolf, Rush, and Sully—and me!

And I cannot wait for you to read what happens next!

Read Sully, book two in The Brotherhood series, here! Book s2read.com/brotherhood3

Enjoy Rush? Make sure you stay in the loop!

Join my newsletter.

Join my Facebook group, Penelope's Black Hearts.

Follow me on Instagram @authorpenelopeblack

***

I would be honored if you had the time to leave a brief review of this book. Reviews are the lifeblood of a book, and I would so appreciative.

Thank you all so much.

XOXO,

—pen

WHEN IT ENDS EXCERPT

Continue reading for an excerpt from
When It Ends:
A Dark Apocalyptic Romance
Available now on Kindle Unlimited

What if the end is just their beginning?

They stole my heart at fourteen and broke it before we even graduated high school.

It's been five years since I've seen them, and only a twist of fate reunites us when the mountain falls. It's the first disaster in a predicted apocalypse—a string of natural disasters that could be catastrophic.

It's the beginning of the end of everything.

Finis omnibus.

Old feelings reignite and new feelings blossom as the four of us form an unbreakable bond. As the world starts to fall and society fractures, it's a race against time for survival.

WHEN IT ENDS EXCERPT

Available now on Kindle Unlimited
bit.ly/WhenItEnds

CHAPTER ONE

AMELIA

"You come here often?"

I pause the maze I was creating with the condensation on my vintage tumbler. The drinkware is one of the only memorable things about this aging bar-casino on the outskirts of Las Vegas. The overused and uninspired pickup line is the cherry on top of my shitty-day sundae. I've had just enough alcohol and too little sleep in the last two days to reel in my annoyance.

"Do you have a small dick?" I ask over my shoulder without turning around to see the face that goes with such a terrible line.

It's not the first time I've thrown such a crude question at someone. And nine times out of ten, it gets the message across succinctly.

I'm not interested. Move along.

Much to my surprise, laughter greets my question instead of curses or insults. It's a carefree sort of sound, like he just heard a surprising joke. It's enough to pique my interest, and I swivel the barstool to the right and look over my shoulder.

He's tall enough that I have to tip my head back to take him in. Wavy dark blond hair, long enough to pull back. The blinking lights from the bank of slot machines behind us highlights his in flashes, but it's too dim in here to make out the exact color of his eyes. But they're dark, alluring even.

His laughter tapers off, leaving only dimples to wink at me as if to hint at his mischief. He mock-wipes a tear from underneath his eye as he slides his hands into his pockets, leaving his thumbs hooked over the top of his dark-wash jeans.

A charcoal gray tee stretches across his chest, the once-white logo faded. I idly wonder if he bought it purposely distressed or if it's worn from use. I'm not discreet about my perusal, but this mystery man only tips his head to the side. Patiently waiting until I've had my fill.

Heat warms my cheeks, but it's not from being caught. I like that he's giving me space to ogle him, it's oddly endearing. I pause when our gazes connect.

The low lights from the bar don't do either of us any favors, I'm sure. And the blinking lights from the machines to his right give his beard—a day or two past a five o'clock shadow—a tie-dye effect. On any other man, I'm sure it would take down his desirability factor, but he gets another point in his favor because it only heightens everything about him.

He nods and shoots me a secret sort of smile. I almost kick myself when my own lips curl up in response. He takes it as an invitation and slides onto the stool next to me.

My brows hit my hairline at his presumption, but I manage to check myself when I realize that it's one of the only available seats at this little bar. And I did just check him out for two solid minutes.

My new seatmate signals to the bartender with a finger and a friendly smile. I sip my drink, letting the harsh burn of rum and Coke—heavy on the rum—coat my throat as I watch him interact with one of the two men behind the bar of Tennessee Pete's.

You can tell a lot about a person by the way they interact with people in the service industry. I've seen firsthand the way people treat waitstaff and baristas and bartenders. It doesn't matter how attractive this guy is, I'm not going to sleep with him if he's rude.

Wait.

Where did that thought come from? I wasn't—I'm not going home with anyone tonight. I'm just here for a few drinks, maybe a burger and fries, and then I'm crashing for a few hours before I finish driving. I'm on the last leg of my cross-country trek home. Sleeping with some random man I meet in an old casino slash motel isn't on my to-do list for the day.

I suck my bottom lip as the man next to me orders a whiskey sour with a smile and some small talk, gesturing with his hands. He does have nice hands though, big palms with long fingers.

Sipping my drink, I tilt my head and study him. He reminds me of someone, but I can't quite put my finger on who. A celebrity, maybe.

He flashes those dimples at the bartender, and little tendrils of lust sit up and take notice.

I suppose having a little fun never hurt anyone.

He half turns his body toward me. "So, do you come here often?"

"Are we back to that so soon?" I counter quickly with an arched brow. "Should I repeat my question now too?"

He smiles at me and drags his teeth into his bottom lip. "Is that an invitation?"

My nose wrinkles as I stare at him for a moment, mentally chastising myself. Sure, he's good-looking. Okay, so maybe more than good-looking. He's downright hot. That kind of attractive that would make you throw your morals out the window.

Kind of like what I just mentally decided a moment ago.

I am going to be so disappointed if he turns out to be an asshole.

I sip my drink and eye him over the rim of my glass. "Does that line ever work for you—the come here often one."

The bartender, an older man with salt-and-pepper hair, smiles and slides his drink across the lacquered oak bar. The stranger next to me snatches it in a smooth movement, the veins in his forearms popping as he grips the glass. He accepts the drink with a murmured thanks. "I don't really hit on women often."

"Wow. I don't even know how to take that."

"Nah, it's not like that, Blondie. More like I don't really hang out in casinos or bars."

I roll my eyes at the nickname. Having naturally dark blonde hair seems like it would be great, right? Except it's this in between color—lighter and brighter in the summer and darker and moodier in the winter. Or if we're living in a city that actually has seasons like we have for the past couple years. "Blondie, huh? Because I haven't heard that one before."

He dips his chin. "Alright, what's your name then?"

I smirk with just a touch of incredulousness, but it gives me an idea. I've been in a deep '90s movie binge lately. "Cher."

"Damn. What are the odds, Cher? I'm Sonny." He holds out his hand, but since there's not much space between us, his fingertips skim the fabric of my olive green tank top.

I can't help it. He's too charming for his own good. Or maybe mine. "What are the odds," I murmur as I slide my hand into his. His grip is firm but not overpowering, and he pumps our hands for a few seconds too long, his dark eyes twinkling as they hold my gaze.

* * *

"Wait, wait. You're telling me the most embarrassing thing

you've ever done is run around in the snow?" I arch a brow at him, my mouth pinched to the side in disbelief.

"Well, I was thirteen, remember? And they'd dared me to run around the house in my boxers. I still remember feeling that adrenaline rush of doing something dangerous and catching the eye of the hottest girl in the eighth grade. It was a win-win."

I laugh as I point a French fry smothered in cheese sauce at him. "That doesn't sound even remotely embarrassing!"

He grins and pops his own cheesy fry into his mouth. "Well, that's because you haven't heard the embarrassing part yet."

"You tripped! Lost your boxers! Shrinkage!" My voice increases in volume and glee with each guess, laughter tripping over my words.

Sonny shoots me a mischievous side-eye. "Where do you think this story is going?"

I lift a shoulder and swipe another fry through the addicting sauce. "Spill then."

He blows out a breath, his cheeks puffing out to the sides. There's an air of playfulness around him. It's a welcome respite from my usual type. He lowers his head and looks at me from underneath his long, dark lashes. "Well, you see, my granddad came home and nearly had a stroke seeing my lily-white ass running around the house—"

"Ha! You did lose your underwear then!"

He straightens with a smirk. "Did I mention I was thirteen? Jake Thompson bet Carl Hannoc twenty bucks that I wouldn't actually streak. So I doubled-down on both of them and walked out with eighty bucks. And an earful from Pops. He read me the riot act in front of everyone that night—before he let me put my clothes on."

The mental image of an eighth-grade Sonny running around and trying to impress his friends plants itself in my mind, and I can't stop the giggles before they're out. He chuckles along with me as he takes another fry.

We switched out cocktails for soda and greasy food an hour ago. For bar food, it's pretty good. The company helps too.

The cheese sauce drips down onto the edge of my hand. I'm not one for messy hands while I eat, but I'm having too much fun to care right now. I toss the fry in my mouth and halfheartedly wipe my hands on the crumpled up napkin next to me.

I shake my head a little. "I can't even remember anyone's name from eighth grade, let alone memories so clearly like that."

I guess that's not entirely true. There are a couple people I don't think I'll ever forget, no matter how old I am. I take a sip of my Cherry Coke, the bubbles fizzing on my tongue.

"So you were thirteen, and that was ... how long ago?" I squint with a tilt of my head.

"You fishing for my age, Cher?" He smirks. "I'm an open book, baby girl. All you have to do is ask."

I pause at the new nickname, my brows slanting low over my eyes. I don't know how long we've been chatting, but either it's long enough for him to read me—which seems unlikely—or it's a throwaway pet name. One of those things guys use all the time because they can't remember the girl they're on top of.

Disappointment threatens to prick my bubble of fun, but I shove it out of the way at the last second. Two baskets of fries and a handful of drinks doesn't mean anything more than exactly what it is. And I won't be here long enough to find out if he's a player or not, so no skin off my back.

Ready for more? Read When It Ends here!

THE WREN EXCERPT

Continue reading for an excerpt from
The Wren: A Dark Arranged Marriage WhyChoose Romance
Available now on Kindle Unlimited

As the firstborn King, I should be the heir of the Irish Syndicate.

Instead, my father wants to marry me off to the highest bidder to fund a war I don't believe in.

My carefully controlled life starts to unravel, spiraling out of control faster than I can stop it.

And then I meet them and everything stops for a moment.

Tall with perpetual smirks and covered in tattoos, they remind me what it feels like to live.

They remind me that I don't need someone to save me.

I'm a King. I can save myself.

CHAPTER ONE

NICO

"I've found your wife."

I stop in front of the wet bar on the side wall of my office in one of our nightclubs, Violet Oak. I don't bother responding to my father just yet. I need something to settle my nerves. I thought my fucking heart was going to explode out of my chest when my father walked in my club ten minutes ago.

My long-lost sister, Madison, and her men were scattered around the private level of our club and the dance floor. They were here on my assurances that they'd be safe.

Fucking hell—they wouldn't have even been in Las Vegas is I hadn't given my sister's husbands my word that our father was out of town on business. And then that asshole strolls in like he's owns the place, and I looked like a fucking fool.

There's little more in this life than I despise than looking like a fool.

And just when I was starting to build a relationship with her, too.

Fuck.

I exhale and resist the urge to stretch my neck from side to side to release the tension. We're in my office on the third floor of Violet Oak, and it's a sharp contrast to the dimly-lit levels of the club below.

Light gray walls with charcoal gray accents, wrought-iron up-light sconces make the room feel larger with their beams of white light. My desk sits to the right, with two safes behind it, and plush leather seats facing the front.

"Did you hear me, son? I said I've found your new wife."

I nod my head, an acknowledgement that I heard him and nothing more.

"Let's wait until Rome is here." I make sure to keep my voice even. I learned a long time ago it's best not to needle Dad when he's worked up like this. It never ends well for anyone.

I grab four old fashioned glasses from the shelf next to me and line them up. I splash three fingers of my favorite barrel-aged sixty-proof whiskey in all four glasses. I pinch the edges of two glasses between my fingers and thumbs and turn around, handing my father his drink first as a sign of respect.

I set my brother Tommy's glass in his open palm and leave our youngest brother Rome's drink on the edge of my desk. "Rome should be up here in a minute."

Dad sips his drink, but he's unable to wipe the excitement from his face. I haven't seen him this excited in a long time, so it must be something really good.

"And where is your brother, Romeo?"

Sneaking our sister and her men out of the back door.

"Probably fucking someone in one of the private rooms on the second floor," Tommy drawls.

Dad grins, his mouth stretched too wide. "I bet you make a killing on those private rooms, eh, son? This is the city of sin, after all."

I catch his innuendo, but I do my best to not think about my father using private rooms all over this city with his many, many mistresses.

"We do alright." I sip my drink and look out of the tinted window to the levels below. To everyone down there who happens to look up, all they see is an iridescent window.

Dad puffs out his chest, his chin tipped high. "So modest, my oldest son. It's why you're so successful."

I swipe the droplets of whiskey on my lower lip with my tongue, my eyes narrowing at my father. He's untrustworthy on the best of days, and I can count on one hand the times he's ever given me a compliment.

He's buttering me up for something.

Rome walks in, saving us from the silence. It was nearly reaching uncomfortable territory.

"Ah, perfect timing as always, son," Dad says.

Rome closes the door and beelines for the drink on the edge of the desk. "What did I miss?"

"Now we can begin. I came home early to tell you the great news: I've found Nico's wife." He pauses and stares at us with a smile.

My father's face turns redder the longer the silence stretches, but I genuinely don't know what to say. I lean my hip against the wall and watch the anger play out over my father's face.

Maybe I've been a bit overserved tonight, not that I would admit that to anyone, because I'm not nearly as concerned with him right now. Or more likely, Tommy told the bartenders to pour with a heavy hand tonight to celebrate.

"What the fuck does that mean?" Tommy finally asks what the three of us are all thinking.

I'm still stuck on the fact that Dad cut his business trip short by five days. Guilt gnaws at my frayed nerve endings. I would've never forgiven myself if Dad ambushed our sister tonight.

Dad hates being questioned, and Tommy's tone was laden with derision. He glares at my brother as he sinks his one hand in his pants pocket and cradles his drink to his abdomen with his other. He strolls around my office, pausing next to me by the window and perusing the club-goers shedding their inhibitions on the dance floor.

It's all a ruse.

He doesn't care about the people, and he doesn't care about the club. We own and run it ourselves, one of the few legitimate business ventures we have. And he's always taken it as a personal offense, as if we should desire to be under our father's thumb forever.

"It means that I've secured an alliance for us. One that's going to expand our operations tenfold," he says with his back to us, his gaze still out the window.

Now I know that I've had too much to drink, because it takes me longer than it should to connect the dots.

"An arranged marriage. That's what you meant about a wife." It's not a question.

Dad spins on his heel, his face lighting up with genuine glee. About the prospect of *more*—as if we need more money or men or territory or fucking stress in our lives. We have enough wealth to last us several generations over.

But Vito Santorini is a selfish, greedy man. And the boss of the west coast Syndicate. It's a deadly combination.

"Yes, son. Think of all we can achieve together once we cement this alliance." His eyes dance with excitement, and I can't recall the last time I saw him this excited. Not even when he recently saw our sister—his daughter—for the first time in fifteen years.

"You've never pushed this before. Why now?" Tommy asks.

Dad clenches his jaw and glares at Tommy before switching

his gaze to me. "Arranged marriage isn't uncommon in our life, you know that."

I nod a few times. "Aye, I do. But Tommy's right. Why now? What else is going on?"

His greed and desire to grow the family business? Sure, that I buy. But this sudden arranged marriage proposal that isn't needed to grow? I'm not buying it.

He waves a hand around the air in front of him, batting our questions away like they're gnats. "As I was saying, negotiations went exceptionally well, and in two months' time, our two families will be joined. Then, my son, we'll be one step closer to unstoppable."

Rome sits forward in his chair. "Which family?"

"Is there a contract?" I ask at the same time.

Uneasiness churns in my lower gut. The idea of Dad brokering some deal with someone that involves my life has me feeling a little murderous. It's an unexpected feeling.

"Of course. But before you ask, no, you don't get to see it."

I tense. "Why?" I can't think of one good reason why he'd keep the contract—the name of my soon-to-be wife—from me.

"Eager to find your bride?" He leers at me, and that earlier feeling of apprehension rises.

So I do what I always do and play along.

I force my expression into something closer to his and lift a shoulder. "You know me, Dad."

He claps me on the shoulder. "All in due time, son."

The Wren now available on Kindle Unlimited
bit.ly/theWren

ACKNOWLEDGMENTS

Thank you to my readers! I still pinch myself that I even *have* readers! I'm so grateful that you took a chance on me. I hope you're not too angry with me for that ending. I promise that Sully's book will be here before you know it!

To all the bookstagrammers and bloggers and readers that send me messages and create beautiful edits for my books—I'm still in awe. Thank you.

Thank you to my husband who's always the first one to champion me. I'm so grateful for you—and your delicious food!

To my tiny humans: I love you both more than all the stars in the sky.

To my wonderful family who's encouraged and supported me —thank you, thank you! And thank you to each and every one of you who read my books—I'm lookin' at you, Grandma!

To my amazing beta readers Claire, Tracey, and Savy. I'm so thankful for each of you. Your kindness and support means the world to me.

And I want to thank each and every author who has been so kind and wonderful while I asked a million questions. There are far too many of you to thank, and for that alone, I'm forever grateful. There are a lot of wonderful people in this community, and I'm so glad to be apart of it.

***

ALSO BY PENELOPE BLACK

THE BROTHERHOOD SERIES

Wolf

Rush

Sully

THE FIVE FAMILIES SERIES

Gilded Princess

Twisted Queen

Vicious Reign

Fractured Dynasty

THE BLUE KNIGHTS MC SERIES

Coming Spring 2023!

STANDALONES

When It Ends:

A Dark Apocalyptic Romance

THE KING SISTERS WORLD

The Wren

The Wild

Made in the USA
Las Vegas, NV
28 February 2024

86449463R00204